D1151794

Big and Clever

To Carey, Alex,
Lily, Mum and Dad

With thanks to my agents Penny and Jennifer Luithlen, my publisher Ross Bradshaw, my family and friends and everyone who helped and supported me along the way.

Big and Clever

Dan Tunstall

Five Leaves

Big and Clever
Dan Tunstall

Published in 2009
by Five Leaves Publications,
PO Box 8786, Nottingham NG1 9AW
www.fiveleaves.co.uk

ISBN: 978 1 905512 68 3

Five Leaves acknowledges financial support
from Arts Council England

Five Leaves is a member of Inpress
(www.inpressbooks.co.uk),
representing independent publishers

Typeset and design by
Four Sheets Design and Print
Printed in Great Britain

one

As far as I know, Jamie Oliver has never been to Parkway College. If he ever did drop by, he wouldn't make it out of the place alive. He'd take one look at what was being served up in the canteen and pass out. And if the shock didn't kill him, a couple of weeks of eating the stuff would finish him off. It's Fat Bastard City round here.

I'm halfway along the queue in front of the serving hatches, pushing my tray along the metal runners. My plate's already filling up nicely. Decent sized portion of chips. Two sausages. Couple of bits of bacon. Big spoonful of baked beans.

Right behind me in the line, my mate Rakesh is getting stuck in. He's got the chips and the bacon and the beans but he's gone for three sausages, and he's got some mushrooms too. I don't know where he puts it all. He's about the same height as me, five eight, but while I'm quite broad, he's built like a pipe cleaner. I carry on along the line, grabbing a bread roll and a foil-wrapped pat of butter, a jam doughnut and a can of Coke.

Without looking up, the woman at the till totals up the items on my tray, picking up my bread roll and checking underneath.

"One ninety-five," she says. She couldn't sound any less enthusiastic if she tried.

I fish in my pocket, get out two pound coins and collect my change.

"Thanks."

She still doesn't look up.

I stand by the wall waiting for Raks and then we scan the dining area for somewhere to sit.

"Not looking good, Tom," he says.

I puff out my cheeks and glance down at my watch. Twenty-five to one.

"We've hit the middle of the rush hour. Seems to be worse on Mondays."

The people who were behind us in the queue are filing out into the hall. They don't appear to be having any difficulty finding somewhere to have their lunch. Everyone seems to know everyone else.

"Ever get the feeling we're missing out on something?" Raks says.

I nod. He's read my mind. It wouldn't be so bad if it was just the older kids who were sorted, but it's the Year Tens too, people our age. Everyone seems right at home. Everyone except Raks and me.

Most of the other Year Tens have come to Parkway from schools here in Letchford. Me and Raks haven't. Everyone's a bit sharper than us.

We've lived out in Thurston since the start of primary school. It's eight miles out in the sticks. Not many kids from Thurston opted to come to Parkway. It's the 'didn't fill your form in on time' option. There are a few familiar faces here, but they're not really what you'd call mates. At least Raks got put in the same tutor group as me or we'd really be struggling. Most of the people we used to knock around with have gone to Letchford Grammar or Townlands or Alderman Richard Martin. That's where Zoe's gone. Right on the other side of town. I miss Zoe. I still get to see her two or three nights a week, and in the mornings before the school buses leave Thurston, but it's not the same.

Two girls brush past us, trays in hand. As if by magic the group at a table on our left reorganise themselves and two places miraculously appear. The girls sit straight down, crack open their cans of drink and start eating. Simple.

Raks smiles.

"That's the way to do it, then," he says.

We set off across the polished wooden floor. Out in the middle of the hall, we stop again. I can see people from our tutor group dotted about, but nobody's beckoning us over. Nobody's even noticed us.

"This is doing my head in, man," Raks says.

I'm about to say something back, but then I'm almost knocked flying by a big lad in an army jacket jostling past. He stops, turns and looks me in the eye. He's got shaggy hair and bad skin. Still looking me in the eye, he pinches one of my chips and wanders off.

I shake my head.

"Bastard."

There's a flash of movement over on the far right side by the double doors leading to the foyer. A couple of girls have finished eating. They're taking their plates and cutlery back to the stacks by the serving hatches. It's what we've been waiting for. Raks hasn't noticed. I nudge him and we head for the two grey plastic chairs and unload our trays.

I open my can and nod at the bloke across from me. He's in our year. Tall thin black geezer with braided hair. The kids call him Snoop. I recognise him from Business Studies and ICT. If he recognises me though, he's keeping it to himself. He puffs out a breath and gets up, closely followed by the other three lads at the table. All of a sudden we've got the whole place to ourselves.

I laugh and shake my head.

"Have we got BO?" I sniff my armpits. Nothing to report but the smell of Lynx Africa.

Raks stuffs a forkful of mushrooms into his mouth, flicking his eyes around the dining hall.

"Everyone seems to belong to some sort of group, don't they?" he says. "The indie lot, the popular ones, the swots, the townies, the chavs. It's like a safari park here. All sorts of different species."

I can see what he means. We've all got roughly the same outfits on, the same dull greys and blacks, but already people have started accessorizing and adapting school colours to show which gang they're in. The hip-hop lot with the hoodies sticking out of the back of their pullovers, the big trainers and the low waist-bands. The townies mixing in expensive gear and designer labels. The emo kids, the Goths, with dyed-black hair and studded belts, big built-up boots with three-inch soles, pewter bangles and necklaces.

"Question is," I say, "what species are we?"

Raks shrugs. He picks up his Coke and leans back in his chair.

"Dunno mate. Never had to think about it before. It wasn't like this back in Thurston, was it? Thurston's The Village That Style Forgot."

I butter my bread roll and make a chip butty. As I'm shoving it into my mouth I catch sight of our reflections in the glass of the double doors. Slouched on either side of the table, same nondescript black shoes and trousers, same nondescript grey jumpers, same nondescript hair, Raks's black and mine brown. Maybe I'm being a bit hard on us, but the overall package isn't exactly screaming *Top of the Pecking Order*. We're not nerds. I wouldn't go that far. We just look a bit *insignificant*.

During the first week of term there was a tutor group meeting. Mr Green sat us all down in a circle. We each introduced ourselves, said a bit about the sorts of things we were interested in. I went first. Told people about my Thursday paper round, football training on Tuesday nights and how me and Raks go fishing on the canal. Nobody said anything. A few people laughed. A couple of girls shook their heads. Everyone else was into music or gaming or clothes. I'm fifteen in just over a month, but seven weeks at this place and I feel like I'm five all over again.

We carry on eating. All around us groups are coming and going. Laughing, joking, playfighting. Raks and me are like outsiders, staring through a window at other people having a good time.

I mop up some juice from my baked beans with the half-eaten end of a sausage, looking around again at the wildlife. Over on the far side of the hall, next to the noticeboards and the disabled toilet, two tall white lads with blond crew-cuts are sitting hunched over a bulging Nike rucksack. As I watch, three black lads walk up to them. Money changes hands, and then something DVD-shaped appears from out of the rucksack. In the blink of an eye, it's disappeared again, inside the jacket of one of the black lads.

To our left, there's a bunch of emo kids — big black coats, facial piercings and dodgy eye makeup. Judging from the guitar cases propped against the edge of the table, they're in a band. They're having a discussion. Apparently the band needs a new name. Two of them want Nocturnal Emission, but the other two are going for Prolapsed Colon.

I look at Raks.

"Tough one."

Raks laughs. He's started eyeing up two girls sitting by the fire exit. He's always fancied himself as a bit of a ladies' man, and I suppose he is quite good looking. He's got a sort of Amir Khan thing going on, minus the sticky-out ears. Good skin, strong jaw, white teeth, straight nose, big doe eyes, long eyelashes. Bit of a pretty boy. A couple of Zoe's mates fancy him. I give him a kick under the table.

"I know what your game is."

He laughs again, then turns his attention back towards the girls. They're both blonde and pretty, taking it in turns to check themselves out in a hand-held mirror, touching up their hair and their make-up. Popular types. Me and Raks wouldn't even register as a blip on their radar.

"They're right out of our league."

Raks shakes his head.

"Speak for yourself, man," he says. "Anyway, what do you mean *our* league? You're spoken for. Under the thumb big-style. Mr Faithful."

I tut.

"I'm still in the game." I'm trying to convince myself more than anything else, but he's right. I've known Zoe since the infants, and we've been together since the start of Year Eight. I'll window-shop but I'd never go behind Zoe's back and Raks knows it.

"Still in the game?" he says. "You announced your retirement long ago, you sad bastard."

I laugh. There's no point in arguing.

"Wonder what she's up to at the moment?" I say.

Raks shrugs.

"Busy getting to know some of the Sixth Formers." He's grinning. "You know, the big ones with their own cars."

I know he's only pissing about, so I laugh, but I'm

not as laid back about it as I make out.

"She *might* be hanging out with Sixth Formers though," I say.

Raks shakes his head.

"Give it a rest man. Stop talking about her. You'll just end up making yourself miserable."

I smile, embarrassed. He's right again. I *should* stop going on about her, but it's easier said than done. We spent virtually every day together in the summer. Last week was good too. October half-term holiday, the sun shining, like August all over again. Now though, winter's coming. I'm stuck in this place and it all feels like a thousand years ago.

I pick my doughnut up and start scanning around the hall again, trying to find something to focus on, something to take my mind off negative thoughts. There's a lad sitting at a table over to the right. He looks familiar but I can't quite place him. Tall, white kid with short dark hair. Blue zip-up tracksuit top and jeans. Not a big fan of dress regulations by the looks of it. Feet up on a chair, black Adidas Samba trainers. He's on his own, but you can tell he's not bothered. He's eating a hot dog and reading a magazine, listening to music on an MP3 player.

"Who's he then?" I ask, nodding towards him.

"That's Ryan. Ryan Dawkins I think his name is." Raks takes a gulp of Coke. "He's in a few of our classes. English Lit. French. I think he's in Business Studies and Art and Design too."

I've got him now.

"That's right. He's in Sankey's tutor group. Hardly ever turns up though, does he?"

Raks shakes his head.

"No. It's just the odd lesson here and there. I heard he's a bit of a nutter. Lives up on the Blue Gate

Fields Estate. You know what it's like up there."

I nod. I don't know much about the Blue Gate Fields Estate, but I know the reputation. The Bronx, it's known as. I've been through there in my dad's car once or twice. It's on the other side of Letchford. All concrete roads and derelict cream and grey council houses with brown metal shutters on the windows to keep the crackheads out.

"They call him ASBO Boy."

I laugh and stuff the last bit of doughnut into my mouth.

"Who's they?"

"Just people. I was talking to that Bradley Ellis at registration last week. He went to the same school as Ryan Dawkins last year. The teachers didn't know what to do with him."

"Do you reckon he has got an ASBO then?"

"God knows, mate, " Raks says. "There's loads of rumours about him though. He had to retake a year, and they reckon it was because he'd been in a Young Offenders place."

It's nearly ten to one. I reach into my bag and find my timetable. Monday afternoon. Biology and ICT. My heart sinks. I look up and see five lads making their way across the hall. They're older than us. Year Elevens. Three white kids and two Asians. The haircuts and low-slung trousers mark them out as part of the hip-hop fraternity. Budget variety, judging by the cheap-looking trainers.

Raks has seen them coming. He grins.

"Check it out," he says, flicking his eyes in the direction of the hip-hop crew. "Hanging With The Homeboys."

"Straight Outta Letchford, muthafucka."

We clench our fists and knock them together, Fifty

12

Cent-style. We laugh, but it doesn't last long. The gang are heading for our table.

"You two are done here, right?" one of the Asian lads asks, pushing his tray against Raks's elbow. He's got facial hair that looks like it's been drawn on with a felt tip.

It's a rhetorical question. Raks and me both know it's time to go. It's one thing making smart-arse comments about people, but they aren't much use in situations like this.

"Yeah, we're just on our way," I say, taking a last swig of Coke and piling things back on my tray. I stand up, trying my best to act casual.

The biggest white lad pushes past me, hooking my chair round with his foot and sitting down. Making himself at home. Raks is getting the same treatment from one of the Asian lads. Ten seconds ago we were just letting our dinner go down nicely, and now here we are standing around like a pair of fools. I can feel my face going red. I look at the kid who shoved me out of the way. He's got a pudgy, freckly face and lines cut into his hair. Around his wrist there's a bracelet. A pair of jewel-encrusted handcuffs. It looks like the sort of thing you get for 20p in a plastic egg from a lucky dip machine in Wilko's. He's the most unconvincing gangsta I've ever seen. He's about as likely to bust a cap in a brother's ass as my gran. The thing is though, he's just made us look like idiots. And there's nothing we can do about it.

Raks leads the way back towards the canteen to dump our trays, then we head for the exit doors, past the table we'd been sitting on. The lads who chucked us off certainly don't look like they're suffering any attacks of conscience. They're stuffing their faces, paying no attention to us at all. A couple of them are squinting at the screen of a phone, watching a video clip of a bloke getting his head cut off.

"Wankers," Raks says, keeping his voice low.

We're just about to push through the doors to the foyer when it occurs to me that the lads didn't need to kick me and Raks out. There were five places going spare on Ryan Dawkins' table. There still are. It's like he's got some sort of invisible exclusion zone around him. Just as I'm looking across, Ryan glances up. He raises his eyebrows in acknowledgement, and nods in the direction of the lads at our old table, circling his thumb and forefinger and cranking his hand backwards and forwards in the air.

My stomach flips over. ASBO Boy's on our side. I'm shocked, but I'm slightly chuffed too. It's like the feeling you get when a big dog runs up to you and licks your hand instead of chewing your arm off. I laugh and nudge Raks.

"He agrees with you," I say, jerking my thumb in the direction of Ryan Dawkins.

By the time we look back across though, he's stopped the hand gestures and he's reading his magazine again.

two

Dad's had a rough night again by the looks of it. It's only five past seven in the morning and he's up and dressed, which isn't usually the case. Thing is, he's in the same clothes he was wearing yesterday, food stains, creases and all. Added to that, the coffee table in the living room is covered with empty beer cans and a half-full bottle of Costcutter's own brand vodka. You don't have to be Sherlock Holmes to deduce that he passed out on the sofa last night and never made it to bed. It wouldn't be the first time.

"Morning Tom," he says, coming into the kitchen, trying to sound bright and cheerful. His chin is covered in stubble and his eyes are pink. "Can I get you anything?"

I take a bite of my toast and shake my head.

"No, it's alright Dad." I point towards his mug. White and blue with a union jack on one side and *I LOVE GREAT YARMOUTH* on the other. Me and my mum bought it for him one summer holiday. "I've made you a coffee. Do you want some toast?"

Dad runs his hands through his hair. He's forty-three next year and he's going grey fast. Forty-three going on sixty-three. In the past, people have said I look like him. I hope that's not what I've got in front of me.

"Would you mind?" he says. "I've got a bit of tidying up to do."

Dad takes his coffee and goes back into the living

room and I stick a slice of bread in the toaster. I flick the radio on. Letchford Sound. *Letchford's Best Mix of Music and More.* That's what it says on the bumper stickers. I've never really been too sure what there's *More* of. Phone-ins probably. People moaning about binge drinking, dogshit and the lack of disabled parking spaces round the precinct. It's *The Toby Collins Breakfast Bonanza.* The Tobemeister, he calls himself. I saw him once, doing a roadshow in the Ainsdale Centre in Letchford. He's about fifty.

The toast pops up. I butter it, spread on some honey and take it through to Dad. His tidying hasn't got started yet. The TV's on and he's slumped into the sofa.

"Oh, thanks Tom," he says. "Have you got time to sit down for a bit? Keep me company?" He's smiling at me hopefully.

The clock on the mantelpiece says it's ten past seven. I should be making a start on getting ready, but a couple of minutes won't do me any harm.

I sit in an armchair. *GMTV* is on. It's a report on celebrity cosmetic surgery gone wrong. The report ends and it's on to an ad break. Two different products to end the misery of constipation, amazing new pictures of Jordan in *Heat*, and a CD of Power Ballads.

Dad's gazing intently at the screen, but he's not really taking anything in. He's wrecked. I look at him and shake my head. It's hard to believe he was quite a handsome bloke a few years back. Mum said he looked like Jeff Bridges. Same dark blond hair, same jawline, same mouth. Apparently, his mates at work used to call him *Hollywood Tony*. Film-star looks, they reckoned. I don't think there's much chance of that nickname seeing any use in the near future. The bone structure is still there, but you just don't notice it any more. The skin hanging off it is grey and lifeless. All the spark has gone.

I stare at the mess on the coffee table. The blue material of the sofa is covered in toast crumbs. I'm getting the urge to start clearing up, but I don't want to offend Dad. I don't want him to think I'm implying that if I don't do the tidying, it'll never get done. That's not too far from the truth though. Cooking, cleaning, generally sorting things out. I seem to do most of it.

It's almost quarter past. Dad and I still haven't said anything. It's like we both want to have a conversation, but neither of us knows how to start. The adverts end and the *GMTV* logo comes back on screen. I stand up.

"I'd better be making a move."

Dad nods. He opens his mouth like he's about to say something, then closes it again.

Fifteen minutes later, I've showered, got my school gear on and I'm standing in front of the bathroom mirror trying to sort my hair out. Since I've been at Parkway it's becoming a bit of a preoccupation. Everyone seems to have hairstyling off to a fine art.

I've been having the same haircut every couple of months since the age of four or five. The women at Talking Heads do it on autopilot. Number four round the sides, a bit longer on top. In damp weather it goes fuzzy, like an old tennis ball. I'm coming to the conclusion that I need to be moving on now though. I need to develop a bit of a *look*. The thing is, I'm not quite sure what the *look* should be. A couple of minutes of poking and prodding with a comb, teasing up a few strands here and there with gel, and I'm still no better off.

I click off the bathroom light and cross the landing to my bedroom. Sitting on the edge of my bed, I look around. Blue and white quilt cover, matching striped wallpaper, a few posters dotted about. Oasis. Kasabian. An Airfix Lancaster on a piece of fishing line is slowly twirling by the window. My stereo's on the bedside table and my knackered old TV and video are on top of the chest of drawers on the far side, jostling for space with my PS2 and stacks of books, videos, DVDs and CDs.

I look down at the shoes piled up at the bottom of my wardrobe. My new Nikes, the ones I saved my paper round money for, blue and white with a red swoosh, are sitting next to my school shoes – big, black and clumpy. I know which ones I'd rather be wearing today. The question is, would I get out of the house without Dad seeing?

I weigh up the options for a few seconds. Dad's settled down in front of the TV. It's not a Friday. He won't be going up to Costcutter to get the week's shopping in. He probably won't be getting up off the sofa for hours. He'll probably still be there when I get back this evening, fast asleep or watching some crap film on *Channel Four*. A true story starring Brian Dennehy, something like that. I should make it through to the front door this morning without getting collared.

I get my Nikes out, lace them up, grab some folders off my desk and cram them into my bag. Then I make my way out onto the landing and look out of the window. Through the gloom I can see Raks coming down the road.

Back downstairs, I poke my head into the living room. Dad's hardly moved a muscle since I last left him. He's eaten his toast and drunk his coffee, but that's it. It's another ad break on TV. A fat bloke in a shiny grey suit is explaining how easy it is to claim compensation for injuries when they're not your fault. Trip over a loose kerbstone, and you're sorted.

"I'll be off in a minute," I tell him.

Dad looks across and then down. I pull my foot back further into the hallway, but it's too late. He's seen my trainers.

"Tom," he says. "School shoes."

My heart sinks.

"Do I have to? Nobody else wears school shoes." People *do* wear school shoes, but in general they're not the A-List of the student population.

"Well, Rakesh wears proper shoes," Dad says. "And you know, I'm not bothered what other people wear. The Parkway brochure said black shoes and that's what you've got. They cost forty quid. That's a lot of money. If you don't wear those shoes at school, when will you wear them? I'm not shelling out forty quid for something that's going to gather dust on your bedroom floor."

I'm not going to win this one. The doorbell rings and I let Raks in. I'm secretly pleased to see that he's got his big school shoes on. If anything, his are worse than mine. The soles look like waffles someone's left in the toaster too long.

Raks heads into the living room while I go off to change.

Back downstairs I poke my head into the living room again.

"Let's get moving," I say.

Raks stands up and I notice my dad flicking his eyes down at my shoes. I give him a little twirl and he smiles. I should put that on the calendar. He hardly ever smiles these days.

19

"See you, Mr Mitchell," Raks says.

Dad looks like he's going to heave himself up off the sofa but he thinks better of it.

"See you, Raks," he says. "Have a good day, the pair of you."

Outside it's cold and dark. The clocks go back this Saturday night, which means it should be a bit brighter in the mornings next week, but today it's pretty depressing.

"Your dad looks a bit frayed around the edges," Raks says, as we walk to the bottom of Dale Road and turn left towards the centre of Thurston.

"Yeah." I sniff. "He's pretty low at the moment. Boozing a lot. You know how he gets."

Raks nods, then drops the subject. He knows it's difficult for me. Nobody wants to think of their dad just rotting away.

At the corner of Wolverton Road we head right, then cut through the alley to Carlisle Street. Halfway down someone's dumped an old sofa. It's maroon crushed velvet with yellow foam rubber spilling out of rips in the cushions. As we turn into Carlisle Street I notice the police Scientific Support van parked on the pavement and two coppers dusting the window frames of one of the pebble-dashed granny bungalows for fingerprints.

"What were we saying about Blue Gate Fields the other day?" I say.

Raks laughs.

"Yeah, it's not exactly posh here is it?"

Up at the junction with Blakely Road, old Mr Curran is looking out of his front room window. It's Thursday, so he's probably lying in wait for his *Letchford Argus*. By my reckoning he's got about ten hours to go.

The sky is getting lighter. We carry on along past Costcutter, the Chinese, the bookies and Talking Heads until we arrive at the corner of Lindisfarne Street by the Bulls Head. Swinging my bag off my shoulder, making sure I don't put it down in the pool of sick someone's left behind last night, I push myself up onto the low brick wall that surrounds the beer garden.

Four buses pass through Thurston every morning, one for each of the schools in Letchford. It's like we stand in ascending order of respectability. Down at our end, there's the rag-tag mob who go to Parkway, then there's the Townlands kids, a little bit higher up the sliding scale. Further along, near the entrance to the pub car park, there's the Letchford Grammar school students in their blue and purple, and then last but certainly not least, the Alderman Richard Martin lot, all black blazers and smart trousers and skirts. The kids from the nice part of Thurston. There's not much mixing between the groups but luckily Zoe doesn't let things like that bother her. So far, there's no sign of her this morning.

"Where's the wife?" Raks asks.

"Dunno." I check my watch. It's nearly quarter to eight.

From where I'm sitting I can see Thurston Community College up at the top of the hill. Looking at the low red brick buildings, windows glinting as the sun slowly rises, it's hard not to get a bit nostalgic. I spent three years there. Happy times. I wasn't always the first one picked for games, or anything like that, but I wasn't the last either. I *was* someone at TCC. At Parkway, I'm nothing.

I look up again just in time to catch sight of a familiar figure coming down past the war memorial, shoulder length blonde hair blowing in the breeze. My stomach gives a little flutter. Zoe.

My dad might not have his Hollywood looks any more, but Zoe has. Think Keira Knighley's nose and mouth on Sienna Miller's face shape, and you're starting to get somewhere close. She's five five, fit body, smooth clear skin, blonde hair and pale green eyes. Even the way she moves is nice. She does a lot of swimming, dancing and gymnastics. There's a sort of natural grace about her. People stare at her. Lads and girls. I've got used to it now, just about.

She cuts across the road and comes straight over, smiling. She gives me a kiss. Zoe's not ashamed to be seen with the Parkway misfits. Things have brightened up no end.

"Hello, you," she says. "Sorry I didn't call yesterday. I was really busy. You didn't worry did you?"

I shake my head, doing my best not to look at Raks who's raising his eyebrows and dropping his jaw.

"No," I tell her. "No worries. Are you still coming round tonight? I'll have finished my papers by about six-thirtyish."

She scrunches her face up, looking awkward.

"I can't. Not today. I'm really sorry. I've joined the drama group and we're putting on *Oliver* at Christmas. The auditions are tonight, so I'm not going to be back in Thurston until half past eight, nine o'clock. I'll have to give it a miss."

"Oh, right," I say. I feel slightly crushed, but I know I shouldn't blow things out of proportion. I smile but I'm sure it looks pretty unconvincing. "Which part are you going for?"

"I'm going to try out for one or two," she tells me. "Nancy, Mrs Bumble. See how it goes. I know lots of

22

people are going to audition. I'll just see what happens."

I nod. I can't really think of anything else to say. For the first time I notice that she's wearing make-up. Just a bit of foundation and some eyeliner. I'm still surprised though. Zoe never wore make-up at TCC. She puts her head into my chest and I stroke her hair. We don't say much for the next few minutes, but it's still the most enjoyable part of my day.

It's nearly five to eight. The Townlands and Letchford Grammar buses have come and gone, but the other two are late. I'm just starting to toy with a fantasy where the Parkway and Richard Martin buses don't turn up at all, and I get to spend the whole day with Zoe, but then the Preston's coach rolls up at the crossroads, green and white with added rustpaint. Our bus. It grinds to a halt at the kerb and the doors hiss open.

I kiss Zoe, grab my bag and make my way over to the bus, following Raks up the steps. The driver has got Letchford Sound on. There's no getting away from The Tobemeister this morning. The bus is already half-full with the kids from Rushby and Collinsby. We find a couple of spare seats and Raks lets me take the one by the window so that I can wave. Zoe has wandered down towards the other Alderman Richard Martin kids, but she still blows me a kiss as the bus pulls away. I'm just feeling good about that when Raks jabs me in the ribs.

"You didn't wish her good luck with her audition, you bastard," he says.

A wave of guilt sweeps over me.

"Fuck," I say, quickly sending a text.

The journey is the usual route through the villages, picking up the odd passenger here and there, then out into the countryside, brown fields stretching away as far as you can see. A couple of the big kids on the back seat have been passing a half bottle of whisky around, and the driver's started casting a few glances in their direction, but that's about all. Some days it's a madhouse, upholstery being torn, the fire door getting opened every thirty seconds, graffiti scrawled on the seats, people chucking cans at passers-by. Not today though.

We come through the outskirts of town. Boarded-up tattoo parlours and kebab shops, plastered with faded posters for bands and nightclubs and films from years ago. Derelict pubs and half-demolished houses.

It's started raining now. Raks is staring out of the window, shaking his head.

"What a shithole."

I can't disagree.

Letchford's a nothing place, stuck out in the middle of Lincolnshire, miles away from anywhere. When I was little I used to come into town with my mum and dad, Christmas shopping or going to the cinema. It used to seem big and glamorous. These days though, it's a town in serious decline. The only thing the place ever had going for it was lino. Nearly half of the town worked in the lino factories. But a few years back it all went badly wrong. Nobody wanted lino any more. Not the sort of lino they were making in Letchford anyway. Thousands were laid off, and the town never really recovered. My dad definitely didn't. He's been out of work for eight years now, on Incapacity Benefit for the last five. Chronic depression. But that's got more to do with my mum dying.

Raks sighs and turns his attention away from the window.

"We going fishing this weekend?"

"Mmm," I say. "I've got a match for Thurston Dynamo on Sunday, but Saturday will be OK."

"Up the canal again?"

"Yeah. Got some decent-sized perch and roach up there last time, didn't we?"

Raks nods.

"Yeah. Some beauties. And what about that zander I had? It must have been three pounds. Maybe a bit more."

I stifle a laugh. His zander was nowhere near three pounds. It looked like a stickleback on steroids. I'm going to give him some gyp about it but I stop myself. I don't want to wind him up. And it's just nice to have something to look forward to.

The bus is coming past The Tony Mantle Health And Fitness Factory now. We keep going, heading along the side of the school perimeter fence, turning left, then left again through the main gates.

From the front, Parkway College doesn't look like much. It's just a big, single storey, grey block. On the inside though, it's a different story. The whole place has been built as one continuous spiral, gradually winding inwards until it comes to a circular central courtyard. Apparently it won some sort of architectural award when it was built back in the early seventies. There was an aerial photograph of the school in the *Letchford Argus* last week. Unless you looked closely, you could be forgiven for thinking that you were looking at an old, dried, coiled-up dog turd.

We stop and the big kids from the back seat bustle down to the front, barging people out of their way.

I yawn, pick my bag up, and then shuffle towards the exit doors. The rain's getting worse. I pull my hood up. I've got Maths, English Lit and French this morning. Then it's Geography and Biology this after-noon. I puff out my cheeks. It's going to be a long day.

three

"Anyone? Anyone?" Mrs Wetherall looks from one side of the room to the other.

Nobody says anything. Ten minutes into the lesson and English Lit isn't going well.

She has another go.

"Can anyone offer me suggestions for symbols we might find in *Lord Of The Flies*?" Her eyes scan the room one more time. "*Symbols.*" She's emphasising the word, hoping it's going to trigger someone. You can hear the pleading in her voice. "Come on Year Tens. I know it's our first look at *Lord Of The Flies* as a class, but you were all asked to read the text. There must be somebody?"

We've reached a stand-off. Just about everybody in the room could come up with an answer if they really had to. I mean, the whole island's covered with symbols, isn't it? The conch, the pig's head, the glasses, you name it. The thing is though, nobody wants to be the first to break cover. Nobody wants to look too keen. And there's something off-putting about Mrs Wetherall too, with her VW Beetle, *Stop The War* badge, tie-dyed clothes, nose ring and red Doc Martens. The image is all about peace and love but there's a nasty side to her. She's like a hippy with the good bits taken out.

There's still no response. Everyone's got their heads down, trying to avoid catching Mrs Wetherall's eye. Me and Raks are OK. We're sat right at the back, just us two on the table near the brown concertina partition that separates Room 37a from Room 37b.

Mrs Wetherall tries a new tack.

"Emma," she says, focusing her attention on Emma Atkins up at the front. "Perhaps you could start the ball rolling?"

Emma blushes. She'd been happily doodling away on her note pad, not expecting to participate.

"Er, is the conch a symbol, miss?" she says eventually.

Mrs Wetherall looks relieved.

"That's right, Emma," she shouts. "Exactly right." She bounds across to the whiteboard and scrawls up a cloud with the word *SYMBOLS* on it in blue marker pen, and *CONCH* on a line sticking out of the side.

A few hands go up and in no time the *SYMBOLS* cloud has got lines for *BEAST*, *MASKS/CLOTHES*, *FIRE* and *GLASSES*. I'm toying with the idea of tossing in *PIG'S HEAD*, but I'm finding it hard to concentrate because of all the noise coming from the other side of the partition. Mr Gillespie's teaching a Year Eleven Business Studies class next door, and he's getting the runaround.

Mr Gillespie's a Geordie, a real *Why-Aye, Howay the Lads* merchant. The kids are always winding him up, getting him to say words that sound funny in a Geordie accent. Today he's talking about types of competition. Every time he says Monopoly or Duopoly or Oligopoly everyone's pissing themselves laughing. By the sounds of it, things are building up to some sort of crescendo. Gillespie's raising his voice, trying to restore order. I'm just craning my head to the side, near to one of the rips in the partition, trying to hear what he's saying, when the door to our room swings open and Ryan Dawkins appears.

Mrs Wetherall's in the process of drawing another blue cloud on the board, this time with *PIGGY* written inside it. Hearing the door open, she swivels round and catches sight of Ryan.

"Ah. Mr Dawkins," she says. She puts the lid back on her pen with a click and checks her watch. "And only twenty minutes into the session."

I check my watch too. It's just gone ten, so we're fifteen minutes into the lesson really. Every face in the room is turning towards Ryan standing in the doorway. It's like one of those nature programmes where they use time-lapse photography to show a whole field of sunflower heads swivelling round to follow the sun across the sky.

"Sorry," Ryan says. It doesn't look as if he's going to explain his late arrival.

"So pleased you could join us this week," Mrs Wetherall says, voice heavy with sarcasm. "I don't think you actually managed it last week. It's really good of you to grace us with your presence."

A couple of the kids near the front start to laugh, but I'm starting to feel a bit uneasy. Mrs Wetherall looks like she's enjoying herself, taking potshots at a sitting target. It seems a bit unfair. I've seen other kids turn up late for lessons and nobody's said a word. But this is Ryan Dawkins. His reputation precedes him.

Ryan shrugs.

"That's alright, miss," he says. "No problem."

Mrs Wetherall's eyes widen. Suddenly she's furious. It looks like there's going to be a scene. Before anything can happen though, Ryan has turned away and is heading towards our table, swinging his bag off his shoulder, putting his jacket on the back of a chair and sitting down. I get a sudden twinge of anxiety. ASBO Boy's just parked himself across from me. It's one thing feeling a bit of compassion for him, or nodding at him across the dining hall, but this is something else. He's supposed to be a headcase.

"Alright lads?" he says.

We both nod. Mrs Wetherall carries on looking daggers at Ryan for a few more seconds and then turns away and goes back to her *PIGGY* cloud. Ryan fishes an A4 pad and a biro out of his bag and chucks them on the table-top.

"I thought she was really going to go for you there," Raks says.

Ryan waves his right hand in the air, like he's swatting a fly. A don't-give-a-shit gesture. I notice that the two outer knuckles of his left hand have pinkish scar tissue running across them. Up close he's quite intimidating. Taller and broader than Raks and me, black hair shaved down to a number one, pale skin, square jaw, piercing blue eyes and thick, dark eyebrows. He's in the same Adidas trainers and tracksuit top he was wearing the last time I saw him. Raks says the word is he was sent back a year at his last school. It could have been more than that. He looks about twenty.

"Water off a duck's back," he says. "All teachers are the same. Always chipping away, looking to get me to blow up, so they can chuck me out."

"She was bang out of order, though."

Ryan's hand waves again.

"She'll get hers, one day."

"I'd have just told her to piss off." Raks is getting carried away now.

The corner of Ryan's mouth curves up in a grin.

"Would you?"

30

There's a pause as Raks shuffles about in his chair, looking uncomfortable. Telling people to piss off just isn't his style. Luckily for Raks, Ryan leaves it at that.

"I'm Ryan, by the way," he says, stretching his hand out.

"Tom," I say, taking Ryan's hand and shaking it. My anxiety is starting to subside now. He isn't so bad. In fact he seems quite a sound bloke. "And Rambo here is Raks."

Ryan grins again.

"Alright, Raks?" he says. "Anyway, what are we supposed to be up to this morning?"

"*Lord Of The Flies*." I turn my pad round and show him the notes I've scribbled so far.

"Oh right," he says. "William Golding."

Raks and me exchange a glance. Maybe Ryan knows his English Literature.

Ten minutes later the *PIGGY* cloud on the board has all sorts of lines sticking out of it. As a class we've established that, amongst other things, he's *INTELLIGENT* and *PRACTICAL*, that he's a *PROBLEM SOLVER* and a *MEDIATOR*. I'm starting to feel a bit sorry that he ends up getting his brains smashed out on a rock at the bottom of a cliff.

For the last part of the session, Mrs Wetherall wants us to think about the *THEMES* of the novel. I start jotting a few things down, and I'm doing OK to begin with, but after a while I'm running a bit short of ideas. Mr Gillespie's shouting at the top of his lungs on the other side of the partition and it's not helping. I've been keeping a tally of the kids he's sent out to stand in the corridor. I'm up to five so far. I peer over to see what Raks has got. He's done less than I have. I'm about to lean across and see if

31

Ryan's put anything down when I notice Mrs Wetherall heading in our direction.

"Let's see how you're doing, then," she says, pulling out a chair and sitting down in a cloud of Dewberry scent. She looks over the top of her rimless rectangular glasses. "Ryan – are you going to go first?"

Ryan slouches back in his seat, eyes down. I can't help thinking that Mrs Wetherall is trying to put him on the spot again. I can feel the tension in the air. Ryan's saying nothing, staring at his pad and sucking the end of his biro.

Mrs Wetherall is smiling now. It's not a pleasant smile. She's got big receding gums and teeth like a horse, and the smile is getting wider and wider, because she knows she's got him. He's been dossing around, doing sod all, and now she's going to be able to give him another jousting. Ryan looks up. He takes a last glance at what he's written on his pad, and then he's off.

"Well," he says. "There are a lot of themes that cut right across the novel. What I've done is reduced them down to seven major ones. First off, there's the contrast between civilization and savagery — the idea that we're all pretty savage deep down. Then there's the conflict between good and evil. Bad things happen to good people. The world's an evil place. Next up there's the theme of violence. Right through history humans have always used strong-arm tactics to sort things out. After that there's leadership. Some people are born leaders. That's just the way it goes."

He's about to carry on, but Mrs Wetherall's holding her hand up. The expression on her face is priceless. She looks like she's been hit with a baseball bat. When she speaks you can hear the amazement in her voice. Or perhaps it's disappointment.

"Ryan," she says. "That's very good. Very good." She gets up and crosses to the whiteboard without saying another word. It doesn't look like she wants any feedback from Raks and me, which is probably a good thing.

Eventually the lesson trundles to a close. The break time bell rings and people start packing their pads and pens away, streaming out and heading for the canteen and the vending machines. Ryan pulls his bag onto his shoulder and makes for the door. He's about to set off on his own when he stops and turns round.

"What are you two doing now then?"

"Nothing much, really," I say. "Just going up to get a drink and a bag of crisps."

"Mind if I tag along?"

I look at Raks. He nods.

"Yeah, no problem," I say.

Ryan and me stand by the door while Raks packs his things into his rucksack. Mrs Wetherall has been sorting out various bits of paper on a table by the whiteboard and now she comes past us, head down, clutching a Tesco Bag For Life across her chest.

"See you, Mrs Wetherall," Ryan says, bright and breezy.

Mrs Wetherall tries a smile, but this time she can't manage it. She keeps going.

I laugh.

"Gutted," I say.

Raks has finally got himself sorted and we head out into the corridor, where Mr Gillespie's laying down the law to the kids chucked out of the Business Studies class. Judging by the smirks on their faces, it's not having the desired effect. We keep on going, anticlockwise around the curve, in the direction of the canteen. As the three of us walk, I start to feel a strange sort of pride. It's taken a few weeks, but we've made a new mate. There's three of us now. When there's only two of you, you feel a bit exposed, a bit vulnerable. But now we're a gang. Maybe it's just a coincidence, but Ryan's walking one step in front of Raks and me. It's like he's assumed command from the word go.

It's busy in the canteen. People are getting tea and coffee and hot chocolate, lining up at the tills. We get our cans and food and take our places at the back of the right hand queue. In front of us there's a fat girl in a crop top and combats. She's got *BAD GIRL* tattooed across her lower back in Gothic script.

"That was quite something back there, Ryan," Raks says, as we're waiting.

Ryan looks puzzled.

"What was?"

"All that stuff you came out with. All those themes in *Lord Of The Flies*. You weren't even there when Wetherall asked us to read it at home."

"Oh," Ryan says. "I've read it before. I've seen the film too, the old 1960's one, not the crappy modern one."

Raks looks at him. "Shit."

Ryan grins, raising his eyebrows.

"You're surprised are you? Just thought I was some stupid thick bastard?"

Raks looks mortified. In that split second it's dawned on him that he might just have offended someone we had down as a maniac less than an hour ago.

"N-n-no. No. I didn't mean that." He looks at me to help him out.

"He's not trying to be…" I say, but Ryan cuts me off.

"Don't worry about it," he says. His voice is calm. Matter-of-fact. He's trying to put us at ease. "I know what people think of me. I know what people say about me. All that ASBO Boy bollocks. I don't give a fuck though."

I nod. There are one or two things I want to find out. I look at Ryan and take a breath.

"Have you got an ASBO then?" I ask him. As the words are coming out of my mouth I'm already realising what a sad question it is.

Ryan doesn't seem to be bothered. He laughs.

"Not yet," he says.

"So why do people call you ASBO Boy?"

"It's just a nickname, isn't it? People think I'm some sort of juvenile delinquent, because I've been in a spot of bother once or twice."

Raks seems to have got his composure back now.

"What sort of bother?"

Ryan shrugs.

"Just things. Probably nothing like the stuff people think I get up to. I mean I've heard people saying I've been in Young Offenders and all sorts. It's bollocks. I told you though. I don't care. If people are scared of me, they just leave me alone. I can cope with that. To be honest, I'm happy with it."

There's something in Ryan's body language that's saying we should let the subject drop now. Not surprisingly. Raks and me are starting to sound like a couple of little kids quizzing our big brother about the things he does when he's out.

We're getting to the front of the line. I put my Coke and crisps next to the till and reach into my pocket for my money. Before I get the chance though, Ryan's pulled out a fiver.

"I'll get this," he says, putting his own stuff down

and taking Raks's.

"Oh, cheers," I say, surprised.

BAD GIRL is collecting her change. She picks up her tray and wanders into the dining area. The woman at the till looks at us suspiciously. She slowly tallies up.

Ryan hands over the note.

The woman holds the note in the air, narrowing her eyes, checking the watermark. She gives us another suspicious look, then she opens up her till.

We pick up our food and drink and head out into the main part of the hall. As we walk, a couple of older lads, Sixth Formers, nod acknowledgement at Ryan. I've seen them before. Tall lads, short blond hair. One of them is carrying a Nike rucksack. Our local DVD specialists. It's not so mysterious that the hip-hop boys didn't push their luck with Ryan a few days back. He's got connections.

The room's quite full, but we don't have any trouble finding a seat with Ryan leading the way. Sitting down, I rip open my crisps and stuff a couple into my mouth.

"You're going to piss on the English Lit GCSE then, Ryan," I say. I'm looking to get a new conversation going.

Ryan takes a swig of Sprite and shrugs.

"Who knows? Passing exams isn't exactly at the top of my list of important things."

"Don't you want to stay on for the Sixth Form though?" Raks asks, through a mouthful of scampi and lemon Nik Naks. "You know, get a couple of A Levels, go to college, all that stuff?"

Ryan winces.

"What's the point of piddling around till I'm twenty-one, twenty-two, coming out with an armful of certificates?" He takes a chomp of his Mars bar. "This is Letchford. There are no jobs round here. I'll just be bumming around on the dole for the rest of my life. Like I said, passing exams isn't a big thing with me."

"So what *does* get you going then Ryan?" Raks asks.

Ryan laughs. Putting his can of Sprite down, he hooks his thumb under the collar of his jacket, pushing it forward so that me and Raks can see the small enamel badge next to the zip. Orange and black, with the lion crest and the initials *LTFC*.

"Letchford Town," he says. "That's what does it for me." He pulls the badge up and kisses it. "Come on you Tangerines." It's the first time I've seen him properly enthusiastic.

"So you go to the matches do you?" It's a stupid question really. I'm full of them this morning. Ryan looks pleased that I've asked it though.

"Not missed a home game for six years," he says. He brushes down his collar, making sure that his badge is facing the right way.

I crack open my can.

"Who do you go with then?" I ask.

"Just people," Ryan says. "What about you lads? Ever been?"

Raks shakes his head.

"I've been once or twice."

"What about you, Tom?"

"Well, you know," I say. "I've been a few times, with my dad. Not so much in the last couple of seasons though." In truth I've not actually been since I was in primary school. Since before my mum died. Dad isn't too keen on being around crowds of people these days.

Ryan nods. He reaches into his pocket, checking his phone for messages. You can see the disappointment in his face.

I suddenly feel really guilty. Like I've let him down. You're supposed to establish common ground at the start of a friendship, but here are me and Raks admitting that the most important thing in Ryan's world does nothing for us. I'm about to say something, but Raks gets in first.

"How are Letchford doing this season, then?"

Ryan shoves his phone back into his jacket.

"The same old same old, really." He finishes his Mars bar and crumples up the wrapper, shoving it into the top of his empty Sprite can. "Bottom half of the table. Fourteen points from fourteen games. Out in the first round of the League Cup to Leicester. Leroy Lewton's got six goals so far, but Championship clubs have started hovering around, so he'll be off in the January transfer window. Bloody Coventry or somewhere."

I'm thinking of ways I can get things back on track. I start dredging my memory banks, spooling back to last Saturday at ten to five, trying to visualise the League Two classified results on *Final Score*. Like a flash it comes to me. Swindon Town 1, Letchford Town 2.

"Decent win last weekend, though," I say. I'm trying to sound authoritative, hoping that I've got it right. Luckily, Ryan's convinced.

"Not bad," he says, livening up again. "Away form's been pretty good this season. We'd not beaten Swindon for years. And it puts us above Mackworth in the table. That's always nice."

"Are they still the big rivals, then?" I say.

"Oh yeah." There's a stern look in his eyes.

"There's not really anybody else is there? Not since Lincoln went up. I mean, there's Boston, and I suppose Grimsby at a push, but they're miles off. Mackworth's just down the road."

I nod.

"If we could just get the home form going then, we could be thinking about the Play-Offs next May," I say. I'm warming to the task now. I've started referring to Letchford Town as we.

Ryan smiles.

"Not this year," he says, shaking his head. "Not if you'd seen them against Wrexham and Barnet."

Raks has finished his Nik Naks now. He smoothes the packet out on the table-top and opens his can of Coke.

"Bad, were they?" he asks.

Ryan skims his hand across his hair.

"Fucking awful. The thing is, it doesn't matter does it? They're my team. With a bit of luck we won't go down this season, but even if we do, I'll still be there in the Conference."

I look at my watch. It's just after eleven. People are tidying their tables and heading off in the direction of their third lesson of the day. An idea is starting to form in my mind. If there isn't much common ground between Ryan and us at the moment, then we're just going to have to make some.

"So who have Letchford got this weekend?" I ask. I'm hoping to get us an invitation, but I'm trying to be subtle.

"Castleton at home."

"What do you reckon then?" I say. Ryan isn't biting yet. "Three points?"

He shrugs.

"Who knows? They're fourth at the moment. Only

39

two points off the top." He pauses, scratching his nose. "Tell you what," he says eventually, "why don't you two come down this Saturday?"

Bingo. I silently congratulate myself, then I look across at Raks. He's nodding. We were supposed to be going fishing, but we can do that any old time. I turn back to Ryan.

"Yeah," I say. "Yeah. I think we might just do that."

four

As the 84 bus pulls into bay seventeen at Letchford bus station, I check my watch. Just gone quarter past one. We're supposed to be meeting Ryan at half past at the Café Rialt in the Ainsdale Centre, and that's right across town, so we need to get a move on.

Raks has been listening to music on his mobile phone. He's in a little world of his own, slumped against the window.

"Earth calling Rakesh Patel," I say, leaning in close to his ear.

Raks shakes his head and pulls his earplugs out.

"We're here," I tell him. "An hour and three quarters to kick-off."

"Shit," he says. "I've got butterflies, man. I don't know why."

I nod.

"Yeah. I know what you mean." I've got butterflies too, a little tingle that's been building and building since Thursday break time. I could hardly sleep last night.

We both stand up and Raks smoothes down the front of his new replica shirt. Orange with black piping and the logo and slogan of our sponsors, Letchford Borough Council. *Working For You*. He told his mum and dad on Thursday evening that we were going to the match this weekend. By the time he got home from college last night they'd got him all kitted out. If I want a shirt it's going to take me at

41

least three weeks of paper round money, possibly two if I get a lot of leaflets to deliver. Whatever, I'm going to have to earn the money myself. There's no point in asking my dad.

It's chilly outside. Raks never seems to feel the cold. He's strolling along with his coat undone, but I'm shivering. I zip my jacket right up until just the top of my orange and black Letchford scarf is visible under my chin. It's the first time I've worn the scarf in years, and it's quite a strange feeling. My mum knitted it for me. Winding it round my neck this morning brought back a lot of memories.

Halfway up Church Lane we pass a newsagents. There's a notice in the window. *Letchford Town Official Matchday Magazine On Sale Here Price £2.*

"Hang on a minute," I say.

Inside the shop, the programmes are stacked up on a shelf by the door. Picking one off the top of the pile I take it across and put it down by the till. Leroy Lewton's grinning from the front cover, eyebrows notched, diamond ear studs gleaming. The middle aged Asian bloke behind the counter glances up. He's been looking at the ads at the back of *The Daily Sport. Genuine Hard Core Porn Direct To Your Mobile.*

"Anything else, chief?" he says.

I shake my head and pay my two quid.

Carrying on up Church Lane, I start leafing through the magazine, scanning for relevant statistics. Inside the front cover there's a section called *Roll Of Honour*. It's pretty brief. *Founded 1904. Elected To The Football League 1909. Football League Division Four Runners Up 1986. Freight Rover Trophy Southern Area Finalists 1990.* It's not exactly Manchester United.

Raks nudges me in the ribs.

"It's a bit late in the day to start swotting up," he says, pointing at my programme.

I shrug.

"I'm just trying to gen up on a few facts and figures so I don't feel like such an amateur." He's right though. I'm not going to become the Letchford Town *Mastermind* overnight. I close the programme, fold it in half and shove it in the back pocket of my jeans.

We head into the precinct. The whole place has gone downhill the last couple of years. The big M&S was the first to go, and then just about everyone else followed. All that's left are charity shops, Everything's a Pound places, Iceland, and a Wilko's that's so big I swear the far end's in another time zone. Today there's a market in the pedestrianised area between the shops. Fishmongers, a few people selling fresh produce and stall after stall of fake branded goods and bric-a-brac. Everywhere you look there are pensioners picking up second hand clothes, rubbing them for a moment or two, then putting them back down again.

We go under the archway and through the sliding doors into the Ainsdale Centre. It's nice and warm inside and not too crowded. In the background, music is playing. It's a pan-pipe version of *Angels*.

We head up the escalators to the first floor. Outside Kwik Kash three ferrety-moustached lads in shell-suits and Burberry caps are huddled together taking it in turns to peer into the ALDI carrier bag one of them is holding. We carry on past Malc's Menswear making for the Café Rialt up at the far end. Everyone in Letchford calls it the Café Rialt, but it's the Café Rialto really. It's just that the O on the neon sign in the window gave up the ghost years ago.

"What time is it?" Raks asks.

"Half past." My butterflies are going into over-drive.

We're coming to the end of the walkway now, fifteen yards from the café and closing. As I push the door a bell rings. It's quite dark inside. The air smells of strong coffee and burning bacon. Westlife are on the radio. There aren't many customers for a Saturday, just a few old blokes and a couple of women with buggies disappearing under piles of shopping bags. Ryan's nowhere to be seen.

"He's stood us up," Raks says.

I shake my head.

"He'll be here." I'm trying to sound confident.

The next time I check my watch it's nearly quarter to two. I've got myself a can of Coke and a cream doughnut and Raks has got a can, a doughnut and a plate of chips and beans, and we're sitting down in the corner by the window. The Letchford programme in my pocket is digging into my back so I pull it out and put it on the table. The table-top is brown Formica. It looks like it was last given a wipe down in about 1980.

"Still no sign of Ryan," Raks says, making a start on his chips.

"Yeah. What do you reckon? Finish this lot, then have a wander around outside, see if we can see him anywhere?"

Raks nods. He shovels another forkful into his mouth.

"So what did your old man say when you told him we were going to the match this afternoon?"

I sniff.

"Nothing much. Just to keep out of trouble. Your mum and dad OK about it?"

He nods again.

44

Another couple of minutes pass. Raks is getting more and more twitchy. He's finished his chips and beans and he's drumming his fingers on the table edge.

"Is Ryan supposed to be coming here on his own or will he have other people with him?" he asks.

"He'll be on his own," I say.

"How do you know that?"

"Because here he is now." I point over Raks's shoulder to where Ryan's heading down past Argos.

The door opens and Ryan comes in, nodding and raising his thumb in our direction. He gets himself a can of Red Bull and a bag of crisps and then he comes over to our table, pulling out the chair next to Raks.

"Sorry I'm late lads," he says. "Got a bit delayed. Unforeseen circumstances." He sits down and unzips his jacket. He's wearing an Adidas top again, but it's a green one with yellow stripes this time.

"No worries," I tell him.

Ripping open his crisps, Ryan looks first at me, and then at Raks. He shakes his head.

"Raks mate," he says. "You need to get that coat done up. The shirt's a bit too much. You look like a Satsuma. You've got to show your allegiance but don't go over the top. Tom's got it about right. Just a bit of scarf showing."

Raks looks slightly hurt, but he does what Ryan says. I make a mental note not to waste my money on a Letchford shirt. I'm just congratulating myself on instinctively knowing what's expected of a new recruit to the Letchford Town ranks when Ryan catches sight of the programme next to my can of Coke. He laughs.

"I never bother with these any more. Is there anything worth reading in it these days?" He picks it up and flicks through from the back, shaking his head at the league table. "This is the bit I always like," he says as he gets near to the front. "The *Roll Of Honour*. Promotion and Freight Rover Area Finalists. Roman Abramovich eat your heart out."

I smile.

"Yeah, I was looking at that earlier on. It must have been good in the late eighties, early nineties."

Ryan looks wistful.

"Glory days," he says. "Since we got relegated in 1991 we've just been treading water. I'd have loved to have been there when we were on the way up."

Raks makes a start on his doughnut.

"Wasn't there quite a lot of trouble back then though?" he asks. "Letchford Town were known for having a hardcore of pretty mental fans weren't they?"

Ryan nods.

"The LLF. The Letchford Lunatic Fringe. The top firm outside the top two divisions."

I laugh.

"That doesn't sound like much to shout about."

"Oh, I don't know," Ryan says. "They put some big teams to flight. Then there was The Battle Of Southlands in May 1992. The Mackworth lot came over to try and take over the LLF's manor. Dozens of arrests, riot vans, the works. It's gone down in history, that one."

"I've heard about that," Raks says. But it's all died down now, hasn't it, all the fighting and stuff?"

Ryan shrugs, takes a swig of Red Bull then locks his fingers behind his neck, rolling his head from side to side.

"Mmmm," he says.

Raks hasn't finished with the questions.

46

"You've got a season ticket, then, Ryan?"

"That's right." Ryan pulls a plastic wallet out of his inside pocket, running his thumb through the vouchers inside.

"Whereabouts in the ground are you then? Sitting or standing?"

Ryan raises his eyebrows.

"Standing, mate. North Stand Spion Kop." He scratches his nose. "So where were you when you went?"

Raks's eyes roll up as he scans his memory banks.

"I think it was the East Stand," he says eventually.

Ryan laughs.

"The *Letchford Argus* Family Stand, they call that nowadays. It's a sad place. Full of bloody kids. Facepaint and flags and Jester hats." He shakes his head.

Raks looks crestfallen.

"My dad wasn't really up for standing."

Ryan laughs again, but this time he's not taking the piss.

"Don't worry about it. It's better than the Main Stand with the camel-hair coat fraternity. Tartan Thermos flasks and Tupperware boxes of egg sandwiches all round. Polite applause and no swearing."

"So how do we get in this afternoon?" I ask, looking to change the subject. Me and my dad used to sit in the Main Stand. "Can we pay on the turnstiles?"

Ryan nods.

"Yeah," he says. He puffs out his cheeks and checks his mobile. "Anyway, we'd better think about setting off for the ground. It's getting on for ten past two."

We head for the door. Down by the ground floor exits an old bloke is playing Elvis songs on a Hammond organ. He's left the piano case open in front of him, with a piece of card propped inside it. *All Donations Gratefully Received*. He's got about seventy pence so far.

Back outside it seems to have got even colder. We cut through the car park, then we head across the main road and down one of the side streets.

"How long's it going to take us?" Raks asks.

"Not long," Ryan replies. "Fifteen, twenty minutes, something like that. Once we get to the Industrial Estate we're halfway there."

We carry on walking. As we get closer to the ground, the other football punters are getting easier to spot. It's mainly blokes in white trainers and slightly-too-short stone-washed jeans, replica shirts sticking out underneath the back of black or blue bomber jackets, but there are families too, all heading in the same direction. I feel a little twinge of excitement.

We're coming to a junction now. On the left there's a row of shops, the Ayia Napa Fish Bar, Balti Towers Indian Takeaway, Gladiator Cabs and a dodgy looking pub called The Shakespeare, and on the right there's a patch of open ground. Back in the late eighties, when Letchford Town looked like they were going somewhere, the patch of land was set aside for a new, twenty-two thousand all-seater state of the art stadium. They got the planning permission and even started digging the foundations, but then the sponsors pulled the plug. Now all that's left is a big brown hole in the ground, filled with water. We stand and stare for a few seconds, then keep on going, crossing over and heading into the Letchford Industrial Estate.

The Industrial Estate's a ghost town. Since the bottom dropped out of the lino market, most of the factories have been empty. One of the units on the right hand side has been burnt out and now the metal roof joists are hanging down like thick strings of black elastic. Further up on the left, surrounded by a muddy wasteland, I can see Morrells, where my dad used to work. The big digital clock by the gates still says *17:00*. That was when my dad used to clock off. It's like time has stood still since the afternoon the place shut down.

Ryan nudges me, then taps Raks on the elbow.

"Check it out," he says, pointing along the line of pylons marching beside the road.

A few hundred yards ahead, silhouetted against the grey sky, is the Southlands Stadium. It's just as I remember it. Four ramshackle stands, each one a different shape, like a Meccano kit with a few pieces missing. I get another little tingle of excitement. Checking my watch I see it's nearly half past two. The pavements on both sides of the road are packed with people now, and the air is filled with the smell of hot dogs and burgers from the portakabin by the crossroads. Next to the burger van there's a bloke selling non-official merchandise. Scarves, flags and T-shirts showing a skinhead with his trousers down, crapping on a Mackworth top. *Letchford Town Shit On The Mackworth* it says underneath.

"That's a classy piece of kit," Raks says, pointing to the T-shirt.

Ryan and I laugh.

We're just about to cross the road into the stadium car park when there's a bit of a kafuffle behind us. Two police motorbikes sweep past and as I turn round I can see that a group of young lads, kids around our age, are running and shouting and banging on the sides of three tatty coaches that are

49

cutting their way through the crowd.

"What's going on?" I ask.

"Away fans," Ryan says. There's an odd look in his eyes.

Before I have a chance to ask anything else, Ryan has barged his way to the edge of the pavement and he's giving the finger to the Castleton supporters leering and gesturing out of the windows of the coaches. As the third bus comes past I notice two blokes at the back, mooning, hairy arses pressed to the glass. The whole incident is probably over in less than ten seconds. I'm rooted to the spot, heart pounding, too shocked to move.

"Bastards," Ryan says, pushing his way back through to where Raks and me are still standing.

"What was that all about then?" Raks asks. He looks as confused as me.

Ryan shrugs.

"Nothing really. Just ritual. There's a bit of history with Castleton." He's completely back to normal now. It's like someone has flicked a switch and he's gone from one state to another in an instant.

"History?" I say.

Ryan does the dismissive wave of his hand I remember from the English Lit lesson.

"Bit of rivalry from days of old," he says. "They sent us down in 1991. Beat us 3-2 on the last day of the season."

"Ninety-one?" I say. "That's a bit before your time."

Ryan shakes his head.

"It's ingrained in the DNA of all Letchford fans," he says. "Never forget. Never forgive."

My heart rate is slowing down. The away coaches have gone and everything's calm again. We head around the ground anticlockwise, along the side of the Family Stand, towards the turnstiles at the back of the North Stand. The Castleton team bus is standing in a bay on the far side of the car park. *Compton's Luxury Transport, Silloth*. It looks tattier than the supporters' coaches.

I hear my mobile beeping. It's a text from Zoe. *Hv fn tk cr Z X*. I smile. She sounded a bit dubious yesterday when I told her I was going to the football, although to be honest she was more interested in *Oliver* than in what I might be doing on a Saturday afternoon. She got the part of Mrs Sowerberry the undertaker's wife at the auditions on Thursday and she just wanted to talk about that. But at least she's thinking of me now. I'm about to send a message back, but there isn't time. I'm right up at the front of the queue now, at the point where it splits into two.

Ryan and Raks go through Gate 19 and I go through Gate 20. The bloke in the booth is about sixty with dandruff on his shoulders and wispy hair scraped forward to cover his bald patch. A comb-round instead of a comb-over. It looks like a grey snowball has exploded on the back of his head. For some reason I've got this horrible feeling that I'm not going to be let in, but I know it's stupid really. It's not the cinema. There's no certification system, and I'm not going to be thrown out for being too young.

Comb-Round Man looks up.

"Season ticket?"

I shake my head.

"Eight pounds, son," he says. Simple as that.

I hand him the right money, relieved, and click my way through the turnstile. Raks and Ryan are waiting for me on the other side. The concourse smells of beer and cheap aftershave. People are lining up for food and drinks and waiting to put bets on, watching *Soccer Saturday* on the televisions bolted to the walls, swigging pints in plastic glasses. Music is blaring out of the PA system. Harry J All Stars. *The Liquidator*. Same as when I used to come with my dad. The playlist must be stuck in a time warp.

"Anyone need a piss?" Ryan asks.

Raks and me shake our heads.

"OK then. We might as well get out and see what's going on."

Ryan leads the way up a flight of concrete steps. The nearer we get to the top, the louder the sound of the crowd is getting, bouncing down off the low metal roof of the Kop. The music has stopped now and the tannoy announcer is reading out the Letchford team. Each name is getting a cheer apart from Dave Nicholson. He used to play for Mackworth. I can feel the little ball of excitement in my stomach getting bigger and bigger.

The pitch is starting to come into view. It's only the sixth home game of the season and the grass is still looking lush and green. The Letchford players are warming up at our end, doing shuttle runs and taking shots. We climb the last couple of steps and then stand at the top, surveying the scene. The home terracing stretching out in front and behind us. The away supporters in the corner to the right, the orange seats of the Main Stand slowly filling up but the black seats spelling out LTFC still visible. The glass-fronted executive boxes at the far end, scoreboard perched on the top. The corrugated roof and wooden seats of the Family Stand away to the left. Old Trafford it isn't, but it still looks fantastic.

I look at Raks and Raks looks at me. We're both grinning like idiots, swept up in the atmosphere of the occasion.

"Now, this is better than fishing," I say.

five

As the ref blows his whistle for half time, a chorus of boos rumbles round the Southlands Stadium. 0-0. And it's not exactly been Champagne Football. The players troop off towards the tunnel and the PA system cranks into action. *Let Me Entertain You*. Someone's got a sense of humour.

"What do you reckon, then?" Ryan asks.

I smile, picking a few flakes of black paint off the crush barrier in front of us, running my palm over its rough, pitted surface.

"Just like watching Brazil," I say.

Ryan laughs.

"You're going to like it here." He turns towards Raks. "What about you, mate?"

"We should be at least one up, shouldn't we?" Raks says. "How did Leroy Lewton miss that one near the start? He was only about three yards out."

Ryan shrugs.

"That's Leroy Lewton for you. He'll play a blinder if he thinks the scouts are in looking at him, otherwise he couldn't hit an elephant's arse with a banjo."

"At least he's looked like he's interested," I say. "Not like Dave bloody Nicholson. How many times has that left winger gone past him?"

"Don't get me started on Dave Nicholson," Ryan says. "The man's a donkey. Sometimes you wonder if he's only had the rudiments of football explained to him five minutes before kick-off."

"Well you know what his real problem is though, don't you?" Raks asks.

I shake my head.

"He's a dirty Mackworth scumbag, isn't he?"

We all laugh.

Let Me Entertain You is abruptly brought to a halt and the tannoy announcer starts to give out the half-time scores. Grimsby are winning at Swindon and Boston are drawing at home to MK Dons, so there's not much to get worked up about. The best news has been saved for last though. Mackworth are two nil down at Accrington Stanley. A big cheer rings out.

"See?" Ryan says. "It's not all doom and gloom."

We make our way back up the terracing and go down the steps to the concourse. I head for the toilets while Raks and Ryan join the back of the food kiosk queue.

As I'm waiting for my turn at the urinals, doing my best not to inhale the smell of shit that's filling the air, I see a couple of familiar faces coming towards me. It's the two sixth formers who acknowledged Ryan in the canteen the other day. The DVD boys. As they come past, they both make eye contact and nod in my direction.

"Alright, mate?" one of them says.

I feel a sudden surge of pride. They know I'm a Letchford fan. They know I stand on the Kop. It feels good.

By the time I've finished, Raks and Ryan have been served. Ryan's balancing three polystyrene cups of coffee on top of each other, and Raks is clutching a jumbo hot dog smothered in mustard and tomato sauce. He's already eaten half of it.

As Ryan leads the way back up, Bon Jovi's *Keep The Faith* is coming over the PA. We're still in a musical time warp. Taking care not to spill the coffees, Ryan heads past the green-jacketed stewards and down the terracing. I'm assuming he's aiming towards where we stood for the first half, but instead of stopping when he gets there, he carries on going, eventually coming to a halt by a crush barrier right up against the fencing separating our supporters from the away section.

"This should be a better viewpoint for the second half," he says.

Taking a coffee, I look over Ryan's shoulder and through the mesh towards the Castleton fans. They've come all the way down from Cumbria, but they've brought a decent crowd. Well into the hundreds. A big bald-headed bloke in a sweatshirt catches my eye and raises his middle finger. I quickly look away.

Out on the pitch there's some sort of kids' penalty competition going on at the far end. Letchy The Lion, our mascot, is acting as compere, but there seems to be some sort of dispute over who's taken a kick and who hasn't. It's started raining and everyone looks like they'd rather be somewhere else. The Castleton subs are doing stretching exercises in the centre circle, and the Letchford lot are playing keepy-uppy in our goalmouth.

"Who's that?" Raks asks, pointing to one of our subs. It's a youngish-looking lad with bleached hair and neon blue boots. He's keeping the ball up with just about every body part imaginable, like a performing seal. He finishes off by trapping it between the heel of his boot and his arse, turning to the crowd as if he's expecting a round of applause. He doesn't get one.

Ryan tuts, turning away from the pitch.

"That's Danny Holmes. Our record signing. Flash bastard."

I nod. I've heard of Danny Holmes. He was some sort of whiz-kid striker at Man U, but then he did his cruciate, was out for eighteen months and never really got another chance. We still ended up paying a hundred and fifty grand for him, though.

"Why's he on the bench then?" I ask.

"He's not fully fit," Ryan says. "He never is. If he manages ninety minutes all season we'll be doing well. He's always got a tight hamstring or damaged ligaments, or shin splints. Something niggling. The thing is, if he spent as much time in the gym as he does swanning around town in his Porsche, we might just get our money's worth out of him."

Letchy's penalty competition has ground to a halt. It's starting to get dark and the floodlights are slowly flickering into life. I take a swig of coffee and check my mobile. No more messages from Zoe. There's a squeal of static from the PA system and then the opening bars of *The Boys Are Back In Town*. Another chorus of half-hearted booing breaks out and I look up to see the teams straggling back out onto the pitch. The ref blows his whistle and the second half gets under way.

Letchford are attacking our end now and almost straight from the kick-off a long diagonal ball from Tony O'Neill sails into the Castleton box. Leroy Lewton slides in from our left flank just as a Castleton defender slides in from the opposite direction. There's a collision, the defender flies in one direction, Leroy flies in the other and the ball harmlessly trundles out for a goal kick. When the players have finished picking themselves up and jogged back towards the halfway line, there's a huge muddy cross left behind in the penalty area. It looks like the site of buried treasure in a kids' pirate book. X marks the spot. Somewhere behind us a bloke's voice pipes up.

"Someone should get out there with a spade," he says.

Everyone laughs. Unfortunately that's just about the entertainment high spot for the next thirty-five minutes. Dave Nicholson's still having a shocker. As the digital timer on the scoreboard flicks over to 80:00 he launches himself into a flying tackle on the Castleton number 16, misses, and demolishes the advertising hoarding for Silk And Satin Table Dancing Club. It's his most useful contribution to the afternoon.

"Ten minutes to go," Ryan says. "It'll start to get interesting soon."

I blink, wondering what he means. It looks to me like it's heading for a 0-0 draw. Both teams have settled for it.

"I don't mean on the pitch," Ryan says. It's as if he's read my thoughts. "That's bollocks. I mean here. Look around you."

I've been too busy watching the match to really take notice of what's been happening in the stands, but now for the first time it registers. Groups of youngish lads are starting to form, gradually edging towards our side of the terracing, nearer to the away fans. Looking behind me, I spot the DVD boys. They nod at me again, then grin at Ryan. Further up I can see some other lads I recognise from the back of the school bus. Without realising it, we've been absorbed into a gang too. All of a sudden there's excitement in the air. It's an odd feeling I can't quite put my finger on. A bit scary. But good.

I glance across towards the away section and see almost a mirror image of what's going on in our part of the ground. Gangs forming, advancing towards the fencing. It's probably nothing sinister. Just part of a ritual that I'm not used to yet. Still, it's hard not to conjure up the image of soldiers manoeuvring before a battle. But football violence died out years ago didn't it?

I look at Ryan. There's a sort of half-smile on his lips.

"Told you it would be a better viewpoint from here, didn't I?" he says.

Strange things are starting to happen. The match is still going nowhere, but the crowd seems to be getting more and more animated. The chanting is getting louder, building and building as each set of fans taunts the other.

Shit Ground No Fans from Castleton.

Your Support Is Fucking Shit from our lot.

You've Never Won Fuck All from Castleton.

You Dirty Northern Bastards from our lot.

There's real vitriol in some of the stuff that's being bandied about, but we're right in there, belting out each of the songs like our lives depend on it. Things get cranked up another notch when the Castleton fans start bringing up the history between the two clubs.

Did You Cry In Ninety-One? they're goading over and over again.

At first there's just booing from our section but then a chant of *Wankers, Wankers, Wankers* breaks out. It's not the wittiest response, but it's having the desired effect, drowning out any sound that's coming from the Castleton lot.

By the next time I look at the timer, it's showing 87:00. The chanting is dying down. Over to the left I notice something going on in the technical area. John Whyman, the Letchford manager, is waving his arms around like a windmill, trying to get a message across, and the fourth official is heading towards the touchline flashing up the numbers 16 and 22 on his digital board. Leroy Lewton is being substituted.

"Oh shit," Ryan says, as Leroy starts trudging off.

I turn towards him.

"What's up?" I ask.

"Have you seen who's coming on?"

I look across to the dugouts just in time to see Leroy shaking hands with his replacement. Blond hair. Blue boots. Danny Holmes. As the details of the substitution come over the PA system, the response from the Letchford fans is roughly fifty-fifty cheers and boos. The Castleton fans are a lot more certain about how they feel, launching into *Rent Boy, Rent Boy*.

Danny doesn't have much impact on the game. In fact for the first three minutes he's on, he doesn't even touch the ball. The scoreboard is showing 90:00, yellow digits glowing in the gloom. I didn't see how much stoppage-time the fourth official put up, but the tannoy announcer has just given it as two minutes.

Carl Butterworth has got the ball midway inside our half. The Castleton players are backing off, looking to run the clock down, and they're letting Butterworth advance towards the centre circle. All of a sudden there's movement in front of him. Danny Holmes spins away from his marker and hurtles into the Castleton box just as Butterworth launches a long ball over the top. Garry Puncheon, the Castleton goal-keeper, sensing the danger, comes flying off his line, then stops. He's stranded. The ball arcs through the air, skims off Danny Holmes's head, sails over Puncheon and nestles in the back of the net.

There's a moment of stunned silence, then pandemonium breaks out. A huge roar erupts as a tidal wave of bodies crashes down the terracing towards where Danny Holmes is standing, back to the crowd, thumbs pointing to the name on his shirt. In a split second I'm lifted off my feet and carried over to the left, then the right, then finally back to where I started. I'm vaguely aware that I've cracked my kneecap against the crush barrier but it doesn't matter. We're 1-0 up in stoppage time. As the roar dies down I look around for Raks and Ryan. Ryan's on my right, but Raks has been carried further down to the left. He's making his way back up, eyes wide.

"Danny Fucking Holmes!" he laughs.

I start laughing too, but Ryan looks serious.

"Don't count your chickens," he says.

The game kicks off again. Castleton are attacking in desperation now, raining balls into our box, everyone apart from their keeper in our half, blue shirts everywhere. Worryingly, Letchford are defending deep rather than trying to keep things up at the Castleton end. It's a dodgy strategy, but it looks like it's going to work. The ref has checked his watch a couple of times.

One last ball is hoofed into our penalty area and Tommy Sharp rises to nod it clear. He's misjudged his jump and he heads it straight up in the air.

"Razor, you daft bastard," someone moans.

The ball drops in slow motion. As it lands, spinning in the mud, a huge melee breaks out in our six-yard box. For some reason we just can't get it away. Paul Hood tries, but his clearance cannons off Tony O'Neill's backside and skids across the goalmouth. Jimmy Knapper dives to his right but it's too late. Mark Young, the Castleton number 18, stabs it home. 1-1.

A deafening cheer goes up from the away support. Some of them were already heading for the exits, but now they're spilling back down towards the front of the stand, dancing around, chanting *Going Up, Going Up, Going Up*.

My head is spinning. Ninety minutes of garbage and then two goals in thirty seconds.

"Bastards," Raks whispers.

I look at Ryan. His eyes are closed and he's shaking his head.

Right next to where we're standing, a Castleton fan in his twenties starts hurling insults at us. He's gripping the wire fencing so hard his knuckles are going white. As he pulls the wire mesh backwards and forwards, his eyeballs are bulging and his neck tendons are sticking out.

"You wankers," he's screaming. "You fucking wankers."

There's a blur of movement as three lads from our side of the barrier charge across aiming kicks at the wire and sending the bloke back a couple of paces. I'm shocked, but before I have a chance to do or say anything, another group of Letchford lads barges past me, squaring up to the mob that's rapidly forming on the other side of the fence. I'm about to say something to Ryan when I notice that he's not there. He's jostled his way through the crowd until he's standing virtually nose-to-nose with the Castleton fans, shouting and gesticulating.

All hell is breaking loose. A phalanx of stewards is arrowing up the slope towards us. Some of the Castleton lads are trying to climb over the barrier into our section, while fans from both sides are tearing at the wire, trying to pull it down. The ordinary punters, the old blokes and the young kids, are taking evasive action now, backing away across to the left hand edge of the terracing. Out on the pitch the final few seconds of the match are being played out, but nobody's watching.

I'm just turning towards Raks when there's a sudden jolt of pain at the side of my head, just above my ear.

"Fucking hell," I shout, hunching over, clutching my hand to where a lump is already forming on my scalp.

"What's going on?" Raks says.

There's a jingling noise and something lands on the concrete in front of me. A two pence piece. Things start to make sense.

"Bastards are coining us," I say, rubbing my head, checking my fingertips for blood.

"You OK?"

I nod. Adrenalin is surging through me now. My heart is pounding and there's a strange metallic taste in my mouth. I feel dizzy and out of breath. The pain in my head is fading away and being replaced by something else. Anger. Raw anger. Looking past the scrum of bodies on our side of the fence and into the Castleton fans I swear I can see a bloke pointing directly at me, coin poised between his thumb and forefinger, laughing.

As another penny whistles past my ear, some sort of primeval instinct takes over. Before I can think of the implications, I've vaulted over the crush barrier and charged towards the fence. I'm down past Ryan, kicking out, aiming at the hands of the Castleton fans still gripping the wire mesh. I'm completely out of control.

Somewhere, through the chanting and the swearing, I hear the sound of the referee blowing the final whistle. Shooting a glance towards the pitch I see the players heading for the tunnel. The other three stands are already almost empty. It's just the Kop that's still heaving with bodies.

As I swing another kick towards the barrier I feel a hand on my shoulder. I spin round. It's Ryan. Raks is right behind him.

"Come on," Ryan says, yanking at my arm. "Got to get a move on."

The tannoy announcer is thanking us for coming and telling us that the attendance has been 5,988. He's wishing us a safe journey home. We're not interested. We've got other things to think about. We sprint back up the terracing and bundle down the stairs. All around us the gangs of Letchford lads are spontaneously joining together now, like regiments forming themselves into an army. As he pushes his way to the front, it becomes pretty clear that Ryan's one of the generals. The exit gates are open and we charge straight out, heading left towards where the away fans are starting to spill into the car park.

The battered old supporters' coaches we saw on our way in are standing over to the right, doors open and engines revving, but there's a no-man's land of about fifty yards between the exits and the buses. Some of the Castleton fans are making a run for the coaches, but fifty or sixty are standing their ground as we advance towards them. Stewards are starting to appear, but there's nothing they can do. The two sets of fans are twenty yards apart and closing. Everything seems to be happening at about a million miles an hour. Ryan's up ahead and Raks is next to me.

"Fuck," he says. "What are we doing?"

There's no time to answer. The first punches are

being thrown and Ryan's throwing them. A couple of the lads in front of me are hesitating, holding back, but I'm on autopilot. I barge my way through and run straight into a kick in the stomach. The funny thing is, I feel the impact but it doesn't actually hurt. I double over slightly and then look up at the bloke who kicked me. He's a bit older than I am, about the same height, chubby with short blond hair. Nothing special. He grins at me then swings his left fist into my cheek. There's a thud and the taste of blood in my mouth, but again, it doesn't hurt. In an odd sort of way I quite enjoy the feeling.

I'm grinning now, and the bloke who's been hitting me has an uncertain look in his eyes. I take a step forward, swinging my right fist towards him, but he puts his arms up and I hit his elbow. Straight away I launch another right and this time I connect with the tip of his nose. There's a squishing sound and blood spurts, black under the orange car park lighting. It looks unreal, like a bad special effect. I shift my weight across to the other side, driving a left upper-cut into the bloke's face as he lurches forwards, trying to fend off the punches. One more whack to the back of his head and he's on the deck. It's an almost indescribable sensation. I suppose deep down every lad wants to know if he could handle himself in a fight. Well now I know. I can.

I'm about to aim a kick at the blond kid but I'm knocked sideways by a big bloke in a denim jacket, flailing backwards, trying to keep his balance. Fists and feet are flying everywhere. The air is filled with the sound of trainers scuffling on wet tarmac. In that split second I don't know if the big lad is Castleton or Letchford. Just to be on the safe side, I hit him in the side of the head. Another body comes flying past me, and this time there's no mistaking the identity. It's a Castleton fan in a replica shirt, ducking and diving, trying to avoid a volley of haymakers from a skinny Asian lad. Raks.

The whole area is in complete chaos. Trying to take it all in is like watching random frames from a film projected at five times the normal speed. I whirl round on the spot, dodging under a left hook from a gangly kid with black gelled hair, swinging my elbow at him as he stumbles to one side. I miss and nearly touch down as someone falls against the back of my legs. Spinning to my left I catch sight of a tall red-haired lad, a lad I've seen on the Parkway bus, landing a forearm smash into the face of a big bald-headed bloke. It's the chap who gave me the finger at half time. As the bald bloke staggers away, the Letchford lad sees me and winks.

The fighting is over in seconds. The Castleton lot are outnumbered and coming off worst. One by one they're breaking away and scattering towards the coaches and we're chasing after them, raining punches and kicks on anything that moves. I'm just starting to think that we're actually going to follow the Castleton fans onto the buses when a police riot van screams around the corner from the back of the Main Stand. The back doors fly open and a team of coppers in helmets and visors and body armour starts charging towards us.

Now we're the ones running. Back along the North Stand, round the corner and along the side of the Family Stand, zigzagging through the lads and dads and the family groups, our army breaking up, trying to get lost in the crowd. As I run I look around, hoping to catch sight of Raks and Ryan, and sure enough there they are, keeping pace as we sprint across the final few yards of the car park and head towards the Letchford Industrial Estate.

By the time we're a hundred yards up the road, there's no need to run any more. The coppers gave up the chase long ago. Raks bounds across towards me, gasping, out of breath, laughing like a hyena. He jumps up and puts me in a headlock.

"Tommy Boy," he says, ruffling my hair and letting me go.

Ryan steps in between us, throwing his arms round our shoulders and squeezing, like a father with his two favourite sons.

"What did you think of that then lads?" he says.

Raks shakes his head.

"Fucking amazing," he says. His eyes are sparkling. He looks completely off his head, high on violence.

Ryan looks at me.

"What about you Tom?"

My lips move but no sound comes out. The lining of my throat is ripped and sore from all the chanting, but that's not the reason why I'm saying nothing. I'm completely lost for words. All sorts of thoughts are swirling through my mind. I think of Zoe's text before the game. Have fun. Take care. I think of my dad this morning, telling me to keep out of trouble. I think about what's just happened. The sights. The sounds. The feelings. It's just mad. I've never experienced anything like it.

Twenty minutes ago, ten minutes even, I was a completely different person. But now everything's changed. And I just don't know how I could possibly describe what I'm feeling. One thing I do know though. I'm hooked.

six

It's bright today. Late October, just gone half past seven on Monday morning, but the sun's in the sky and the birds are singing. It feels like it's going to be a good day. I heave myself up onto the wall of the Bulls Head beer garden and Raks boosts himself up next to me.

"Come on then," he says.

I look around. We're earlier than usual and hardly any of the other kids have arrived at the bus stop yet. I reach down into my bag and get out the newspaper I've just bought. *The Sun*. The headline says *NEW PRISONS FIASCO*, but it's not the news I'm looking for. Opening the paper to the middle pages, I pull out the *Super Goals* supplement. *28 Pages. Britain's No 1 Pullout.* Wayne Rooney's on the front cover, snarling and looking aggrieved about something, but I'm not interested in that. I'm flicking through the Premier League reports and the Championship reports and the League One reports, back towards the League Two news.

"Anything?" Raks says.

"Not yet." I keep on scanning, across the pages and down the columns. The League Two table is on page 24. Letchford are down to 18th.

"Come on," Raks says. "You must have gone past it." He reaches across me, pulling the edge of the paper up so that he can look too.

I turn over another page, and there it is.

WHYMAN RUES DEFENSIVE LAPSE
Letchford Town 1 Castleton Rovers 1
Letchford boss John Whyman fumed as his League Two strugglers failed to hold onto their lead.

In a match that sprang to life in second half stoppage time, record signing Danny Holmes shook off his injury woes to head the Tangerines ahead, only for Mark Young to level for Castleton after a scramble in the Letchford goalmouth with literally seconds remaining.

Whyman said : "To say the least I'm truly disappointed. It was two points thrown away.

"I thought we defended well all match. We showed great control but a momentary lapse has cost us dear."

In a final blow for Whyman, on an afternoon he'll want to forget, Letchford and Castleton fans clashed in ugly scenes in the minutes after the final whistle.

I look at Raks. He looks at me.

"We're in!" I shout.

We both start laughing. We were there. We were involved. And now it's here in black and white. In *The Sun*. Validation. In the oddest sort of way it feels like the biggest achievement of my life.

"Unbelievable," Raks says. He takes the paper out of my hands and reads the last sentence out loud. "*Fans clashed in ugly scenes in the minutes after the final whistle.*"

We both laugh again, and we're still laughing when a voice I recognise cuts in.

"What's so funny?" It's Zoe.

Instantly I'm embarrassed, caught unawares. I grab *Super Goals* back from Raks and shove it into my bag. It's like cramming porn mags under the bed when I hear my dad coming up the stairs.

"Oh, nothing much," I say. I slide down from the

wall and give Zoe a kiss. She smells nice. Freshly washed hair and body spray. "You OK? I've not seen you all weekend."

She nods.

"I tried to call you yesterday afternoon but your phone was off. Was the match good on Saturday?"

I sniff. I'm calmer now.

"Yeah. It was alright."

Zoe smiles. She's wearing lipstick today.

"I looked out for the result on *Sky*," she says. "It was a draw wasn't it?"

"Yeah. One-all. We should have won though." I look at her and notice that her eyes are being drawn down towards my feet. Or to be more precise, my shoes. Blue and white Nikes with a red swoosh.

"No school shoes today?" she asks.

"Nah." I try sound offhand. In truth my school shoes are stuffed in my bag. I took them off and changed into my Nikes the minute I got round the corner into Wolverton Road. Raks did exactly the same. We'll be putting our jeans on as soon as we get into the toilets at Parkway.

"Your dad not mind?"

I shake my head.

"Nah," I say again. But of course my dad doesn't know.

Zoe's looking at my face now. There's a flicker of concern in her eyes. She reaches up with her hand, running her fingers over the bump on my right cheek. It's where I got punched by the blond lad, outside Southlands on Saturday.

"What's happened here?" she asks. Her green eyes are watching me intently.

"Bloody hell," I say. "It's like *Twenty Questions*. I got elbowed yesterday morning, playing for Dynamo." I thought she might ask about my face so I already had my answer lined up. I hope it doesn't sound too rehearsed.

"Looks sore," she says.

I shrug.

"It's alright." I push my tongue into the side of my mouth, into the rough patch where my teeth mashed against the inside of my cheek. At the same time I reach up to feel the lump on the side of my head where the coin hit me. The lump's still there, but I don't think Zoe can see it. "Anyway, am I going to see you tonight? Mondays are usually good for you aren't they?"

She shakes her head.

"Not tonight. I've got *Oliver* rehearsals after school, right through until seven o'clock, so I'll be whacked out by the time I get home."

I raise my eyebrows.

"Rehearsals already?"

She nods.

"We've not got long you know. It's only six weeks, so I'm going to be staying late at college quite a lot this half term. I've got pages of dialogue to learn, and I have to sing a song too. *That's Your Funeral*. Well, not just me. Simon too."

"Simon?" I say, trying to keep the concern out of my voice.

"Simon Matthews," Zoe says. "Mr Sowerberry. He's really nice. You'd like him."

"Right," I say, as cheerfully as I can.

"Actually, I can give you the date of the performance now." She dips into her shoulder bag and brings out her diary. "Friday December 15th. Eight o'clock in the drama studio. You're definitely coming, aren't you?"

"Course," I say.

"You too, Raks?"

Raks nods.

"Count me in."

I check my watch. It's just gone quarter to eight. There's a hiss of air brakes and I look up to see our bus at the crossroads.

"Right then," I say, picking up my bag. "Got to go."

Zoe stands on tiptoes and gives me a peck on the lips.

"See you then." She pulls a strand of hair out of her eyes. "And sorry about tonight. It'll be hard this next few weeks, but I'll make it up to you, yeah?"

"Yeah," I say.

The bus stops and the doors swing open. I climb on board and follow Raks along the aisle. I wave to Zoe, she waves back and then the bus pulls away.

We sit down. We're behind the Dalton twins. Matching blue parkas, matching telephone-directory-thickness sci-fi novels. I put my bag at my feet and fish out *Super Goals*, flicking through to page 27 again.

"Is it still there?" Raks asks, grinning.

I laugh.

"It's still there."

We don't say much for the next ten minutes. The Tobemeister's playing *Three From The Eighties* on Letchford Sound but I'm not really listening. I scroll up and down the menu on my phone and think about the History assignment I was supposed to be working on yesterday. Raks is staring out of the window, at the leaves swirling in the breeze and the rubbish rattling in the hedgerows. As we turn onto the Medstone road he takes a deep breath and puffs out his cheeks.

"So what did your dad say when you got back on Saturday evening?"

I wrinkle my forehead.

"Not a lot. Asked how it was. Said he might come to a game one time."

Raks laughs.

"What did you say to that?"

I shrug.

"Just said I didn't think it would be his cup of tea."

We watch the countryside flashing past for another couple of minutes. Every now and again Raks is shaking his head, the way he does when he's trying to get something straightened out in his mind.

"It was one hell of a day, wasn't it?" he says eventually.

I push my tongue into the ripped inside of my mouth.

"You could say that."

"I couldn't sleep," Raks says. "Saturday night, I just lay there, thinking about everything that happened. I don't mean the match. I mean what happened afterwards. It was going over and over in my head."

I nod.

"Yeah. I didn't get a wink on Saturday night either. Yesterday morning, playing for Dynamo, I was like a zombie. I spent ninety minutes trundling up and down the right wing, but I hardly touched the ball. I wasn't into the game at all. Same as you, things were just going round and round my brain."

The bus stops outside the chip shop in Medstone and two girls get on. Year Elevens. Good-looking and self-confident. Our eyes follow them as they pass by, heading towards the back, but they don't notice us.

"The whole thing was weird though, wasn't it?"

73

Raks says, as the bus draws away from the kerb again. "When it all kicked off, something came over me. I was punching and kicking people, but it didn't seem like it was *me* who was doing the punching and kicking. I just didn't feel guilty about it at all. It's like because I was part of a crowd I wasn't responsible for what I was doing."

"Yeah," I say. "I know what you mean."

Raks has got a faraway look in his eyes now.

"And I felt like I had all this power, like there was danger all around but nothing could hurt me. It was this amazing buzz. It was..." his voice trails off, and he shakes his head again.

I just nod. I know that he probably wants me to help him put things into words, but there's no point. I couldn't do it on Saturday, and I still can't. It was a complete overload. Too intense. But brilliant.

The rest of the journey into Letchford seems to pass more quickly than normal. It only feels like a couple of minutes since we left Medstone, but already my watch is saying it's quarter past eight and we're heading along towards the Parkway all-weather football pitches. I'm just thinking about getting my bits and pieces together when someone heaves themselves into the seat behind us, sticks a hand between the headrests and ruffles my hair. Ducking out of the way, I twist round to see what's going on. A pink, freckly, grinning face looms over me. It's the big, red-haired Letchford lad who laid out the bald-headed Castleton fan on Saturday. The one who winked at me.

"Well, well, well," he says, looking at me, then at Raks. "It's the fucking Kray twins."

We all laugh.

"I'm Gary," he says. "Gary Simmons."

Raks and me shake Gary's hand.

"I'm Raks," Raks says. "And this is Tom."

"You two are mates of Ryan's, right?" Gary says.

We both nod.

"You're dark horses, you are," Gary says. "I'd never have had you two down as Letchford lads, but you're a right pair of fucking yobbos."

I smile, shaking my head. I've never been called a yobbo before.

Gary looks out of the window. We're coming through the gates now.

"You should sit up the back with us," he says. "Not down here with all these muppets." He looks around to see if anyone's going to object to being called a muppet. Nobody does.

"Yeah, thanks Gary." I try to keep it low-key, try not to show how chuffed I am.

Gary stands up. He's said his piece. He nods at us both, then heads for the front of the bus. His mates from the back seat pile down after him. They look like a team of debt-collectors. Gary, another white lad, and a massive black kid who virtually blocks out the light as he comes past.

"I wouldn't want to spill his pint," Raks says.

I laugh. We watch the lads disappear down the stairs and then we stand up. By the time we're out on the pavement, heading down towards reception, Gary and the rest of the gang are long gone.

Five minutes later we're sitting in our tutor room waiting for Mr Green to turn up. When it's not being used for registration or for tutor group meetings, Room 16 is the GCSE Art and Design studio. The whole place stinks of oil paint and PVA glue. All sorts of artworks are balanced on shelves or against the radiators, drying or waiting to be mounted. Up against the far wall there's an eight-foot rowing boat made from papier mache. Apparently, some of the Year Elevens did it for a project last year. They never got to try it out though. Health and Safety issues.

The place is packed this morning and everyone seems to be talking at twice the normal volume. At least three types of music are competing for air space, blasting out of mobile phones in different parts of the room. There's some hip-hop, some indie and some slit-your-wrists dirge about wanting to commit suicide coming from the direction of the black trench coat brigade.

Usually I'm a bit self-conscious at times like this, a bit aware that me and Raks are slightly out on a limb. But I'm feeling more confident today. Over by the stationery cupboard, Susie Black and Carly Watts are locked in conversation. Susie and Carly are what you'd call popular girls. Well dressed. Quite fit. Pretty bright. Every so often, one or the other of them shoots a glance at me and Raks. They're gossiping about us. And judging from the way Carly's just smiled at me, what they're saying isn't too terrible.

I nudge Raks.

"Don't make it too obvious," I say. "But check out Susie and Carly."

Raks takes a quick look. He raises his eyebrows.

"See what I'm getting at?"

"Yeah." Raks shakes his head. "It's a bit of a first isn't it? Those two normally look at us like we're something they've just scraped off the bottom of their shoe. What's changed?"

"Well it can only be one thing," I say. "They've got wind of what happened on Saturday."

Raks frowns.

"Already?"

I shrug.

"You know what the bush telegraph is like round here. Everyone knew that David Riley had shagged Louise Wilson before she did." I'm exaggerating, but not much. "People know who we are now. We're going to start getting some respect."

Raks smiles. All sorts of possibilities are starting to occur to him.

"Susie and Carly eh? Which one is going to be the lucky lady? Or maybe I'll have them both on the go."

I pull a face.

"You couldn't handle one of them, let alone two."

"Well, I'll have to," Raks says. "I'm not going to be getting any help from you, am I?"

I laugh. I look towards Susie and Carly again. Susie sees me. She flicks her eyes down towards the ground then back in my direction. A little twinge of guilt goes through me. Flirting behind Zoe's back. Bad boy. Still there's no law against it. It's harmless. Window shopping. And it's just nice to be noticed again. I'd almost forgotten what it felt like. I lean back in my chair and smile. All of a sudden life is good.

There's a bit of a commotion over to the left. Looking across I can see Mr Green coming through the door. Grey hair with a side parting, moustache, glasses perched on the end of his nose, England One Day International cricket shirt, keys on a chain on his belt.

"OK then guys," he's saying. "If we could just have people sitting down, we'll make a start."

A couple of kids giggle. The music gets turned down, but nobody makes much of an effort to find a chair.

Mr Green tries again.

"OK. Come on guys. Chop chop."

Once more, no real response. Mr Green's looking slightly edgy now. The shaving rash on his neck is starting to glow bright red. I feel a bit sorry for him really. He's not a bad bloke. He's fiftyish, a Geography teacher of the old school, a throwback to the seventies and eighties. You'd get fairly short odds on him owning a corduroy jacket with elbow patches. Anything goes with Mr Green. On the first day of the autumn term he let it be known that he wanted us to call him Alan, and it's turning out to be a bit of a rod for his back.

"Guys..." He's trying to disguise the desperation in his voice now.

Joe Humphrey pats him on the shoulder.

"Chill out, Alan," he says.

Another minute passes. People are still milling around, so Mr Green decides to press ahead anyway.

"Right," he says. "We won't bother with the formalities. Just a quick head count. Hands up if you're not here." It's the same joke he cracks every few days. Nobody laughs.

Ten minutes later and Mr Green's finally winding things up. He's gone through his usual motivational monologue, and he's given out a list of messages as long as my arm. Don't drop chewing gum on the carpets. Don't wear jewellery in the science labs. Please stop smoking cannabis in the toilets. Students are expected to attend *all* their classes, not just those that fit in with their social diary. Mr Barnard the Principal would like to remind people not to bring mobile phones to school, or if they must, keep them switched off. The bell rings and people stand up, stretching and yawning, slowly heading for the door.

I look at Raks. His eyes are glazed, staring into space. I click my fingers in front of his face.

"Come on. Get in gear."

Raks blinks.

"I was miles away. What have we got first thing?"

"Business Studies."

Raks pulls a face.

"Gillespie."

We both laugh.

Room 37b is already filling up by the time we arrive. Mr Gillespie's nowhere to be seen, but he's definitely been in the vicinity. There's a Newcastle United mug full of milky tea steaming on a table near the front, and he's written *ASSETS AND LIQUIDITY* in big black letters on the whiteboard.

"Shit," Raks says. "*Liquidity*. How's that going to sound when Gillespie says it?"

"Dunno," I reply. "But I'm sure we're going to find out."

I'm just looking around for somewhere to sit when I see a familiar face grinning at me from a table in the far corner. Ryan. Cutting through the crowd, we pull out a couple of chairs and sit down.

"How's it going lads?" Ryan asks.

"Not bad," I tell him. I reach into my bag and get out *Super Goals*. "Have a butcher's at this. Page 27."

Ryan takes it from me, leafing through towards the back. Finding the right page, he squints his eyes, whizzing through the text and nodding. He smiles.

"Nice one. It got mentioned on *Lincolnshire Today* last night too, when they were showing the goals. *Police are concerned about the recent escalation of violence in and around the Southlands Stadium.* That was what they were saying."

I nod. I pick a piece of loose skin from along the

side of my thumbnail and look at Ryan.

"You knew there was going to be trouble on Saturday, yeah?" I'm pretty sure that I've read the situation right, but I just want to be certain.

Ryan laughs, handing back *Super Goals*.

"I had a reasonable suspicion," he says. "Just recently it's been taking off again. Started the second half of last season, and then carried through into this one. We've been getting a bit of a firm together. It's lads from all over town, but there's quite a few from this place. Jimmy and Scotty in the Sixth Form. Then there's the Year Elevens — Gary Simmons and his mates on your bus. Rob Miller and Big Jerome Thompson."

Raks shakes his head.

"But when we were in the café on Saturday, and I asked you about trouble at Letchford games, you said it had all died down these days."

Ryan shakes his head.

"You said that. I just didn't contradict you."

Raks frowns. He still needs a few things sorting out.

"So if you were fairly positive there was going to be a bit of a ruck, how did you know me and Tom would be able to handle ourselves?"

Ryan holds his hands out, palms upwards.

"I just felt confident. I could see you had it in you."

"That right?" I say. Not for the first time today, I'm chuffed. *I* didn't know I had it in me.

Ryan nods.

"Yeah," he says. "And I was spot-on wasn't I? You did good, lads."

I'm beaming. I feel about two foot taller.

Ryan carries on.

"You're part of the crew now. We're away the next

couple of Saturdays — Hereford in the league and then Kidderminster in the first round of the FA Cup — but then we've got Ashborough at home on the 18th. You're coming, yeah?"

Raks is nodding.

"Too right."

I don't say anything, but I don't need to. I'll be there. It's nearly three weeks away, but already there's a churning in my stomach. A craving. Until Saturday I didn't realise how dull my life really was. And now I can't wait for Saturday to happen all over again. To experience all those sensations one more time. The adrenalin rush. The taste in my mouth. The breathlessness and the light-headedness. The feeling of being one step from the edge of disaster.

Up at the front of the room, something's happening. People are sliding their backsides off the tables and sitting themselves down. Mr Gillespie's here. Tall and thin with spiky black hair. He picks up his Newcastle United mug and takes a slurp of tea.

"Right then," he says. "Today we're going to talk about assets and liquidity."

A ripple of laughter goes round the room. The Geordie accent has done the trick again.

"Mr Gillespie," Kelly Fox says. "What's Lick Widdity?"

The next fifty minutes or so seem to pass me by. Mr Gillespie has had one of his better mornings classroom-behaviour-wise and I'm sure he's given out plenty of good, useful information but I've not really been taking it in. I look at my notes and see lots of stuff about cash flow, liability and fixtures and fittings, but it doesn't make much sense to me.

As the bell goes to end the session and we start to pack our things away, a mobile phone goes off.

Everyone freezes. A few people start looking guilty. Others are glancing around, trying to work out where the sound is coming from. Slowly but surely it begins to occur to us all that there's only one person who would have Geordie anthem *The Blaydon Races* as his ringtone. Mr Gillespie.

The room is deathly quiet. Mr Gillespie looks mortified. He reaches into his pocket and mutes his phone.

"Mr Barnard will have you for that," I say.

It's not the best joke I've ever cracked. In fact it's not much of a joke at all. But suddenly there's laughter. One second the room was in silence, and now people are pissing themselves. Looking at me and guffawing like I've just come up with the funniest gag since *My Dog's Got No Nose*. It's not everyone of course. The emo lot and the swotty ones and some of the indie mob are pretending not to have noticed, but plenty of kids are having a good old laugh. The popular ones, the chavs, the townies, the hip-hop crew. Even Snoop's joining in, and I've never even seen him smile before.

For a second or two I'm puzzled. This time last week nobody would have noticed me if I'd painted my arse blue and danced naked on the tables. But now I'm the centre of attention. And it's at that point that it all makes sense. I thought the bush telegraph worked fast around here. I just didn't realise how fast. It isn't only Carly Watts and Susie Black who know I've jumped up the Parkway hierarchy. It's everyone. The word is well and truly out. I *am* someone.

I swing my bag onto my shoulder and head down towards the door with Ryan and Raks following. Even out in the corridor I can still hear people laughing. Laughing at my joke, even though it was crap. Because that's what you do when a kid with a bit of influence pipes up. Confidence surges through me. It's a great feeling. For the very first time, I'm completely at home at Parkway College. 100% settled. There's no doubt about it now. I've arrived.

seven

It's just gone quarter past one. The bell for Wednesday afternoon registration is going to go in five minutes and me and Raks are heading into the toilets for a quick pit stop. The urinals are busy so we use the cubicles. Raks goes into trap one and I go into trap three. Whoever's in trap two isn't a well man. The walls between the cubicles are paper-thin and you can't avoid the sound effects. There's a squealing, like air being slowly released from a balloon, followed by rapid splashing and a final burst of what sounds like gunfire. To round things off, a low moan comes floating over the partition.

"Nobody smoke!" somebody shouts.

I zip up my fly, pull the chain and unlock the cubicle. The toilet is clearing out now, as people start making their way to their tutor rooms. I cross to the sinks, squirt a glob of pink handwash into my palm and push down the hot tap. I rinse my hands, then dry them on a paper towel. Back in trap two there's the sound of frantic bog-roll-dispenser use. Raks's cubicle door swings open and he steps out, clicking the cap on a big black permanent marker.

"Been busy?" I ask.

He grins.

I push past him and stick my head round the cubicle door. In four-inch letters on the left hand wall it says *LTFC – PRIDE OF ENGLAND*.

I tut.

"Naughty boy."

He shrugs.

"Makes a change from the ejaculating cocks or offers of gay sex you usually get in bog stalls," he says.

I laugh. He's got a point.

The door to trap two opens and a big emo kid emerges. He's got a fringe over his eyes and a huge black leather jacket that's only prevented from dragging on the ground by his stack-heel shoes. I recognise him from the canteen last week. One of the band members. *Nocturnal Emission* is stencilled onto his rucksack. Looks like the Prolapsed Colon boys got voted down.

"You want to eat more fibre," I tell him.

Emo Boy grunts and shuffles off.

Raks goes across to the sinks. While he's washing his hands, I look at our reflections in the mirror. Not for the first time this week, a thought crosses my mind. A lot has changed over the last few days. Me and Raks are different people now. But on the outside everything still looks the same. We need to do something about it.

"Raks," I say. "I've come to a decision."

Raks grabs a paper towel.

"Shit." He raises his eyebrows, smiling. "That sounds ominous."

I laugh.

"No. I'm being serious."

Raks chucks his paper towel into the bin.

"What's up then?"

I run my fingers through my hair and look into the mirror again.

"The hair's got to go," I say. "We look like a pair of kids. We've got to sort it out."

Raks has stopped smiling.

"What are you suggesting, man? A proper bone-head?"

I nod.

"It's got to be done. You think of the people we knock about with now. Ryan, Gary, Jerome, Rob – they've all got short hair. Neat and sharp. And then there's us two. First and second place in the Tim Henman look-alike competition. We just don't look the part."

Raks glances at the mirror.

"You could be right," he says.

"It's got to be done," I tell him again. "I've got about a tenner on me. What about you?"

He checks his pockets, counting the coins into the palm of his hand.

"About eight fifty."

"Right then. You and me are going to be stopping off at Talking Heads on the way home."

Raks nods.

"Right you are," he says. He swings his rucksack onto his shoulder and we set off for our tutor room.

Afternoon registration with Mr Green is the usual shambles. By the time he's cracked his 'hands up if you're not here' joke and done his head count there's a full-scale argument raging in a corner of the room. Sophie Reed and Tanya Fielder are both convinced that the other one's been shit-stirring and saying things about them. As Raks and me pick up our bags and head off round the curve for ICT in Room 22, Mr Green's started trying to sort out Sophie and Tanya's problems. It sounds like it's going to be quite a long process.

The corridors are busy but it doesn't take us long to reach Room 22. The Computer Suite. A group of lads have got here before us and they're standing just inside the doorway. Two are on phones and the other three are just milling around. As we come in they step out of our way. We trudge up to the back and pull two chairs in front of one of the tatty PCs, watching as the Parkway College logo bounces around the screen. As I get out my pad and pen, I notice that someone has scratched *HAYLEY IS A DOG* onto the work surface.

People start arriving in dribs and drabs. The Dalton twins. Cassie Morton and Nita Parmar. Four girls in black puffa jackets. Snoop and a couple of his mates. The room's filling up and Mr Dickinson has appeared. He's sitting up at the front, fiddling with a laptop, one buttock perched on the edge of a table, foot swinging backwards and forwards.

I tug at Raks's sleeve.

"Look at the state of Dicko," I say.

Mr Dickinson is in his early forties. Today he's in ripped jeans and a body-hugging khaki T-shirt with *US ARMY* embroidered on the left sleeve. His shoes are a kind of halfway house between trainers and something more formal. Light brown leather with a row of stitching up the middle, pointed at the toes. They look like Red Indian canoes. The remains of his hair has been dragged forward and sprayed into a sort of fin.

Raks shakes his head.

"There's a man having a mid-life crisis if ever I saw one," he says.

Mr Dickinson's foot stops swinging. He looks around the room and nods.

"Alrighty then folks. Lets have a bit of decorum in the forum."

Thirty seconds of chair-rattling later and most people have got themselves sorted. One or two are still ambling about aimlessly, but Mr Dickinson has obviously decided he's got enough of an audience to make a start.

"Alrighty then folks," he says again. "We're starting on our Communications module this afternoon. We're going to be looking at the terminology associated with the Internet first of all, and then later, we're going to actually go on-line."

An ironic cheer goes up. The Dalton twins are shaking their heads. Bradley Ellis leans over towards me and Raks.

"It's a feast of entertainment," he says.

We all laugh.

Mr Dickinson finishes off his introduction and then gets things underway with a PowerPoint presentation on the interactive whiteboard. *The Internet And You*. You can see he's very proud of it. It's all fairly basic, but I have to give him credit, it certainly looks good. There's plenty of information to help us distinguish our *.coms* from our *.cos*, our *.orgs* from our *.govs*, and our *IPs* and *ISDNs* from our *ISPs*, but by the time we've trundled through *browsers* and *filters* and staggered onto the *advantages and disadvantages of the internet* there are quite a few glazed expressions about the place. The last page of the presentation swishes off the screen and Mr Dickinson scans the room.

"So are there any questions?"

The silence seems to go on and on. Over to the right someone makes a hollow whistling sound. All we need now is some tumbleweed blowing across the floor.

Mr Dickinson takes this silence as a good sign.

"Alrighty then. It's up to you now. First, choose a topic, maybe something that could help you with your studies in other subjects. Geography, say. Next, choose a search engine. Then finally, enter some keywords, and see what you can come up with." He slides his buttock down from the table and scans the room again. It's time to get started.

I look at Raks.

"What's it going to be then?" he asks.

"Dunno." I'm not feeling too inspired. I look at my watch. It's already gone two o'clock. Dicko's been talking for half an hour.

"Come on, man," Raks says. "Guns? Porn? On-line gambling?"

I shake my head.

"You're not going to get any of that stuff on the school network," I tell him. "There'll be all sorts of filters."

Bradley Ellis starts laughing. Glancing across I see that he's managed to find a dogging website. Joe Humphrey has got an amateur strip show on YouTube. Further over, Snoop's screen is showing a photo of a bloke in a leather mask with spikes attached. I'm not sure what it's all about but it's not Geography. I think it's fair to say the filters aren't working.

Raks clicks on the *Internet Explorer* icon and types in *Google*. The cursor flickers in the empty search box.

"Any ideas?"

I shrug. Sitting up in my chair I pull the keyboard across. Something's just occurred to me. A flash of inspiration.

"I just want to give this a go," I say.

I take the mouse from Raks and select *Pages From The UK*. I type in the keywords *FOOTBALL+ HOOLIGAN*. Then I click on *Google Search*.

Half a second later the results are in. 238,000 matches found.

Raks laughs.

"Nice one," he says. "But looking through that lot will take us until Christmas."

I nod.

"Yeah. We need to narrow it down a bit." I delete *FOOTBALL+HOOLIGAN* and try *HOOLIGAN+FIRMS*.

Another click of the mouse and we're down to 25,000 hits.

I scroll down the first ten, selecting one or two at random. To be honest it's all a bit disappointing. It's mostly anti-hooligan stuff. Highbrow articles about disenfranchised youth and the inner motivation of the thug, from *The Guardian* and *The Times*. Stuff about *The Psychology of Violence*. Messageboards full of daft comments.

I think violence spoils football. I want to keep the beautiful game beautiful.

Raks tuts.

"This is all a bit dull and worthy," he says. He grabs the mouse and leans over to type in *+LEAGUE TWO* after *HOOLIGAN+FIRMS*.

This time we've got 5,500 matches. Three down from the top of the list of the first ten is a site called *LOWERLEAGUELADS.CO.UK*.

Firms League table/Latest Odds/Your Views/ Newsdesk/Previews/New And Archive Photos And Video.

I get a little jolt in my stomach. Somehow I just know this is the one.

Another click of the mouse and we've struck gold. Rolling straight onto the screen, superimposed over a CCTV image of a broken-chair-wielding pitch invasion, is a league table. A League Two table. But it's not the usual table, with Letchford struggling down in 18th. It's a hooligan table, and in this one we're 5th. Right up in the Play-Off places.

"Fucking hell," I say, trying but failing to keep my voice down. "Check it out."

"And just look at this." Raks is pointing. "Last week's positions are in brackets. We're up four places, and Castleton are down from 5th to 10th."

"Yeah. Because we ran the bastards out of town on Saturday."

We both laugh. A few people glance in our direction, trying to see what we're up to. Mr Dickinson has started circulating, so we need to watch out. He's loitering around the girls as usual though, so we're probably in the clear for the next couple of minutes. Over by the door, Nita and Cassie are squirming in their chairs as Dicko leers over them.

Raks is still looking at the monitor. He clicks on the Letchford logo and selects the *Latest Odds* option. We're in at 3/1.

Mainly youth firm. Don't travel in numbers but home form very promising. Need 2 prov their not just gobby kids.

"*Gobby kids?*" I say. "Fucking cheek."

Raks clicks us back to the league table.

"There's just one problem with this," he says.

"What's that?"

Raks points at the screen again.

"Look who's leading."

I hadn't noticed it before. I was just so pleased to see where Letchford were. But there, at the top of pile, is the worst team of all. Mackworth.

"Shit," I say.

Raks shakes his head. Two more clicks and he's

found Mackworth's *Latest Odds*. 6/4 favourites.

Top mob in this division can pull 100+ lads for awaydays. A match 4 anyone.

We stare at the screen in silence for a few seconds.

"A hundred plus fans?" Raks says eventually. "That doesn't sound like many."

"It doesn't mean a hundred plus fans," I tell him. "It means a hundred plus lads. Fighters."

Raks nods, catching on.

"So when are we playing them at Southlands?"

I narrow my eyes, trying to visualise the fixture list in the back of the programme.

"It's not long. Middle of next month. December 16th, I think."

Raks nods again.

"That's the day we go top of the league then."

I smile. I get another churning sensation in my stomach. December 16th. It sounds like a date with destiny. I take the mouse from Raks again. I'm just about to select *Latest News*, when Mr Dickinson calls a halt to things.

"Alrighty then," he says, hitching his backside onto the table again. "I know you've not had long, but we're going to have to shut the network down now. We've got a bit of a problem." There's a slight edge of panic to his voice.

People stop what they're doing, shrugging at one another, looking puzzled. Bradley Ellis leans across.

"The Dalton twins have hacked into some sort of US Government site," he whispers. "Something to do with the Pentagon. Dodgy stuff."

I'm not sure if that's what's really happened, but Dicko's definitely rattled. Beads of sweat have sprung out on his top lip and patches are spreading out under his armpits. He certainly bears the haunted look of a man who just knows he's going to get a visit from MI5 in the not-too-distant future.

There's about fifteen minutes of the session left, but Mr Dickinson lets us go early. Usually that would be good news, but today I feel cheated. Still, I've jotted down the *LOWERLEAGUELADS* website address for future reference. We go down to the canteen for a bit, then make our way to Room 16 for the last session of the day, Tutor Guidance.

Tutor Guidance is a chance to have an informal chat with Mr Green, sort out any problems you might be having, that kind of thing. Most weeks it's fairly pointless, but today it's a total washout. Alan's not finished dealing with Sophie Reed and Tanya Fielder yet. If anything, the situation's getting worse. Even as the bell rings for the end of the afternoon, both girls are still red-eyed and tearful, bickering and jabbing their fingers at one another, while Mr Green sits between them shaking his head.

"Shit," I say, as Raks and me make our way out into the corridor. "I hope Greeny never tries to join the Samaritans."

The Preston's coach is already waiting as we go up the slope from reception. The driver is standing on the pavement smoking a cigar. It's the same bloke as always. In his fifties, greasy grey hair, beer gut and a burgundy jacket with the sleeves rolled up. *I FOUGHT THE LAW* is tattooed on his left forearm. It looks like he did it himself. As we go past, he gives us a sideways glance and coughs.

Clambering up the steps, we head towards the back. The Year Eleven girls from Medstone are halfway along the bus on the right hand side. Seeing us coming, they nudge one another and giggle. Raks looks at me and smiles.

"I'm liking this popularity lark more and more," he says.

Gary Simmons and the other lads are already in place on the back seat, so we slide ourselves in, one row down, nodding in their direction. It's usually quite rowdy up at the back, but today there's a middle-of-the-week feeling in the air and nobody's really in the mood for saying anything.

By twenty-five to four the bus has filled up. The driver has finished his cigar and we're heading out through the gates. As we go down along the perimeter fence there's some activity up ahead. They're having an emergency drill at The Tony Mantle Health And Fitness Factory. The fire alarm's ringing and the car park is full of orange women in velour tracksuits clutching energy drinks and mobile phones.

After that, the journey is pretty dull. It's warm on the bus, and as we come through the outskirts of town I can feel my eyelids getting heavier and heavier. Before long I'm spark out, dozing with my chin on my shoulder. The next thing I know, Raks is digging me in the ribs.

"Rise and shine, Sleeping Beauty," he says. "We're home."

I blink and look out of the window. The Bulls Head is coming into view. I must have been asleep for twenty minutes or so. The bus trundles to a halt and the Thurston kids start standing, making their way down to the doors. Raks gets up and I heave myself out of the seat, hoisting my bag onto my shoulder.

"See you tomorrow," a voice says.

I turn round. It's Gary Simmons.

"Yeah," I say. "See you Gary." I nod towards Rob and Jerome and follow Raks down the bus.

As I step onto the pavement I check my watch. It's just gone five past four but the sun's already on the way down, a big orange ball sinking behind the outline of Thurston Community College away to the left. Somewhere in the distance I can hear someone letting fireworks off. The bus pulls away and we head across the road, round the corner by the pub and down Lindisfarne Street towards the shops. Ahead of us, the front of Talking Heads is lit up. I suddenly remember what we were talking about in the toilets at dinnertime. Haircuts. I'd almost forgotten. A flicker of anxiety goes through me. I look at Raks.

"Scalping time," I say.

Raks looks uncertain.

"You sure about this?" he asks. "I don't know what my mum and dad are going to think about me turning up with a skinhead. I mean, what's your old man going to say?"

I snort.

"God knows," I say. "But he can hardly give me lectures on the subject of grooming can he? Half the time he looks like he's just stumbled out of a bus shelter."

Raks nods.

"What about Zoe?"

"Oh, she'll be alright about it." I sound a lot more confident than I actually feel. Zoe's always telling me I should grow my hair.

Talking Heads isn't busy. It never is. The sign in the window says *Appointments Not Always Necessary*. It's a bit of an understatement. I push through the door and sit in one of the red plastic chairs dotted along the right hand wall. Raks sits down next to me. The radio is playing quietly in the background. *The Danny Morrissey Drivetime Show* on Letchford Sound. There's only one woman working this afternoon, doing what she can to what's left on an old man's head. She's in her late twenties, good looking, with black shaggy hair tinged red at the tips. She did my hair the last time I came in. She's wearing a low-cut black top and a short black skirt over a pair of red leggings. Right on cue, Raks starts tugging at my elbow, raising his eyebrows, nodding towards the hairdresser.

I laugh.

The woman looks over in our direction.

"Be with you in a few minutes, yeah?" she says.

We nod.

I take my coat off and hang it on the back of my chair. There's a low table to the right covered with dog-eared magazines. I hand Raks a *Cosmopolitan* and get myself a copy of *Heat*. On the front cover there's a photo of some former girl band member, still trying to cling onto the arse hairs of celebrity. *My New Man's A Bad Boy. But We're Trying For A Baby.*

By the time I've flicked through the magazine, the hairdresser is brushing clippings off the old chap's shoulders and dusting his neck with talcum powder. She helps him put his coat on, he pays and he makes his way to the door. The hairdresser turns towards Raks and me.

"Who's first then?" she asks.

I glance across at Raks. He's sitting rigid, eyes glued to *Cosmopolitan*. Something about Posh's new diet. It looks like I'm going to have to take the lead. I cross to the chair and sit down as the hairdresser puts a grey vinyl gown over my shoulders. I look straight ahead, at my reflection in the mirror. My cheek still looks slightly swollen. On the shelf in front of me there's a set of clippers. My stomach twists.

"Right," the hairdresser says. "What's it going to be?"

I flick my eyes towards Raks. He's finished with *Cosmo* now, and he's looking at me. Daring me.

The hairdresser runs her hands through my hair, pulling up my fringe between her first two fingers.

"Four round the sides, some of the length and weight from the top, yeah?"

I swallow.

"No," I say. "I want to go for something different this time. Something not so long. Number two all over."

The hairdresser stops what she's doing. She stares into the mirror, right at me.

"Are you sure about that?" she asks. "Compared to what you've got, number two will seem very short. It'll be totally different."

I nod.

"Yeah, I know." I look across at Raks. He's giving me the thumbs up.

"Well," the hairdresser says, "if you're sure that's what you want."

I look into the mirror at my fluffy, little boy's haircut for a final time. It's the haircut I've been having since primary school. Since the days when it was my mum sitting behind me reading magazines. I feel a bit sad and nostalgic. But things have moved on. There's no going back now.

"Go for it," I say.

The hairdresser plugs the clippers in and switches them on, moving round until she's directly behind me. The sound of buzzing fills the air, and then a heap of brown hair falls onto my shoulder, skittering down across the front of the gown like a mouse running for cover.

The heap of hair looks massive. For a split second, a horrible thought starts to gnaw away at me. I've done something really stupid. Then I catch sight of Raks. He's shaking his head, with his hands over his mouth, making out that he's horrified by what's happening to my barnet. But I can see from his eyes that he's only pissing about. From that point on, everything is fine.

Five minutes later the hairdresser puts the clippers back on the shelf. Bringing her eyes down level with the top of my head, she brushes away loose hairs, checking that nothing has avoided the clipper blades. She straightens up and smiles. She's happy with how it looks and so am I. It's a transformation. There's no other word for it. The hairdresser picks up a mirror and shows me the back and the sides, smooth, sleek and brown, a hint of scalp showing through, giving it a bit of edge. It's not a boy's haircut any more. I feel like I've got my *look* at last.

"How's that for you?" she asks.

"Brilliant, thanks," I say, but that doesn't really do it justice. It's perfect.

The hairdresser puts the mirror down. She tears open the Velcro fastenings on the gown and pulls it forwards so that all my hair falls in a pile by my feet.

I stand up and follow her towards the desk at the back of the shop.

"That'll be £6.50 then, please," she says.

I fumble in my pocket and bring out a handful of change. I count out six fifty and hand it over, putting another pound into the tips jam jar.

"Thanks very much," the hairdresser says.

I smile and head back towards my seat. As I sit down, Raks stands up.

"It looks fucking good, man," he says. He runs a

hand through his own hair.

I grin.

Raks makes his way over to where the hairdresser is waiting.

"What's it going to be then?" she asks.

Raks doesn't hesitate.

"Number two all over."

eight

I wanted a lie-in today. Saturday is the only day when I can really have one. I deliberately didn't set my alarm clock, and I was hoping that when I opened my eyes it would be nice and late. Nine o'clock, ten o'clock. Something like that. I should have known better. Twenty-five past seven it was, when the bloke next door started hammering on his extension. He's been building the thing every weekend since before I went to primary school. That's about eleven years. I think it took less time to build the Taj Mahal.

I've been upstairs all morning. I had a shower earlier on, and since then I've been listening to music, playing on my PS2, just rattling about. Dad's in the living room, but he was on the beer again yesterday evening. It's not too much fun being around him the morning after the night before. I went down for a bowl of Rice Krispies around ten, but Dad was flaked out, drooling on the arm of the sofa, so I just left him to it.

It's getting on for five past twelve now. Zoe's coming round at quarter to one. We're getting the bus into town to have a look round the shops. Letchford are away at Kidderminster in the first round of the FA Cup this afternoon, so I'm not going to Southlands. I check myself out in the mirror on the wardrobe door, then I head for the stairs.

As I come into the living room, Dad's just waking up. He yawns and stretches and tries to give me a smile.

"Morning Tom," he says.

I sit down and snort.

"Not any more," I say.

Dad looks guilty. He wriggles himself upright and blinks a few times. He reaches for the remote control, flicking the TV on. It's a kids' show on *ITV*. Two young lads, a sort of poor man's Ant & Dec, are trying to whip a crowd of bored-looking under-tens into a frenzy. They're not having much success.

A couple of minutes pass. Neither of us is saying anything. The bloke next door has taken a break from crashing about. Now he's having an argument with his wife. It's hard to work out exactly what they're shouting at each other, but every now and then something comes through loud and clear. *What the fucking hell do you expect me to do? What do you think I am? Fucking psychic?*

I look across at Dad. He's taken his socks off and they're lying on the floor like a pair of discarded snakeskins, black against the dirty cream of the carpet. On the TV, the poor man's Ant, or it could be Dec, is sitting in a glass tank having green gunk poured over him. The cameraman cuts away to a shot of a kid in the crowd. The kid yawns and picks his nose.

I check my watch. Ten past twelve. I've only been downstairs for five minutes, but already it feels a lot longer. Dad pushes himself up off the sofa. He stretches again, rolling his head from side to side until his neck clicks.

"How's about me making us some dinner?" he says.

I shake my head.

"No, it's alright," I say. "I'll get something in town. Zoe's coming round in a bit."

He looks a bit disappointed.

"What time's she coming?" he asks.

"About quarter to one," I say.

Dad nods. He looks at the clock on the mantelpiece.

"You've got plenty of time then. I'll rustle us up an omelette and some beans. We can eat it in here, watch *Football Focus*. What do you reckon?" He looks at me, eyes all wide and hopeful.

I shrug.

"Go on then," I say.

He heads off towards the kitchen and I turn my attention back to the kids' show on TV. The final credits are rolling now. A boy band in matching beige leather jackets are miming to their latest single and the poor man's Ant & Dec are dancing with two blokes in dinosaur costumes. I shake my head and flick over to *BBC1*.

Ten minutes later Dad's back in with two purple plastic plates of omelette and beans.

"I had to use the picnic set," he says. "Nobody did the washing up last night."

I raise my eyebrows.

"Well, it was Friday yesterday. It was your turn."

Dad sniffs. He hands me my plate and a fork.

"Thanks," I say.

"Is it OK?" he asks. He's got that hopeful look in his eyes again.

I poke at the omelette with my fork. It's burnt to a crisp around the edges, but it's still runny in the middle. Frazzled brown pieces of onion are floating in the uncooked egg. The beans look like they've been stuck to the bottom of the pan. A smell of burning is starting to waft through from the kitchen.

"Yeah," I tell him. "It's fine."

We don't say much during the time it takes us to eat our dinners. There's nothing very interesting on *Football Focus* either. News from the Premier League and Europe. Some stuff about sports nutrition and the latest scientific training methods. I can't imagine much of that going on at Southlands. Letchford do get a mention at one point, but only as potential victims of a giant-killing in the Cup this afternoon. I laugh. To call Letchford Town *giants* is a bit of a piss-take.

I'm just wiping up the last of my bean juice with the final bit of omelette when I realise Dad's been staring at me.

"What?" I say.

He strokes his chin. There's getting on for three week's worth of stubble on it now.

"I just can't get over your new hairdo," he says. "What would Mum think?"

I pull a face. Dad's hassling me about my appearance. That's some joke.

"Dunno," I say. I run my hand over my cropped hair. It's ten days since I had it done. I was actually thinking it was about time I got myself down to Talking Heads again. It's starting to get a bit long.

The conversation looks like it's ground to a halt. I pick up the plates and take them into the kitchen. I brush onion skins off the chopping board and into the bin, then I make a start on the dishes. Today's and yesterday's.

I'm just wiping down the work surfaces and trying to get the egg splashes off the hob when the doorbell rings. I toss the sponge back into the sink and make my way down the hall. I open the door. It's Zoe. Her hair's tied back and she's in a navy blue army-style jacket, long multicoloured scarf, skin-tight jeans and a pair of green Converse All Star. If we were at Parkway, I'd have her down as an indie kid. She seems have a different look every time I see her. She's smiling brightly.

"Hello you," she says, stepping up and giving me a kiss.

I close the door and get my jacket down from the pegs.

"We might as well get going," I tell her.

"Tom?" Dad shouts from the living room. "Who is it?"

"It's Zoe," I shout back. "We're off into town."

I can hear him getting up. I don't really want Zoe seeing him in his present state, so I start pulling on my jacket as quickly as I can. I'm not fast enough though. Dad's in the doorway. Unwashed. Bloodshot eyes. Wild hair. Bare feet. Crumpled clothes.

"Hi Zoe," he says.

She smiles.

"Hi Mr Mitchell."

Dad shakes his head.

"Call me Tony. No need to be formal. You never know. I could be your father-in-law one day."

My heart sinks. Dad's trying to be charming. And what a thought. Having him as your father-in-law. An offer no girl could refuse. Luckily Zoe takes it all in her stride.

"You never know, Tony," she says, smiling again.

I've got my jacket on now. I check that I've got my wallet, keys and phone. I have.

"Right then," I say. "We're off."

Dad nods.

"Yeah," he says. "See you then. You take care, the pair of you." He looks a bit sad. Nothing more to look forward to than an afternoon in front of the TV and a few cans to make the time pass more quickly.

For a brief second I feel a twinge. I'm not too sure what it is. Affection? Guilt? An idea occurs to me. We could stick around for a bit, cheer him up. We're not in any rush and I know Zoe would be alright about it. I'm going to say something, but then I change my mind. There would no point in sticking around. We'd all just sit there like bookends.

I open the door.

"Right then Dad," I say. "I'll see you later." I smile as reassuringly as I can.

Zoe steps out onto the path. I shut the door behind me and we head off into the village.

It looks like it was pretty lively in the middle of Thurston last night. There's a trail of bloodspots along the pavement in front of the shops on Lindisfarne Street, coming in the general direction of the Bulls Head. Someone's smashed all three of the glass panels on the back of the bus shelter outside Costcutter, and the litter bin on the bus stop pole has been set on fire. It's still smouldering now, gradually oozing down towards the pavement in yellow plastic blobs like lumpy custard.

After a couple of minutes the number 84 turns up. We crunch our way through the broken glass, pay the driver and head up the stairs to the top deck. It's a nice trip into town this afternoon. A proper autumn day. The sun is bright and low in the sky and it's lighting up the leaves on the trees, all yellows and oranges and reds. Zoe seems happy, one hand on my knee, snuggling into my shoulder. We don't do a lot of talking, but it feels OK.

It's about twenty to two when we pull into Letchford bus station. We get off the bus and wander up towards the town centre. Glancing into the newsagents on Church Lane, I see the Asian bloke who sold me the programme the other weekend. He's reading the back pages of *The Daily Sport* again.

I look at Zoe.

"Where do you fancy going then?" I ask. I've not been shopping with her for a while. Usually, she goes with her mates from Alderman Richard Martin. I'm not too sure where she likes to go these days.

"I thought we'd have a look around The Lanes," she says.

I'm surprised.

"Letchford Lanes? Those funny little cobbled streets behind the Town Hall?"

She smiles.

"Yeah. Lots of lovely little boutiques, cafes, vintage clothing shops. Things like that. It's really nice."

I nod, not convinced. Boutiques, cafes and vintage clothing shops aren't really my thing. The thing is, I didn't think they were Zoe's either.

"Thought you were more of an Ainsdale Centre sort of girl."

She shrugs.

"A few of us from the *Oliver* cast came down on Wednesday, before evening rehearsals. I told them I'd never really had a proper look round The Lanes, so they took me into all the good shops, showed me where everything was."

"Oh yeah?" I say. "Who was that then?"

Zoe takes a breath.

"Oh, just some people I know. Lucy. Melissa. Simon Matthews."

I nod. Simon Matthews. That name again.

We head into the underpass to The Lanes. There was an article about the underpass in the *Argus* last week. The council has been trying to tidy it up, make it a bit less of a piss-smelling muggers' paradise.

106

They've steam-cleaned the chewing gum off the floor, moved all the tramps out and put up a tile mosaic on the wall. Two workmen in overalls, linking arms. Celebrating the town's rich industrial heritage. It looks like it was designed by a four year old. As we go past, I notice someone has drawn an enormous dick on one of the men and there's a huge pair of tits on the other. The place still smells of piss. We come back up the slope until we're at street level again. The Lanes zigzag off in different directions in front of us.

"Right then," Zoe says. "Let's make a start."

Three quarters of an hour later and I've lost count of how many shops we've been in and out of. I'm trying to put a brave face on things, but I've looked at enough hand-carved soapstone animals, ethnic-design rugs and dead men's overcoats to last me a lifetime. I'm sure my clothes are starting to smell of joss-sticks.

We're in the St Mary's Hospice charity shop now. Zoe's in the changing cubicle, trying on a T-shirt, and I'm looking through the blokes' stuff, trying to keep myself occupied. It's a pretty unimpressive selection. Sweat-stained white and lime green polo shirts. Donnay and Lotto stuff that's priced up for more in here than it would cost you brand new from Soccer World. The old woman behind the counter is listening to Saga FM. She's looking at me like she thinks I'm about to shove something up my jacket and do a runner. I give her a cheesy grin but she just scowls.

Zoe comes out from behind the curtain with her T-shirt on. It's grey and frayed around the edges, with a faded picture of Mickey Mouse on the front. By the look on her face, I can see that she's quite taken with it.

"What do you reckon?" she asks.

I shrug.

"It's OK."

"I really like it," she says.

I nod.

She rummages on the rack behind me.

"And I think you'd look great in this," she says, smiling enthusiastically.

I look at what she's found. It's a grey and black cardigan. It's about thirty years old. There's a price tag on the left sleeve. £7.99. For a worn-out piece of knitwear.

I stifle a laugh.

"Do me a favour." If Ryan or any of the other Letchford lads caught me wearing something like that, I'd get my head kicked in.

Zoe pushes the cardigan up against me, holding the sleeve along the length of my arm.

"I think you'd look great in it," she says again. "It's a design classic. Timeless."

I smile. I don't want to offend her, but there's no way I'm spending my money on a cardigan last worn by someone's grandad in the 1970's.

"No," I tell her. "It's not for me."

Zoe sighs and puts the cardigan back on the rack. Without saying anything else to me, she goes into the changing cubicle. A minute or so later she's out again. She pays for her T-shirt and we go back into the street.

I look at my watch. Five to three. Zoe still isn't saying anything. There's a bit of an atmosphere building now. I try to think of a way to brighten things up.

"What about going for something to eat?" I say.

She shrugs and checks her watch.

"Alright then. Have you got anywhere in mind?"

"Yeah. What about the Café Rialt in the Ainsdale Centre?"

She rolls her eyes.

"Café Rialt? That's that terrible greasy spoon upstairs near Argos isn't it?"

I nod, but already I know we're not going there.

"No," she says. "I don't really want to go there. We can go to Mrs Brady's Tea Rooms. It's just round the corner. It's lovely in there. Really rustic. Old-fashioned. Simon took us in on Wednesday."

"Good old Simon," I say.

Mrs Brady's Tea Rooms might be rustic and old fashioned, but the prices aren't. Two cups of tea and two cream scones set me back the best part of a tenner. I pick up my tray and make my way across to where Zoe has already parked herself, at a rickety wooden table. There's a mirror on the wall behind her, and I sneak a crafty look at myself as I sit down.

Zoe's noticed what I've just done. She reaches across and runs her fingers over my hair.

"I still can't get used to this," she says. "You look like a football hooligan. Or one of the Mitchell brothers off *EastEnders*. I'll have to start calling you Phil. You've got the right surname. All you need is a black leather jacket and you'll be ready to go down The Vic."

I rub my nose. First Dad, now Zoe. It's Have A Go At Tom's Hair Day.

She carries on.

"You will let it grow back now though won't you? You don't really fit as an East End hard man. I'd love it if you had long hair. What d'you reckon?"

I take a slurp of my tea. It's like dishwater. I wish I'd got coffee.

"Maybe," I say.

109

By the time we've finished in Mrs Brady's it's getting on for twenty to four. I was hoping that a sit-down and something to eat and drink would get the afternoon back on track. Now I'm in the doghouse because I keep checking for Letchford Town updates on my mobile.

Zoe piles our cups and plates back on the tray and stands up.

"It's not much fun being with you if all you're interested in is the football scores," she says.

I have another look at my phone. It's still 0-0.

"Sorry." I get up. "Where do you want to go now?" It's a final effort to save an afternoon that's dying on its arse.

"I suppose we might as well go to the Ainsdale Centre," Zoe says, without much enthusiasm. "Not that there's anything to look at in there."

We leave Mrs Brady's and head back down The Lanes. We go under the underpass, across Town Hall Square and through the precinct. For someone who wasn't particularly keen on the idea of going to the Ainsdale Centre, Zoe certainly wastes no time getting stuck into the shops.

By quarter to five we've been round Primark, Peacocks, Republic and New Look, and she's got herself two new belts, a pair of suede gloves and a canvas bag that looks a bit like a satchel. I had a look at a couple of things in JJB Sports and got myself a poppy from the old chap by the shoe repairers, but that's about it.

I'm standing outside the changing rooms in H&M now. Zoe's trying on a pair of jeans. I seem to have spent a fair amount of time standing outside changing rooms this afternoon. The good thing about that, of course, is that it gives me the chance to check the

Letchford score on my mobile without being nagged. Five minutes from time and it's 1-1. Tommy Sharp put us in front on 65 minutes, but we let Kidderminster equalise almost straight from the restart. It's looking like a replay back at Southlands.

Zoe's coming out of her changing booth, heading my way, jeans on.

"What do you think about these?" she asks.

I glance down at my phone. *Kid'ster 2 L'ford 1 Nicholson o.g. 87.*

"Bollocks," I say.

She blinks.

"What?!"

I shake my head.

"Sorry," I say. "It's the football. We've just gone behind. To Kidderminster Fucking Harriers."

She tuts.

"The jeans," she says. "What do you think?"

I look her up and down. They look identical to the ones she came into town wearing.

"They look OK," I tell her.

She sighs and strides back down the corridor to her changing booth. By the time she comes back out again, it's full time at Kidderminster. Letchford have been knocked out of the FA Cup by a non-league team. It's not a good feeling. I think about texting Raks and Ryan, but I don't know what I could say.

I stand by the doors while Zoe pays for her jeans. When she's finished, we go out into the centre again, heading towards River Island. Up ahead, there's a group of lads standing outside Harris's Amusements, chewing gum and generally looking hostile. A couple of them are staring at me. Zoe grabs my hand and I can feel her trying to guide me across to the other side of the walkway. I'm not budging though. As we come level with the arcade, one of the lads lunges out towards me.

"Tom, you wanker," he says.

I grin. It's Gary Simmons. Rob and Jerome are hovering in the background.

"Alright, Gary?" I say.

Gary shakes his head.

"Fucking Kidderminster cocksuckers," he says. "And what about Dave Nicholson? Mackworth reject twat."

"Yeah," I say. "What a tosser. I'm off home now to put my head in the fucking oven." I start to laugh.

Zoe pulls at my hand again. I glance across and see concern and confusion on her face. I feel really awkward. I've got a nasty feeling I'm going red.

"Er, Zoe," I say. "This is Gary, my mate from Parkway and from the football. Gary, this is Zoe, my missus."

Gary grunts and Zoe gives the sort of smile you might use if you were forced to sit bare-arsed on a pinecone at gunpoint. She's not impressed. There's a hard, staring look in her eyes now. The awkwardness isn't going away. It's getting worse. I'm embarrassed, but I can't quite work out what I'm embarrassed about. Is it because Zoe's seen the sort of people I hang about with? Or is it because Gary's caught me playing happy families? I don't know if it's Gary's opinion or Zoe's that's more important to me.

I try to bring things to a close quickly.

"Anyway Gary," I say. "We'd better get off now. See you on Monday."

Gary nods.

"Right. See you Tom. See you Zoe."

Zoe just grimaces.

As Gary heads back towards Harris's, Zoe puffs out

her cheeks.

"You know Tom," she says, "I actually can't be bothered to look in River Island. Let's just go home, yeah?"

I shrug.

"If that's what you want to do."

We walk back to the bus station in silence. We've still not said anything when the number 84 rolls into the bay at twenty past five. We pay our fares and climb the steps. I fiddle with my phone and pick at threads on the seat. Zoe just stares blankly through the window as the bus heads out of town. We didn't say much to each other on the way in, but that was different. That was a happy silence. This isn't.

Just as we're coming through Medstone, she starts up.

"I'm worried, Tom," she says, turning to me. "Something's definitely happened to you in the last couple of weeks."

I shrug.

"Like what?" I ask.

She takes a breath and launches into long list.

"This sudden preoccupation with Letchford Town. Your Phil Mitchell hair. Going around with dickheads like that Gary. I mean, where did this all come from? You surely can't have anything in common with him? And what about this Ryan Dawkins you're always on about? What's he like? I bet he's worse than Gary."

I shrug again.

Zoe carries on. She's getting sarky now and cocking her head from side to side like a chicken does.

"But hey, maybe it's me that isn't up to speed with things. Perhaps I should just get with the program. Get used to being your *missus*. Start hanging around in the Ainsdale Centre. Polish up my swearing. What do you fucking think?"

I start to laugh. I don't mean to, but I can't help myself.

She's not amused. The sarcasm's gone now.

"It's not funny Tom. There really is something happening to you."

I say nothing. I'm changing alright, but Zoe doesn't know the half of it.

She shakes her head.

"I'm worried," she says again. "What's this hard edge that's come over you? You're so…, so unfeeling. Just what are you turning into?"

I look out into the darkness, at the orange streetlights swishing by.

"To be honest," I say, "I don't really know."

nine

Ryan looks at Raks, then he looks at me.

"Hands up who wants to go to French, then?" he says.

I check my watch. It's just after eleven, Thursday morning. The dining hall is starting to empty out. We're due in Room 42 in less than five minutes.

Raks leans back in his chair.

"I quite like French," he says, stretching his arms above his head.

Ryan laughs.

"You just think you're in with a shout with Miss Amis."

Raks grins. Miss Amis is fit.

"Paul Darwin reckons she's shagged one or two of the students," he says. "So you never know."

"Paul Darwin's full of shit," Ryan says. "Anyway, we're getting away from the point. Hands up who *really* wants to go to French?"

"Well, I'm not too keen," I say. I put my feet up on the edge of the table. I've got a suspicion that Ryan's about to suggest a spot of skiving. "What about you, Raks?"

"Dunno," Raks says, shrugging. "Do you think we'd get away with missing it?"

"Well what do you think they'd do?" Ryan asks. "Send us to the Head? Smack our little bottoms?"

We all laugh. It's starting to look like we'll be giving French a miss.

I brush my fingers over my hair. It's been over two weeks since I had it cut now. It definitely needs another trim. Zoe won't be happy, but that's nothing new these days. We had another run-in last night. She said how she'd like it if I was a bit more caring and considerate. A bit more like Simon Matthews. I had to laugh at that. From the sounds of him, Simon wouldn't last two minutes at Parkway.

"So if we're skipping the next lesson, what are we going to do?" I ask.

Ryan brushes crisp crumbs off the table-top.

"There's some blokes I want you to meet," he says. "On Thursdays they're down The Shakespeare. Well, they're there most days really, but I told them we might drop in today."

"The Shakespeare?" Raks looks surprised. "Isn't that the rough-looking place near the Industrial Estate?"

"That's the one."

"Shit. That's miles away. It's right on the other side of town. It'll take us ages."

Ryan tuts.

"You lazy sod," he says. "We're young lads. Not pensioners. A walk will do you good."

Raks laughs.

"Who are these blokes at The Shakespeare, then?" I ask.

"Terrace legends, my son," Ryan says. "Members of the original Letchford Lunatic Fringe."

Raks and me nod. It sounds interesting.

"So are you up for it, then?" Ryan asks.

"Yeah," Raks says. "Let's go for it."

We leave the dining hall, heading into the foyer and reception area. We go out through the front doors as casually as we can, then set off up the path.

Mr Sankey, Mr Khan and Mrs Flanagan are standing under a tree having a crafty fag. We go right past them but they're not paying any attention.

Up near the main gates, Ryan makes a sudden detour to the left, cutting across the car park. At first I'm not sure what he's up to but then I get it. Over by the caretaker's bungalow, next to Mr Dickinson's turquoise soft top, is Mrs Wetherall's VW. It's hard to miss it. It's bright yellow. Without breaking his stride, Ryan brushes along the driver's side. There's a scraping sound and he keeps going, arcing back round to join up with Raks and me again.

"Fuck," he says, grinning. "I'm a right clumsy bastard. Look what I had in my hand." He holds up a Yale key on a Letchford Town key fob.

I glance across at Mrs Wetherall's VW. A jagged black line has appeared across the width of the door. I laugh and shake my head.

"You're going to get us into some serious bother."

Ryan shrugs.

"Maybe. But I told you she'd get hers one day, didn't I?"

We're right at the gates now. We have a final look around, making sure we've not been spotted, and then we go left, down the hill, over the river towards town.

Twenty minutes later we're in the centre of Letchford. It's quite busy. In the precinct, council workmen are shimmying up and down ladders putting up the Christmas decorations. The usual shabby stars and angel shapes in red and green light bulbs strung between the buildings. Glowing plastic icicles dangling from the ledges. Letchford Borough Council. *Working For You*. We cut through the Ainsdale Centre. Raks is getting twitchy in case he runs into his mum doing the shopping, but by the time we get to the back doors he's calming down again. We cross the car park and start heading out of town.

The side streets are deserted. There's just the occasional old couple shuffling along, sidestepping the wheelie bins and dogshit on the pavements. We keep going and pretty soon we're at the junction by the Industrial Estate. Up past the shops is The Shakespeare. It's a tall, red-brick building with a stained slate roof. The pub name is painted on the end wall in peeling gold paint on a blue background, and a concrete bust of Shakespeare himself sits in an alcove above the front door. A cross of St George flutters from a pole bolted next to him.

Instead of heading for the front door, Ryan leads the way through the car park towards another entrance.

"They'll be in the back bar," he says.

We follow him round the corner. Over a low brick wall to our left is the *Family Beer Garden*. It looks like a prison exercise yard with picnic tables. We carry on along the back of the pub, coming to a brown wooden door with frosted glass panels. Ryan grips the handle.

"Come on then," he says.

I hesitate for a split second, then follow him through the doorway.

The room is in near-darkness. In front of us is the bar, polished wood with brass beer pumps and drip trays. Three old men in donkey jackets are sitting on stools, nursing pints and peering at the TV bolted to a bracket up on the left. Horse racing. The barman is cleaning glasses with a white tea towel. He glances in our direction. If he's noticed that some schoolkids have just wandered in, he's not letting on. Looking around, I can just about make out that the walls are papered in burgundy and gold striped paper. The ceiling is high, with nicotine-stained plaster light fixtures. Dim bulbs give out a faint glow through the haze of fag smoke.

I look across at Raks and he looks back, raising his eyebrows.

"I thought you weren't allowed to smoke in pubs nowadays," he says.

Ryan grins.

"Loophole in the anti-smoking legislation." He nods towards the right hand wall.

Squinting through the gloom, I see there's a section knocked out of the brickwork with a sort of metal awning jutting out into the car park. I didn't notice it on the way in. It looks like a glorified serving hatch.

Ryan carries on.

"It's a bit of a piss-take, but technically this counts as a semi-open area, so you can still spark up."

I laugh.

"Nice one."

Ryan's scanning the room now, flicking his eyes over the groups sat at tables around the edge, heads buried in *The Sun*, *The Star* and the racing papers. He turns round with a smile on his face.

"Come on lads," he says, jerking his thumb towards the corner. "They're here."

Narrowing my eyes again, I can make out the shapes of four blokes sprawled around a circular table, piled high with empty glasses and bottles. They've all got short-cropped hair and suntans. Two of them are wearing golf jackets. The other two are in polo shirts. All of them are festooned with gold jewellery. My stomach flips over. These aren't young lads like us. These are heavy-duty geezers, blokes in their forties. Like Ryan said. Terrace legends. The funny thing is, though, I don't recognise any of them. You'd have thought we'd have seen them at the Castleton game, especially when it all kicked off, but they weren't there. I haven't got time to think of anything else though, because Ryan is already striding across the stained carpet, and his mates have seen him coming.

"Ryan, you little shit," the biggest bloke shouts. It's meant as a compliment. He stands up and gives Ryan a bone-crunching handshake. He's virtually as wide as he is tall and his head seems to be joined direct to his shoulders. His hair's shaved so close you can see the ridges of his skull. This bloke really does look like a Mitchell. Phil and Grant's much bigger, much madder brother.

"Alright, Trev," Ryan says. "How you been keeping?"

"Mustn't grumble," Trev says in an 80-a-day growl. "Mustn't grumble."

Two of the others stand up and more handshakes are exchanged. Listening in I hear that their names are Steve and Chris. The fourth man is still slumped in his seat. He's got a sort of Neanderthal look about him. Hair low on his forehead, jutting brow. He's missing a couple of his front teeth too. He downs a shot of whisky and slowly shakes his head.

"I'm fuckin' lost here, Trev," he says. "Who's this little bastard?"

Trev coughs.

"You've met him before, Dave. It's Ryan. Ryan Dawkins."

"Fuckin' hell," Dave says, standing to attention by

his chair as if a member of the royal family has just come into the room. He laughs nervously, a wheezing hee-hee-hee sound like the dog in *Dastardly And Muttley*. He brushes his hand across the stubble on his chin, wipes the palm on the front of his shirt and stretches out to shake. "Ryan fuckin' Dawkins. Fuckin' nice to see you, mate."

While Ryan and Dave get re-acquainted, me and Raks exchange a glance. It looks like Dave's got a touch of Tourette's.

The formalities look like they're coming to an end. The blokes are taking their seats again. No-one seems to have noticed Raks and me yet. I'm starting to feel a bit out of place.

"Trev," Ryan says, half turning so that he's not blocking us from view. "These are the lads I was telling you about. Tom and Raks. Good Letchford lads. Helped give the Castleton bastards a good kicking."

Before Trev can say anything, Chris intervenes. Looking us up and down, he starts to laugh. He points a sovereign-ringed finger at Raks.

"You ain't serious? A Paki football hooligan?" There's astonishment in his voice. "Black lads, I can get my head round that, yeah? But Pakis?"

"Don't call him a Paki." It's out of my mouth before I can think of the possible consequences. I glance across at Raks, but no emotion shows on his face. Ryan looks like he wants to say something but he can't get the words out.

Chris carries on. He's smaller than his mates, and the most aggressive looking. Judging from his flattened nose, he's carried it through on a few occasions.

"So how do you manage to get to the matches then

Osama? You take time off from the Mosque, yeah?"

There's no answer to a question like that. Everything goes quiet.

Steve seems a bit more sensible than the others, a bit less intimidating. His hair is marginally longer and he's got sideburns down to the angle of his jaw. He puts his hand on Chris's arm.

"Fucking leave it, Chris," he says. His voice is soft and low, hard to hear above the clink of pint glasses and the beeping of the fruit machine.

Chris ignores him. He's warming to the task. His weasely little eyes are glinting with a primitive cunning.

"So they do burqas in club colours then, yeah? Nice veils with the club crest embroidered on them?"

Ryan's looking very uncomfortable now. He's shaking his head, rubbing his nose. I've never seen him like this.

"Chris…," he says, but no-one's listening.

Raks gives a little laugh. More of a snort really. He must be crapping himself, but it's not showing.

"You know mate," he says, voice low-key, "I can take my racial abuse as well as the next man, but if you must start all that bollocks, at least get the religion right. You're talking about Muslims. My family are Hindu."

There's a horrible silence as Chris takes this information in. It probably only lasts a few seconds, but it feels like hours. I'm just starting to suss out the odds of being able to make it back to the door without a bottle sticking out of my head when Chris starts laughing.

"I like this lad," he says. He stands up and thrusts his hand in Raks's direction. "I were only pissing about, mate. No offence intended, yeah?"

Raks grips Chris's hand and they shake.

"None taken," he says. "It's just typical of us Pakis isn't it? Come over here, take all your jobs, and now we're taking over the football violence too."

There's another silence, and then Chris laughs again. Raks has judged it just right. The ice has been well and truly broken.

Two minutes later we've all been properly introduced and we've moved to a bigger table under an oil painting of a Spitfire in flight and a hand-written poster on fluorescent green card. *Floor Show Stripers Every Fri Lunch 12-2*. I'm assuming it means *Strippers*. Steve has gone to the bar to get a round in, and Dave is demonstrating his party piece, punching holes through beer mats with his ring finger. He's managed it with one mat and two mats and he's just about to attempt three when Steve comes back with the drinks.

"Carling OK?" he asks, plonking a pint down in front of me.

I nod.

"Yeah, brilliant," I say, although I'm not exactly a connoisseur of beers, wines and spirits. I've pinched a few cans of my dad's lager and necked the odd bottle of White Lightning behind the pavilion on Thurston Rec but that's about it. Two quick swigs of the pint and I'm already feeling a bit spaced out. It's fair to say the Carling is OK.

By the time I'm three quarters of the way down, there's a warm fuzziness spreading through me. Any anxiety from earlier on has melted away now, and I'm starting to feel right at home, confident enough to take the piss out of Dave when he retires hurt from his attempt to puncture three beer mats. I look around the table at Trev and the other lads, and the thought that crossed my mind earlier starts to nag away at me again. Why haven't I seen them at Southlands? Before I can consider whether or not it's a good idea to ask, I've already put my mouth in gear.

"There's something I was wondering," I say.

Trev glances at me.

"What's that, then?" he rumbles.

"Well, if you lot are the proper geezers, the original LLF, then why weren't you at the Castleton match?"

Trev and Steve start to laugh. Dave is wheezing away like Muttley again. Chris is making his way back from the toilets. He starts laughing too.

"What?" I say, looking at Ryan. "What have I said?"

Ryan smiles.

"Let's just say that this lot are known to the Police around here," he says. "And the coppers wouldn't be impressed if they found them in the crowd at Southlands."

Chris has stopped laughing now. He sits down and takes a swig of his pint.

"You see me, Dave and Stevie Boy, yeah? We're banned from all Football League and Conference grounds until 2022."

"Shit," I say. "How come?"

"You've heard of The Battle Of Southlands, yeah?"

I nod.

"Well, a matter arising from the events of that afternoon led to one or two legal difficulties, yeah? I'll leave it at that."

I raise my eyebrows.

"God, that's a bit of a bastard then, isn't it?"

"Mmm." Chris stuffs a fag in his mouth and lights it, throwing the dead match into the ashtray. "I've been trying to convince this lot we ought to start going to tennis matches or lawn bowls, seeing if we can start some aggro there, yeah? But no-one's going for it."

I laugh.

"So that's you, Steve and Dave. What about Trev?"

Dave leans forward. His gold identity bracelet jangles against the table-top.

"Oh, Trev's the real fuckin' naughty boy," he says. "One of the ringleaders, they said in court. Trev has to report to the fuckin' Police station every Saturday afternoon during the football season, and on all other Letchford match days. Isn't that right Trev?"

Trev grins. Dave carries on.

"And that's not the whole fuckin' story is it, Trevor?"

I look at Trev and he shakes his head.

"Nah," he growls. "I ran into a spot of bother at Euro 2000. Got arrested in Charleroi. Spent a bit of time in the Belgian nick. So now I have to surrender my passport whenever England are playing abroad."

"Bloody hell," Raks says. "So you're banned from all football. Domestic and international?"

Trev nods. Just for a second, his huge frame slumps forward. For the first time he actually looks a bit sad.

"Yeah. But I'll always have the memories." He smiles, straightening up again, confidence instantly restored. Leaning back in his chair, he pushes his hand into his jeans pocket and brings out his wallet. Flipping it open, he pulls out a dog-eared photograph and lays it on the table, taking care to avoid the beer splashes.

Craning my head round, I look at the photo. It's five blokes, early to mid twenties by the looks of it. They're all in shorts and white trainers. Four are wearing red England tops and the fifth is in a white T-shirt with a bulldog on it and *These Colours Don't Run* across the bottom. They're all badly sunburnt. I squint, looking more closely, and then things start making sense. I recognise four of the faces. Trev, Steve, Dave and Chris. They're much younger and much thinner, but it's definitely them. The other face, I don't know. It's a big bloke, built like a brick shithouse.

Trev picks the photo up again. He coughs, clearing his throat.

"England versus Holland. Cagliari, Sardinia, June 16th 1990." He recites the date like it's something that's indelibly etched onto his heart, like a special birthday.

Dave takes the picture from Trev and shakes his head, a faraway look in his eyes.

"Fuckin' hell," he says. "What a day. Fuckin' Eye-tie police with rifles. Baton charges, tear gas...." His voice trails off and he shakes his head again.

"So was the match any good?" Raks asks.

Chris laughs.

"The match were shit. 0-0. Stuart Pearce scored a free kick right near the end but it were disallowed. The thing is though, it didn't matter, yeah? The day were about much more than just the football."

Steve leans across, looks at the photo and then sits back again.

"And we had the big fella with us back then, too. Letchford's Top Boy."

"So who was he, then?" I ask. I glance at Trev's picture again, assuming that Steve means the fifth bloke.

"Mickey," Steve whispers. "Mickey Dawkins."

I blink.

"Dawkins?" I say. "So he's…"

Ryan finishes the sentence for me.

"My dad."

Nobody says anything for a while after that. I look across at Ryan, but he just stares at the floor. Trev puts the photo back in his wallet, and the wallet back in his pocket.

"You see lads," he says eventually, voice deeper and growlier than ever, "that's what it's all about. Times like that, experiences like that. The Battle Of Southlands, representing Letchford at Italia 90, Euro 2000. Those were the days of our lives. There's not much else on offer when you're a dosser from Letchford. But those times, those memories, they'll stay with you forever. The LLF was something to have a bit of pride in." There's real conviction in what he's saying. I swear I can see a tear in his eye.

Dave takes up the theme.

"And you boys are the next fuckin' generation," he says. "It's a young man's game these days. You've got to carry the fuckin' torch for us now. We were the Letchford Lunatic Fringe. You lot are the New Letchford Lunatic Fringe."

Spontaneously, everyone picks their pint up, slamming them together in the air above the table.

"Here's to the NLLF," I say.

"The NLLF," everyone echoes.

The rest of the afternoon passes by in a blur. Trev and the lads keep us well supplied with beer while giving us a blow-by-blow account of the chequered history of the LLF. In their heyday they seemed to have had a run-in with every major firm in the old third and fourth divisions, not to mention a few skirmishes with the big boys in cup competitions. Scars on knuckles and eyebrows are pointed out. Dave

127

shows us an indentation on the back of his head caused by a flying chair leg in a pub in Cardiff. Ryan's probably heard it all before but me and Raks are hanging on every word.

We're chipping in with more and more way-out accounts of what happened after the Castleton match. By the fourth or fifth telling, it's sounding like a scaled down version of World War Two. If Dave or Chris or anyone knows we're bullshitting though, they don't mention it.

By ten to three I've put away nearly four pints of Carling. It's easily the most I've ever drunk in one session. On an empty stomach too. I'm starting to think I could quite happily curl up into a ball and go to sleep in the corner of the pub, but it's not really an option.

"We need to think about getting back to Parkway," I say to Raks. "We're going to miss the bus back to Thurston if we don't get a move on."

Raks rubs his eyes, trying to focus. He shakes his head from side to side. I'm pissed but he looks shit-faced.

"What?" he says.

"Parkway. We need to get back to Parkway to get the bus. It's Thursday. I've got the *Argus* to deliver tonight."

Ryan looks at me.

"I'm staying here," he says. "And I don't think I'm going to bother with Parkway tomorrow. So I'll just meet you in the Café Rialt at about quarter to two on Saturday."

I nod.

"Okay. One forty-five, Saturday."

Ryan nods. He looks pleased with how the afternoon's turned out. We've not let him down in front of his mates. I'm pleased that he's pleased. It's a strange thing, but Ryan looks more at home here than I've ever seen him before. With Trev and the lads, he fits right in. It's like he's a middle-aged man trapped in a teenager's body.

I take a breath and stand up. My legs feel like they want to go in different directions. Raks starts levering himself out of his seat, steadying himself against the edge of the table. For a split second it looks like he's going to fall over, but Chris pushes him upright.

"Careful there, Raks lad, yeah?" he says.

Raks grins a pissed grin. Him and Chris have been getting on like a house on fire since their rocky start.

"See you then lads," I say, looking at Trev, Chris, Steve and Dave. It takes a fair bit of concentration not to slur my words. "Good to meet you."

Trev, Chris and Dave hold their hands out and I shake each one. As I turn towards Steve I notice that he's looking at me closely, tilting his head to one side.

"I've got to ask you mate," he says. "Do I know you from somewhere? It's been nagging away at me all afternoon."

I shrug, puffing out my cheeks. I'm pretty sure I've never come across him before, but it's hard to think with this amount of lager sloshing around inside me.

"Dunno."

Steve shakes his head.

"I know your face. I'm sure I do…" His wispy little voice trails away and he furrows his brow, trying to make the connection in his mind.

I shrug again. There's nothing much I can say. I feel like I'm letting him down in some way.

"What's your surname?" he asks.

"Mitchell."

Steve sits bolt upright. He clicks his right thumb

and middle finger and points at me.

"I knew it," he says. "Your dad's Tony Mitchell."

I nod, surprised.

"Yeah. Tony Mitchell. *Hollywood Tony.*" Steve's smiling now, relieved to have made the breakthrough. All of a sudden he's speaking three times louder than normal. "I used to work with him at Morrells. Good bloke. You're the absolute spitting image."

I stifle a laugh. Steve can't have seen the state of my dad recently.

"So how is he, your dad?" he asks.

"Oh, you know, he's surviving," I say. "He's still not working. My mum died a few years back and he's been in a bit of a bad way."

Steve runs a thumb down one of his sideburns.

"Shit. I'm sorry to hear that," he says. "Still, you tell him Steve Fisher said hello."

"Will do." But of course I won't. It would take far too much explaining.

I'm about to start heading for the door when Steve puts his hand on my elbow. He's not finished with me.

"And Tom," he says, voice dropping right down again, "you take care with this football violence thing. It's not for everyone. I've seen people get hurt. Fucking *badly* hurt."

Before I can say anything, I'm interrupted by a burst of laughter from Chris.

"Give it a break, Steve. Don't start getting fucking sentimental. You're pissing about with him, yeah?"

Steve ignores him.

"You're just at the entry level now," he says. "Cracking a few heads, that sort of stuff. It seems like a bit of harmless fun, yeah? The shallow end of

130

the hooligan pool."

I nod.

"Well, just be careful that you don't get pulled into the deep end before you're ready."

I look into his face and I see that he's serious.

"OK Steve." I nod again. "Thanks for the tip."

ten

Saturday November 18th. Kick-off against Ashborough Town is about an hour and a quarter away, and we're in the Café Rialt, sitting at the corner table, waiting for Ryan to turn up. I've got myself a Danish pastry and a can of Red Bull, and Raks has got himself a can of Coke and a plate of chips and beans again.

"He's late," Raks says.

I roll my eyes.

"Don't start all that bullshit. He'll be here. You know what he's like."

Raks shrugs and sticks another forkful of beans into his mouth. I take a swig of Red Bull and look around. The café is much busier than it was last time. It's three weeks nearer to Christmas and the rush is on. The buggy-pushing mums with their heaps of shopping bags are really out in force today. On my left, a fat family in matching Lonsdale sportswear are tucking into all-day breakfasts. On the next table along, an aggressive-looking woman in a long oatmeal-coloured cardigan is trying to feed a Greggs pasty to a kid in a high chair. A sign on the wall says *Customers Must Only Consume Food Purchased On The Premises*. It doesn't look like anyone's going to say anything.

I notice someone's left a copy of *The Sun* on our table. I flick through to the middle pages and find *Super Goals*, scanning through the League Two match previews.

Letchford boss John Whyman has no new major injury worries for the visit of high-flying Ashborough. Visiting boss Tony Jagger could be without defender Ady Samuel.

I put the paper down and look up. Ryan's arrived. He gets himself a bag of crisps and then comes across to our table, pulling his earphones out and sitting down next to me.

"Alright lads?" he says.

We both nod.

Ryan glances up at my hair, then across to Raks's.

"Another trip to the barbers?"

I laugh.

"Yeah. Expensive business, keeping your hair short. Got it done on a number one this time, so it should last longer."

Ryan grins. He reaches over the table and pulls down the zip on the front of Raks's jacket. Raks hasn't got his replica shirt on today. Ryan's grin gets wider. He picks up his crisps and squeezes the bag until the top pops.

"So did either of you go to college yesterday?" he asks, pushing the first couple of crisps into his mouth.

Raks nods.

"Anyone say anything about Thursday?"

I sniff.

"Greeny had a go, said how concerned he was, all that bollocks. Nothing major."

Ryan nods.

"I doubt Sankey'll say anything to me," he says. "He's always happiest when I'm not there."

I take another swig of my Red Bull and bite into my Danish pastry. It's not the freshest cake I've ever tasted.

133

"I felt dog rough on Thursday evening," I say.

Ryan laughs.

"I bet you did. You were putting it back like there was no tomorrow."

"And I had to deliver the *Argus* when I got back to Thurston. By the time I'd finished I was dying. Then I had my missus coming round."

"Bet she was well chuffed when she saw the state of you."

I grin, shaking my head.

"She wasn't too pleased." That's putting it mildly. She took one look at me and went home.

"Still," Ryan says. "It was a good laugh, wasn't it, Thursday afternoon?"

Raks pushes his plate away.

"It was sound. They're good lads aren't they?"

Ryan crunches into another crisp.

"Yeah. They're alright. Chris is a bit of a twat, but it's just because he's so thick."

We all laugh.

My watch says nearly ten past two. I finish off my cake and my drink, then lean back, stretching my arms above my head, yawning. The fluttering in my stomach, the feeling that's been there more or less all the time since the last home match, is getting too big to ignore. It's time to get going.

We head down the back stairs of the centre. The old bloke with the Hammond organ isn't here today. In his place is a stall selling dogs, cats and vintage cars hand-crafted from British coal. Over to the left, one of the empty shop units is being converted into Santa's Grotto.

"Are Ashborough any good, then?" Raks asks, as we push our way through the doors and go out into the car park.

"They went up to second in midweek," Ryan says. "Beat Walsall away. Three points today and they could go top."

Raks nods.

"We could do with a win this afternoon though, couldn't we? Losing at Hereford and then getting knocked out of the FA Cup by Kidderminster Harriers. It's a fucking joke."

"Mmm," Ryan says. "I don't think John Whyman's going to be getting Manager Of The Month for November."

Ryan and Raks are talking football, but my mind is wandering. I'm thinking about events off the pitch. Post-match entertainment.

"What are the Ashborough fans like?" I ask. I've been trying to think where they were in the hooligan league table, but it's not coming to me.

Ryan waves his hand in the air.

"Nothing special. Don't usually bring very many."

I feel a twinge of disappointment.

"So there's not much chance of any trouble then?"

Ryan shrugs.

"Who knows? There are always some opportunities if you know where to look for them. Every club's got a firm, even if it's just a few enthusiastic amateurs. Ashborough might have got some boys together this season."

I give a half-smile. It doesn't sound so bad after all.

Winter's definitely in the air today. As we head down the side streets it's noticeable that padded overcoats are outnumbering bombers now. Woolly hats are starting to appear too, but there are still a few short-sleeved orange Letchford shirts on show. There's three blokes up in front. Two *LEWTON 16*'s and a *SHEEDY 7*. It makes me cold just looking at them. I pull my scarf up a bit closer to my chin and keep walking.

It takes us about twenty minutes to get to Southlands. We've missed the away supporters' coaches, so we just head straight past the merchandise stalls and the burger vans and the programme kiosks and make for the turnstiles at the back of the North Stand. For the sake of superstition, I go for Gate 20 again. Comb-Round Man takes my eight quid and I click my way into the concourse to wait for Raks and Ryan to come through Gate 19. Right on cue, *The Liquidator* comes on the PA. I smile. I feel like a veteran now.

There's still about twenty-five minutes until kick-off. It's too early to go out on the terraces, so we edge our way through the blokes with polystyrene trays of chips until we're in a good position to see the television bolted on the wall next to the toilets. There's a live match today. Man United – Everton. My phone starts beeping. It's a text from Zoe. *HV fn tk cr Z X.* It's exactly the same as last time. Still, it's the thought that counts.

By ten to three, Man U are 3-1 up. There's only a couple of minutes stoppage time left.

Ryan shakes his head.

"This game's as good as over. We might as well make a move."

I lead the way up the steps. As we come to the top, the teams are just leaving the pitch after the warm-up. I look across to the right, to see what Ashborough have brought in the way of travelling support. It's nothing like the turnout from Castleton. My heart sinks.

Ryan jerks his thumb in the direction of the away section.

"Said it might not be too impressive, didn't I?" he says.

We head down the terracing and take up station by the crush barrier we stood behind for the second half of the Castleton match. Down in front of us, a new advertising board has sprung up. *Too Much Bling? Give Us A Ring.* It's a police hotline for people to dob in their neighbours if they've been looking a bit too flush recently. I rest my elbows on the barrier, casting a few glances through the fencing into the Ashborough fans, seeing if I can catch anyone's eye. It's not looking promising.

The clock on the scoreboard gradually trundles towards 14:58. *The Boys Are Back In Town* blasts out and the teams come through the tunnel, hoofing yellow balls towards the goalmouths. Just down to the left someone throws some confetti. It's a pretty half-hearted effort. A couple of torn-up betting slips and a shredded football supplement fluttering through the air. After the formal handshakes, Tony O'Neill and Tommy Sharp head towards the Kop, applauding us for applauding them, while Carl Butterworth leads the mascots into the centre circle for photographs with the match sponsors.

While the players try to keep themselves warm, the tannoy announcer reads out the teamsheets. We greet every Ashborough name with a shout of *Who?*, then cheer the Letchford side one by one. Even Dave Nicholson gets a cheer today. People must be feeling charitable. Eric Emanuel's in for Paul Hood, but apart from that, it's the same eleven who started against Castleton. Danny Holmes is on the bench again.

The niceties in the centre circle are just about over. Letchford are defending our end in the first half, spreading out into their usual 4-4-2. Leroy Lewton is psyching himself up, running on the spot, leaning forward and windmilling his shoulders round and round like a swimmer with no arms.

Up at the other end the Ashborough team are forming themselves into a huddle. They're in all-red today. For some reason their shirts are a couple of shades lighter than their shorts and socks. The kit man must have used the wrong wash cycle. The huddle seems to be going on and on and boos are starting to ring out, getting louder and being joined by chants of *Who The Fucking Hell Are You?* Eventually the message seems to get through and Ashborough fan out across the pitch into their own 4-4-2 formation. The ref signals to both his assistants, checks his watch and then blows his whistle. We're off and running.

Twenty minutes in and it's still 0-0. The ball seems to have spent most of it's time thirty yards either side of the halfway line, in the air. It's like a big game of table tennis.

Raks shakes his head.

"How can Ashborough be second in the table?" he says. "They're fucking useless."

Ryan laughs.

"Everyone is, in this league. There's just crap or slightly less crap."

The crowd has been pretty subdued so far. There's been the odd chorus of *Come On Letchford* and *Letchford 'Til I Die*, but that's about it. Since the last match I seem to have developed a sort of football fan's instinct for knowing precisely when chants are going to finish, but other than that there's been nothing to get worked up about. We've been trying to get some banter going with the Ashborough lot, but without any success. We've not heard a peep out of them yet. We hit them with a blast of *Shall We Sing A Song For You?* but again there's no response.

Looking around where we're standing, the distinctions between the different types of fans are getting clearer to me now. The sportswear and short hair crew, and the ordinary punters. Soldiers and civilians. The civilians are a funny bunch. There's Twitchy Bloke in his camouflage jacket, flinching every time the ball comes into our box. There's Big Fleece Woman, constantly checking scores on her mobile. And there's Pessimistic Granddad, shaking his head and moaning, as if he thinks we should be carving teams up like Arsenal.

Out on the pitch, things aren't getting any better. The goodwill towards Dave Nicholson is wearing pretty thin now. The man just can't pass the ball forwards. Every time it's sideways, safety-first, back to the keeper, or into Row Z. As the scoreboard flicks over to 44:00, Dave slices the ball into touch for what feels like the one hundredth time. Booing rumbles round the ground and a mass exodus starts as people make for the food kiosks.

"Enough's enough," Ryan says, leading the way up to the exits.

My bladder feels like it's going to burst so I head straight for the toilets while Raks and Ryan join the food queues. Another rumble of booing lets me know the half-time whistle has gone. When I've finished in the toilets I stand in the concourse watching *Soccer Saturday*, checking the scores in our division. Mackworth aren't playing, but Grimsby and Boston are both losing.

Ryan brings me a cup of coffee and we follow Raks up the stairs, onto the terracing and back to our crush barrier. We don't seem to have any half-time entertainment today. Even Danny Holmes looks a bit subdued. No ball-juggling this week. Bon Jovi are on the PA again, and the scoreboard is flashing up announcements. *Half Price Sale — One Week Only At The Club Shop. Happy 70th Birthday Ken From Doris And The Kids. Today's Match Is Sponsored By JB Lynex And Sons Butchers.*

Raks has got himself a steak and kidney pie. He lifts the pastry lid with his plastic fork. A musty smell wafts out and he shakes his head. I take a mouthful of coffee and grimace. It's seriously strong stuff. I'm just lifting the cup to take another swig when someone ruffles my hair. Gary Simmons.

"Fucking hell Gary," I say. "You'll have to have to stop touching me up. People are going to say something's going on between us."

Gary laughs. His complexion is pinker than ever.

"Where are you today?" I ask.

"At the back." Gary points up the slope towards Jerome and Rob. Rob's absent-mindedly picking the spots on his forehead and Jerome's just standing there looking huge.

I raise my hand in acknowledgement. Just to the right of them, I notice Jimmy and Scotty, the other lads from Parkway. We've got a full turnout again.

Gary looks across into the Ashborough section. "Piss-poor away support."

Raks nods.

"Ryan still reckons we might get a bit of fun this afternoon, though. That right Ryan?"

Ryan's been looking at his phone. He puts it away and pushes out his bottom lip.

"Well it's not looking good," he says. "But like I said, there are usually some opportunities if you know where to look for them." He raises his eyebrows and leaves it at that.

Gary's face lights up.

"If anyone can sniff out trouble it's Ryan. He's like a fucking bloodhound."

We all laugh, and Gary heads back towards the rest of his crew.

A couple of minutes later, we're into the second half. Dave Nicholson's carrying on where he left off. With his first touch, he miscontrols a pass from Kevin Taylor and then clatters into the Ashborough number 12 as the ball spins loose. The Ashborough lad goes down like he's been shot. Straight away the ref goes charging in, and a chant of *Off Off Off* goes up. But it's not the Ashborough fans, finally waking up. It's us. The ref reaches for his pocket. He flourishes the card in the air like a magician. Yellow. We all groan.

Dave trots back towards our goal, barking instructions to Eric Emanuel and Jeff Hawkins, trying to organise a wall. Before Dave's turned round though, the ref's blown his whistle and the free kick's been taken.

"He's behind you," someone bellows. Twitchy Bloke's got his head in his hands. It looks like it's going to be one of those afternoons.

But then a funny thing happens. Football breaks out. One minute we're hoofing the ball around like it might explode if someone tries to control it, the next we're zipping it around like Tiger Woods with a pitching wedge. Suddenly we're stringing together fourteen passes in a row. During the next move it's seventeen. People start shouting *Ole* every time a Letchford player touches the ball. It's amazing. Carl Butterworth's bossing the midfield, Mark Sheedy is marauding up the left flank and Leroy Lewton is running the defence ragged.

Ryan scratches his head.

"Fuck me," he says. "What's all this?"

On 62 minutes, Tony O'Neill spots Leroy Lewton sprinting diagonally into the Ashborough box and sends a perfectly weighted ball right into his path. What the papers would call a *Slide Rule Pass*. Leroy lets the ball come across his body onto his right foot and then slots it, first time, into the bottom left corner. 1-0.

The usual tidal wave of bodies cascades forwards, but I'm prepared for it this time. As the cheering dies down and we start serenading our number 16 with a chant of *Leroy, Leroy, Leroy*, I'm still right where I started and so is Raks.

"I've got this crowd thing sorted," he says, grinning.

Ryan looks at us both and nods in recognition.

The whole pattern of the match has changed. We're only 1-0 up, but I already get the feeling that there's no way back for Ashborough. They're just not in the game. Even Pessimistic Granddad's smiling now, although I think that's got something to do with the hip flask of whisky he poured down himself at half time.

As we head into the last twenty minutes, the Ashborough fans finally burst into song. A few rounds of *Ashborough, La La La*. It's pretty pathetic stuff. We give them an ironic round of applause for making the effort, and then hit them with *You're So Shit It's Unbelievable, Are You Mackworth In Disguise?* and *Can We Play You Every Week?*

As the timer shows 86:00, Leroy Lewton trots off to a standing ovation, to be replaced by Danny

Holmes, blue boots gleaming under the floodlights. His first few touches aren't up to much, but it's a case of third time lucky. Jimmy Knapper hacks a long kick downfield, it bounces into the area and Danny's onto it like a shot. He turns past the last defender with the ball stuck to his chest and sticks it between Martin Jones's legs, spinning round again to point out the name on the back of his shirt.

We all start to celebrate, but the Ashborough players are running to the ref, signalling for handball. I've got to admit, Danny seemed to have the ball stuck under his arm as he turned. It looked like he was playing the bagpipes. The ref's not bothered though. He's given the goal.

The game's just about done now. A lot of the Ashborough fans are streaming towards the exits and we're sending them on their way with a chant of *We Can See You Sneaking Out*. The strange thing is though, as some of the fans are heading up the terraces, others are staying still. Standing their ground. It's like the tide going out but leaving something dodgy behind on the beach. The Ashborough firm are showing their colours.

Ryan grabs my shoulders and gives me a shake. Then he does the same to Raks. He's seen what's happening. He looks ecstatic.

"Here we go," he says. "Ashborough have grown some bollocks at last."

The atmosphere has shifted into a higher gear. It's not quite as intense as it was at the Castleton game, but it's getting there. A group of about thirty Ashborough fans is heading across the deserted terracing, chanting and threatening us. Straight away gangs are joining together on our side of the fencing. The civilians are retreating and the soldiers are advancing. The adrenalin's pumping now. My heart's pounding and I'm feeling a bit light-headed. This is what I've been waiting for. This is what I've been craving.

The stewards have seen what's going on, and they've started inching up the steps on either side of the wire mesh, doing their best to keep the fans apart. It's all pretty pointless though. We all know this is just the warm-up. The main event's going to be outside, and there isn't going to be fencing keeping us apart out there.

When the final whistle goes, it's like someone firing the pistol at the start of the Olympic 100 metres final. In a matter of seconds, we're up to the exit, down the stairs, across the concourse and through the gates. Just like before, all the Letchford gangs are joining together, becoming one big unit. The NLLF, ready for battle.

But as we turn left and track along the back of the stand, heading for the away gates, it becomes clear that the powers that be have come prepared today. There's a human shield separating us from the Ashborough fans. Sixty or seventy green-jacketed stewards mixed in with half-a-dozen police in riot gear. By sheer weight of numbers we could probably break through. But that would mean tangling with the cops. And that's serious business. We all come to a halt. The battle's not going to happen. I feel completely cheated.

Raks blows out his cheeks.

"Fuck," he says.

Gary shakes his head.

"Fucking pointless," Jerome says.

Rob just looks miserable.

Slowly but surely, the Letchford lads start to drift

away. Jimmy and Scotty have already called it a night. Ryan brushes past me, staring up past the police and the stewards, towards the Ashborough mob. They've cleared the area around the gates, and they're being shepherded out across the car park. A couple of them are starting to feel really brave now that they're out of danger, dancing round under the lights, giving us the finger.

"Wankers," Raks says.

Ryan smiles but then he looks serious again.

"Time to move," he says. Beckoning us to follow, he sets off round the corner and down the back of the Main Stand.

We're travelling faster than the rest of the crowd, and by the time we've got to the other side of the players' car park, cutting through the Range Rovers and Kompressors, the only people ahead of us are the ones who left long before the end of the game. I'm expecting us to turn left, go back through the Industrial Estate via the usual route, but Ryan's got other ideas.

"This way." He's heading up to the right, crossing the road and leading us into an alleyway between two empty factory units.

It's pitch black in the alley, but we keep going. A six-man Special Operations unit on a mission. My heart rate's shooting up again, and it's not just because we're moving quickly. We head right, then left, then right again. I'm completely lost, but Ryan seems to know where he's going. After a couple of minutes of ducking and diving we come out of the maze of factories and onto a lighted street. Over in the distance, across some wasteland, I can just make out the front of The Shakespeare. To the left, I see the digital clock at the front of Morrells. We're almost back at the main road through the Industrial Estate. I know where we are at last. And I'm starting to get an idea of what we might be about to do.

Ryan heads straight for the wasteland, and we follow him again, through the muck and the rubble and the scrubby bushes and the burnt-out cars. Thirty seconds later we're in a position parallel with the main road, under the pylons, hidden from view by a mud bank. Up to the left, black against the glare of the Southlands floodlights in the background, the first of the Letchford fans are heading back towards town. And coming through the crowd, picking up speed, are the Ashborough supporters' coaches. It's just as I thought. An ambush.

We've only got a few seconds to get ourselves set. Just before the coaches pull level with where we're hiding, we break cover, jumping up onto the mud bank like Red Indians cutting off the wagon train at the pass. Instead of bows and arrows though, we're armed with anything we can get our hands on. Ryan starts the barrage, a half-brick bouncing off the roof of the first coach, and then we all join in. Stones and bottles and spark plugs rain down on the tatty buses, denting metal and cracking toughened glass. The Ashborough fans are ducking for cover, putting their arms up over their heads, faces twisted in fear.

It's an amazing scene, but it doesn't last long. Just the time it takes two coaches to travel along fifty yards of road. As the buses disappear into the distance, we run back down the mud bank, whooping and screaming, psyched up to the eyeballs, giving high-fives all round.

Gary Simmons looks like he's going to explode.

"I fucking told you," he screams. "I told you Ryan could sniff out trouble."

Ryan grins and bows, and then we all start laughing like idiots. Totally out of our minds. Totally out of control. It feels fucking fantastic.

As the laugher dies down, I close my eyes and take deep breaths. Savouring all the sensations. Taking everything in. I'm thinking about what Trev said in The Shakespeare. About how the memories never leave you. He's right. I know I'm going to remember this moment, this feeling, for the rest of my life.

eleven

Raks pushes his phone into his coat pocket and shakes his head.

"Full time," he says.

"Still 1-0 to Mansfield?"

"Yep."

"Shit. We just can't get it together, can we? I mean, we looked brilliant in the second half against Ashborough, but then we rolled over at Barnet last Saturday, and now this."

Raks grins.

"At this rate we're going to be playing Burton Albion and Northwich Victoria next season. At least we might win a few games."

I shake my head.

"I wouldn't be too sure. We've already been beaten by Kidderminster this year, and they're just a mid-table Conference side."

Raks nods.

"Yeah," he says. "It's not funny."

The bus stops. The doors swish open and some people get off. Another swish and we're away again. I check my watch. Just gone five o'clock. Wiping condensation off the window, I look out into the darkness. We're coming along the main road back into Thurston. Up ahead I can just make out the orange glow of the streetlights. We should be back in the village in a couple of minutes.

I take my phone out and check it. I'm hoping that

Zoe might have been in touch, but there's nothing. I puff out my cheeks and put the phone away again.

"No text from Zoe today?" Raks asks.

"No," I tell him. "She's round that Simon Matthews's house. Mr Sowerberry. They're rehearsing for *Oliver*."

"Oh yeah?" Raks raises his eyebrows. "Rehearsing, eh?"

"Piss off Raks," I say. He's only trying to wind me up, and I know I should just ignore him, but it's hard. Zoe seems to spend more time with Simon than she does with me these days. I used to see her almost every other night. Now it's hardly ever. We still meet up in the mornings at the bus stop, but that hardly counts. And we seem to spend most of that time arguing, usually about Letchford Town. An unhealthy obsession, she reckons.

Raks knows he's got me rattled, so he lets it drop.

"You still OK for tonight?"

"Yeah," I reply. "The big Patel family knees-up. I'll be there."

Raks laughs.

"I wouldn't get too excited. It'll be exactly the same as it is every year. Just a load of my mum and dad's relatives gossiping and moaning. Bragging about how much they're earning and how big their cars are."

I shake my head.

"It'll be OK."

Raks rolls his head from side to side, then smiles.

"Nanny Patel will be there," he says. "She's over from Leicester. She'll be looking forward to seeing you again."

We both laugh. Nanny Patel's got a bit of a soft spot for me.

"How long do you think it'll take her to ask me about my love life?" I ask.

Raks shrugs.

"Dunno. Ten seconds?"

I grin. Nanny Patel's alright. When we were younger, Raks used to be a bit embarrassed about her, but there was no need. She's like a grandparent is supposed to be. I don't have much contact with my own grandparents. My dad's folks died when I was really little, and we haven't seen much of the other side of the family since my mum died. My mum's parents live in Stourbridge, near Birmingham. It's posh there. According to my dad, my mum's lot never really took to him. Thought he'd taken their daughter down in the world.

The bus is coming up to the crossroads and the war memorial now, turning right and heading down past the shops on Lindisfarne Street. I pick up my shopping bags, then I ring the bell and we go down the stairs. Outside, I zip up my jacket and shiver. We're into December now, and there's frost on the way.

Walking quickly, we're back at Dale Road, fifty yards down from my house, in about ten minutes.

"So you'll be round about seven, then?" Raks says.

I nod.

"And your dad's still coming, isn't he?"

I shrug.

"He's supposed to be." Secretly I'm hoping I might be able to talk him out of it. He's been drinking more than ever just recently. I'm worried he might get pissed and maudlin. Make an arse of himself.

We come to my front gate. I turn down the path and Raks carries on along the street.

"See you sevenish," he calls.

"Yeah. See you mate."

Inside, Dad's had the heating on and it's quite warm. I put my head round the door into the living room, expecting to see him flopped on the sofa, but he's not there. I go back into the hallway and hang my jacket on the pegs. There's music coming from up above. My room, by the sounds of it.

Climbing the stairs two at a time, I push open the bathroom door. Dad's definitely been in here. The air's full of steam and the place stinks of Polytar shampoo. I go back out onto the landing just as Dad's coming out of his room. He's straight from the shower, towel round his waist. He's had a shave at long last, his first in six weeks. That's good. What's not so good is that it doesn't look like I'm going to able to persuade him to stay at home tonight.

"Alright, Tom?" He looks down at the plastic bags in my hands. "Been into Letchford?"

"Yeah."

"Get anything good?"

"Tracky top. Pair of trainers."

He looks surprised.

"Another pair of trainers? You only got those Nikes a few weeks back."

I roll my eyes.

"It was a lot longer ago than that," I tell him. "Anyway, these are Adidas. Adidas Sambas."

"Sambas? God, people were wearing those when I was a kid."

I head into my room and throw my stuff on the bed. Dad follows me in. He's brought one of his CDs upstairs and it's playing on my stereo. Chunky basslines and synthesisers.

"What's this crap?" I ask, laughing.

He pretends to be offended.

"This is proper music," he says. "Level 42. *World*

151

Machine."

I nod. I knew it was Level 42 really. He plays it often enough. He met my mum at a Level 42 concert. March 1987. At the NEC in Birmingham. It was love at first sight, Dad reckons. Sometimes when he plays Level 42, it makes him happy. Other times it makes him sad. I just hope he's feeling happy tonight.

Dad wanders over to my chest of drawers. He picks up a DVD case, holding it out in front of him. *Terrace Warfare*. The cover shows a bloke, covered in blood, clutching a towel to his head.

"Tom," he says. "When I came in here earlier on, I couldn't help noticing this."

I swallow. Suddenly I'm feeling very hot.

"Oh, that's nothing," I say.

He doesn't look convinced.

"Are you sure?" He tilts his head to one side. "You're not getting yourself into any trouble with this Letchford Town thing, are you?"

"Course not," I say, a bit too quickly.

Dad nods. He runs a hand through his hair.

"You know Tom, it can be dangerous at some of these matches."

I laugh.

"It's nothing I can't handle."

He looks at the DVD case again.

"Whatever. You don't want to be spending your money on crap like this though."

I shake my head.

"Someone just lent it to me."

He nods.

"This Ryan character again?"

"Yeah," I say.

Dad frowns.

"I'm not too sure I like the sound of this bloke. He

152

seems like a bad influence. You know, you're a bright lad. You've got your mum's brains. They told me you got the best SATs results in your year last summer. You don't want to let it all go to waste."

I'm starting to get a bit narked now.

"Look Dad," I say. "It's just a DVD. And you don't need to go on at me about bad influences. Like you said, I'm bright enough. I'm in control of what I do. I've got a mind of my own."

Dad puts the DVD down. He's hovering now. Level 42 are launching into *Something About You*.

I don't want to be interrogated any more. It's half past five and I want to get on.

"Right then," I say, pulling my sweatshirt up over my head. "I'm going to go in the shower, and then I said we'd be round the Patels' about seven."

Dad looks at me one more time. I can sense that he's still got things he wants to say, but before he can, I'm past him and onto the landing.

By quarter to seven, I've had a nice long shower, brushed my teeth, sprayed my pits and generally got myself spruced up. Dad's gone now and he's taken his CD with him. I stick on the first Kasabian album to get myself in the mood. I put on clean socks and boxer shorts, pull on my jeans, a T-shirt and my new zip-up Adidas tracky top, then I thread the laces through my new trainers. Sambas in black leather with white stripes. Two minutes later I'm done. I open my wardrobe so that I can see myself in the mirror on the back of the door. I've had a bit of an image overhaul in the last few weeks. I look pretty good.

Downstairs, I check that my phone's in my jacket pocket, then go into the living room. Dad's on the sofa. He's quite smartly dressed. A pair of black trousers and a blue check shirt. I'm just breathing a sigh of relief about that when I notice he's looking at me with guilt in his eyes. Straight away I get a sinking feeling in the pit of my stomach. It's what I was worried about. He's started drinking. There are two empty Stella cans on the coffee table and he's got another can in his hand.

"Just a couple of drinks," he says. "Something to take the edge off."

I take a breath.

"You know, if you're anxious about tonight, you could always stay here. I know you're a bit funny when it comes to being round lots of people."

He shakes his head.

"I'll be fine," he says. "You're not ashamed of your old dad are you?" There's something different in his eyes now. It's not guilt. It's hurt.

I rub my nose.

"Course not."

I sit in one of the armchairs and watch TV for a couple of minutes. It's some sort of talent show. A contortionist in a blue and red catsuit is bending himself into all sorts of positions. At the end of his act, he folds himself into a Perspex box and someone carries him off the stage. My stomach rumbles. I've not eaten since the middle of the afternoon. I think about knocking up a quick sandwich, but decide not to bother. There's going to be food at Raks's house, lots of it. The clock on the mantelpiece says it's getting on for five to seven.

"Best make a move," I say.

Dad stands, picking up the Costcutter bag by his feet. The bag clanks. No prizes for guessing what's in it.

"You don't need to take any drink, Dad," I say. "Raks told me to tell you. His mum and dad will have

154

loads in. You know what they're like."

Dad shakes his head.

"Got to do my bit."

We go into the hallway to get our jackets on. Close up, Dad reeks of booze. He's tried to cover it up with aftershave, but there's no mistaking it. And I can tell it's a lot more than three Stella's worth. He's been drinking all afternoon. I think about having a last go at keeping him at home, but I decide not to bother. He's not going to be feeling anxious about anything now. He's full of Dutch courage.

It's a five-minute walk to the Patels' house. It's properly cold. Stars are shining in the sky and the pavements are starting to turn white. Christmas decorations are everywhere. Every other house on the estate seems to have a couple of miles of fairy lights or an inflatable Homer Simpson in a Santa suit. We come to the corner of Westleigh Road and turn into Cambridge Street. The Patels' house is about fifty yards up on the left. I follow Dad up the path to the front door. We ring the bell and wait.

From the outside, the house looks pretty much the same as ours. Bay-fronted, semi-detached, like all the houses around here. Once you get inside though, the similarities end. We've got three bedrooms and they've got five, but that's not the real difference. Since Mum died, our house has been in a state of suspended animation. Nothing's changed. Carpets, curtains, wallpaper, it's all the same. And it's starting to look a bit dingy. You couldn't call the Patels' house dingy. It's like a palace.

Something's moving behind the frosted glass panels at the top of the door now. There's a rattling sound as bolts are drawn back and then the door swings open. It's Raks's dad, Raj. He's well turned-out as usual, in jeans and an open-collared white shirt. His hair is slicked back and his goatee is neatly trimmed. He smiles and holds out his hand.

"Tony. Tom. Welcome. Glad you could make it."

We step into the hall and start taking our jackets off. Sunita, Raks's mum, sticks her head out of the living room and smiles at me. Dad holds out his bag of cans.

"Something for the party, Raj," he says.

Raj looks into the bag and waves his hand.

"Tony. You shouldn't have bothered. I'm sure we'll find some use for them though."

Both blokes laugh. It makes me feel a bit better. Maybe Dad's going to be OK tonight after all.

I look up. Raks is coming down from his bedroom.

"Alright, Tom?" he says as he gets to the bottom of the stairs.

I nod.

He looks me up and down. The skinhead. The zip-up top. The trainers.

"Shit," he says. "You're turning into Ryan."

I sniff.

"Look who's talking," I say, pointing at Raks's Adidas T-shirt and white Campus. His short-cropped hair looks immaculate, gleaming under the light from the landing above.

He shrugs.

"You could be right," he says. He looks down towards the kitchen. "Come on. We'd better go and see Nanny Patel."

I follow him down the hallway. The dining room and the living room are packed with family members, but Nanny Patel's sitting at the kitchen table. She's in a blue sari, drinking a cup of tea. There's just her and Raks's little brothers Nilesh and Suresh. They're performing a song for her, singing into a green plastic microphone. When the song finishes, they press a button on the mike stand and a sound like machine gun fire comes out. Presumably it's supposed to be applause. Nanny Patel smiles and thanks them. Then she looks at me.

"Thomas," she says, eyes lighting up. "How are you? How is your love life?"

I look at Raks and grin.

"Oh, it's not so bad, Mrs P," I reply. "I'm still seeing a girl called Zoe. Been a few years now."

Nanny Patel nods. She must be in her sixties but she looks a good fifteen years younger. Her skin is smooth and her hair is still shiny and black, scraped up off her forehead. You can see where Raks gets his good genes from.

"You need to find Rakesh a nice young lady," she says.

I shake my head.

"I do try," I say. "But no-one will have him."

We all laugh.

Twenty minutes later Raks and me are heading up the stairs to his room. We've filled up on snacks and nibbles, and we've done the rounds of the relatives. My dad seems alright, deep in conversation with Raks's uncle Arvind. He's onto the spirits now, but it looks like he's in a good mood.

"I've got something to show you," Raks says, as he opens his bedroom door.

On his desk, under the window, is a brand new PC. Shiny, black, slim-line tower. Flat screen monitor. Printer. Swanky-looking keyboard. He's even got a Letchford Town mouse mat.

"Shit," I say. "You jammy bastard."

Raks sits on the edge of his bed.

"Forgot to tell you earlier on. Dad got it yesterday. Staff discount at Curry's. My old one had been on its last legs for months. This one's the dog's bollocks." He gets up and switches it on. "And now I've got a decent machine, my mum and dad have got me broadband."

I laugh.

"Nice one," I say. "Bit of cut-and-pasting and the GCSE coursework's in the bag."

"Too right."

The start-up is finished now. Raks sits at the desk, clicks on the internet icon and finds us the *Google* homepage. He looks at me and grins.

"One more thing." He bends forward and opens a drawer down to the right. Straightening up, he plonks four cans of Carling down next to the monitor. "Sneaked them up earlier on. Dad won't notice. He's got about half an off-licence's worth downstairs."

I'm impressed.

"It's at times like this that I remember why I'm your mate," I tell him.

Raks pulls a can out of the fourpack and cracks it open. He passes it to me and then opens a can for himself. He looks back at the screen. We're both thinking the same thing.

"Are you going to do it, or am I?" he asks.

I pick up the table at the side of the bed and carry it across to use as a chair. Leaning over, and pulling the keyboard towards me, I type in *LOWER-LEAGUELADS.CO.UK*. Straight away, we're at the hooligan table.

"Check it out," Raks says. "We're up to 4th."

"Yeah," I take a mouthful of beer. "But Mackworth are still top."

Raks narrows his eyes, scanning up and down the

league.

"Look where Whitbourne are," he says. "5th. One place behind us."

I nod.

"And we're playing them on Tuesday. December 5th. My birthday. It's going to be a proper crunch match."

Raks looks at the options across the top of the page.

"*Previews*," he says. "Do you think they might have something about Letchford-Whitbourne on there?"

"Probably. Have a look."

Raks takes the mouse and clicks on *Previews*. Letchford-Whitbourne is first on the list. A red rectangle with *Warning:Flashpoint* is superimposed over the text.

Big night at Southlands. Letchfords youth crew come nose 2 nose with Whitbournes old campaigners. Should b tasty. Expect fireworks. Letchford O.B. starting to become a pest, but will need 2b on there toes for this one.

My stomach flips over.

"Fuck," I say. "It sounds like a big one."

"Mmm." Raks clicks us back to the league table, then onto the *Newsdesk* option, scrolling down for references to Letchford. Halfway down the list is *Letchford-Ashborough Match Report*.

Not much action here. Letchford out in force again, Ashborough low in numbers. Didn't really want 2 know. O.B. well on top outside. Good work by Letchford Hardcore, gave away coaches brick broadside.

We look at each other, eyes wide. It's a direct reference to us.

"*The Hardcore*," Raks says. "We're the fucking *Hardcore*, Tommy Boy."

I laugh.

"It's another one for the scrapbook."

Raks nods.

"Yeah. I was a bit pissed off when we didn't get a mention in *Super Goals* last Monday."

We read the report through a few more times. Then I pick up the mouse and get us back to the start.

"What do you reckon *Your Views* is all about?"

Raks takes a gulp of Carling and belches.

"Dunno," he says. "Have a look."

I roll the arrow up and click the button. *Your Views* flashes onto the screen.

Basically, it's a messageboard. But it's not like any messageboard I've looked at before. Straight away, slap-bang in the middle of the screen, is the most recent posting.

Your league table is fuckin shit Castleton full-on would fuck up Whitbourne big-time. BigJon.

Scrolling down, it's more of the same.

Mitcham r still a force dont rul them out will test big guns. Cocky88. Ashborough Crew on home turf will rip Mackworth to shredds. AshyBoy.

Raks blows out a breath.

"Fuck," he says. "It's a hooligan forum. Letchford have got to get a mention somewhere in there."

I finish off my first can of Carling and crack open my second. I get page two up on screen. I shake my head.

"It'll take us ages."

Raks looks at me and grins.

"Better get cracking then, mate," he says.

We spend the next half an hour reading through

160

page after page of threats and boasts from just about every club in our league. Letchford are cropping up all over the place. It looks like everyone wants to have a pop at us. Someone calling himself *Mackworth92* has been spending a lot of time at his keyboard. He's posted at least ten messages.

Letchford soft lads will pay the price. Mackworth rule supreme over Letchford scum.

Raks points at the screen.

"He's a bit keen," he says.

I nod. *Mackworth92*'s most recent contribution rolls into view. Posted yesterday.

Mackworth boys will take over Southlands 16 Dec.

Raks laughs.

"Tosser," he says. "I think we should join the debate. What do you reckon?"

I grin. I take a last swig of my second can of beer, then I click on *Leave A Message*. I'm just about to start typing when there's a knock on the door.

"Rakesh?" a voice says.

We both freeze. It's Raks's mum.

"Shit," Raks says. "Hide the beer."

I start shoving the cans under the bed, while Raks gets the *Google* homepage back up on screen.

There's another knock on the door.

"Rakesh? Thomas? Are you in there?"

Raks clears his throat.

"Yeah, Mum," he calls. "What's up?"

Sunita pushes the door and comes into the room. She looks at me and smiles, but it's not the same sort of smile as before. She looks slightly uneasy.

"Tom, I'm sorry about this," she says. "But I think your dad needs you."

I get a deathly sinking sensation in my stomach. I'm pretty sure I know exactly what she means. I knew Level 42 was a bad sign. All of a sudden the nice warm fuzzy feeling I was getting from the beer has gone. I follow Sunita down the stairs and into the kitchen. Nanny Patel's not there now, but my dad is. He's sitting on a chair in the corner, sobbing. He's saying my mum's name over and over again. Raks's dad is kneeling down next to him. Uncle Arvind is standing by the hob. He looks aghast.

"I feel really awful," Arvind says. "I don't know if it's something I said to him. We seemed to be getting on really well."

"It's not your fault," I say. "He just gets like this. The drink doesn't help. He just gets to a certain point, then it all comes crashing down. I'll take him home."

Dad looks up at me. His eyes are red with tears. I try to give him a smile, reassure him, but it's hard. I'm so embarrassed I actually feel sick. I just want the ground to swallow me up.

Raks has come into the kitchen now.

"Do you want me to walk back with you?" he asks.

I shake my head.

"No. I'll be alright." I look at Raks's mum and dad. "Look, I'm really sorry," I tell them.

They both hold their hands up.

"Don't be silly," Raj says. "It's fine. No harm done. Your dad's had a rough time of it, the last few years, since Clare died. Let me give you both a lift."

"No thanks Mr Patel," I say. "The walk will do him good." I can just imagine Dad puking in the back of the car. That would really round things off nicely.

Raks goes into the hallway and gets our jackets. While I'm putting mine on, Arvind and Raj help Dad to his feet. Sunita gives him a kiss on his cheek and it starts him crying again.

"Come on Dad," I say. "We need to get off now."

Dad starts pulling his jacket on, mumbling apologies to everyone. Eventually he's ready and I lead him down the hallway towards the front door.

I look at Sunita.

"I'm really sorry," I tell her again.

"Don't worry Tom," she says. "It'll all be forgotten in the morning."

I nod.

"Give me a bell tomorrow," Raks says. "Or tonight if you want. And if there's anything you need..."

"Thanks mate."

Raj opens the door and we step out into the freezing night. As the door clicks shut behind us, Dad starts up the path. He catches the edge of a paving stone with his shoe and nearly falls over. He reaches out and steadies himself against me. Without really meaning to, I feel myself pulling away from him. I don't want him to touch me.

"I'm sorry Tom," he says.

Deep down, I know that this is the point where I'm supposed to pat him on the arm and tell him that everything's alright, give him a bit of sympathy. But I just can't. Because everything *isn't* alright. This has been going on for years. And I've had enough of it.

"Just shut up, Dad," I say.

He looks at me and I see a mixture of emotions on his face. Surprise. Guilt. Sadness. I brush past him and open the gate. Then I stride out onto the street and head for home.

twelve

Zoe leans forward and kisses me on the lips.

"Happy birthday, fifteen year old," she says.

I smile and pull her close, squeezing her body against mine. It's chilly at the bus stop this morning and there's a cold wind starting to blow. It's nice to share warmth.

"Thanks."

She unzips her shoulder bag.

"Right then." She grins excitedly. "I want your eyes shut and your hands out in front of you."

I do as she says. There's the sound of rummaging as she goes through her bag. Something flat is placed onto my palms, and then something else is put on top of it.

"OK, I'm finished now," she says.

I open my eyes. In my hands there's a card in a red envelope and a small box, just a couple of inches square, wrapped in orange paper with a black ribbon around it.

Zoe smiles.

"I used Letchford Town colours," she tells me.

I grin. I know Letchford Town aren't really flavour of the month with her, so it's a nice gesture.

"Shall I do the card first?" I ask.

"It's up to you."

I put the box on the wall next to me and tear open the red envelope. It's a *Far Side* card. Zoe knows I like *Far Side* cards. Two deer are standing in a forest. One of them has got a red target on his stomach. The caption says *Bummer of a birthmark, Hal*. I open the card and read what she's written inside. *Happy Birthday Tom. Loads of Love n Hugs Zoe X*.

I show the front of the card to Raks.

"Nice one," he says.

I put the card in my inside jacket pocket, then I pick up my present.

Zoe's looking a bit embarrassed.

"Now, if you don't like it, Tom, I can always take it back and get you something else."

I reach out and touch her hand.

"Hold on," I say. "I've not even seen it yet."

I unwind the ribbon and start to take the orange paper off. Whatever my present is, it's inside a small box covered in burgundy-coloured velvet.

Raks looks at Zoe, eyes wide. He shakes his head.

"It's not an engagement ring is it?" he asks. "You're not going to propose to the sad bastard are you?"

Zoe swings a kick at him.

"Shut up Raks," she says, grinning.

I flick up the lid of the velvet box. Inside, nestled on some black material, is a silver chain with a T pendant. I'm chuffed. I look at Zoe.

"Hey," I say. "It's cracking."

She still seems a bit uncertain.

"Are you sure?" she says, green eyes apprehensive. "I got it from one of those little shops in The Lanes, and I could tell you weren't too impressed by The Lanes were you? You're not just saying that you like it because you don't want to upset me?"

I shake my head. I take hold of her hand and kiss her.

"Don't be soft," I say. "It's cracking. I mean it."

"You'll definitely wear it?"

I nod.

"Definitely." I take the necklace out of the box and undo the clasp. I hand it to Zoe. "You can put it on for me."

She reaches round behind my head and re-fastens the clasp. I pull down the zips on my jacket and on my tracky top, so that the T pendant is next to my chest. Zoe smiles. I've put her mind at rest now.

"So what did you get from your dad?" she asks, sitting up on the wall next to me.

I shrug.

"You know my dad. He's not one of the world's great present buyers. He put a hundred quid in a card."

Zoe wrinkles her forehead.

"A hundred quid? Not bad. You got fifty last year didn't you?"

"Yeah," I say. "It's conscience money though. I'd have got fifty this year too, but he made a berk of himself on Saturday night round at Raks's house. He's trying to get himself back in the good books."

She looks intrigued.

"He made a berk of himself? What did he do?"

I sigh.

"I don't really want to talk about it," I tell her. "Alcohol was involved though."

She nods.

"I hope he's alright."

I change the subject.

"I got a twenty quid note from my grandparents. In a card with a bunch of lilies on the front. They signed it *Best wishes from Margaret and Roger*."

"The personal touch," Raks says, grinning.

"And what about Raks?" Zoe asks. "What did he

166

get you?"

I laugh.

"The tight bastard just brought me six cans of beer he pinched off his dad. I've got them hidden under my bed."

Raks pretends to be offended.

"You ungrateful sod," he says, voice rising. "It's good stuff that. Grolsch. Cost you six or seven quid in the shops. I'll have it back if you don't want it."

I blow him a kiss.

"I'm only pissing around."

We both start laughing.

Zoe tuts.

"Oh," I say. "Raks got me a card, too."

Raks grabs my arm.

"Don't show her the card, man," he says.

I shrug him off. Bending down, I unzip the side compartment of my bag and get the card out, holding it up for Zoe to see. Raks made it himself. Putting his new PC to good use. On the front there's a photo-shopped picture of my head superimposed onto the body of a bloke engaged in an illegal sex act. With a farm animal.

Zoe winces.

"You two are sick."

The Letchford Grammar coach pulls up at the kerb, twenty yards down to my left. It won't be long before the other buses arrive. Zoe brushes some fluff off her blazer. She takes a breath.

"I thought I'd come round this evening after school," she says. "I know you have Thurston Dynamo training on Tuesday night, but that's not until six. If I come round about half four…"

I close my eyes and grit my teeth.

"I can't make it," I tell her. "I'm staying in town

167

tonight after college. Letchford have got a match. Whitbourne Wanderers." My stomach lurches. Just mentioning the game has got my adrenalin flowing.

Zoe looks surprised.

"What about training? You always go to training. I bet you haven't missed a session in years."

I hold my hands out, palms up.

"Dunno. One week isn't going to hurt."

Zoe flicks her eyes down to the ground. She doesn't look happy.

"I could do tomorrow," I tell her. It's an attempt at damage limitation. The last few weeks have been one long rough patch and I know Zoe's made a big effort this morning. I'm trying to do my bit.

She shakes her head.

"Rehearsals."

I nod. I can't complain. I snubbed her and she's snubbed me. One-all.

She looks at me.

"You do know the performance is next Friday night, don't you? You have remembered, haven't you? The date's on the tickets. Eight o'clock in the drama studio."

I nod again.

She looks up. Her bus is coming over the crossroads. She pulls her bag onto her shoulder and gets down from the wall.

"Time to go," she says.

I take hold of her hands and kiss her. The whole situation feels awkward. Now would be a good time to come out with something reassuring, or better still, something funny. Something to lift the atmosphere. My mind's a blank though.

"Sorry about tonight," I say. It's the best I can manage. "But thanks for my present."

Zoe smiles. It looks a bit half-hearted.

"See you Tom." She turns and heads for the bus.

"See you," I call after her. But I don't think she hears me.

Tuesday mornings at Parkway are generally very dull. Today's no exception. Geography with Greeny first thing, then Maths with Mr Wood. And to round things off, English with Mrs Wetherall. Usually, English is made just about bearable by the fact that Ryan's in the class. The look on Mrs Wetherall's face whenever he comes into the room is always good for a laugh. It's been even better, the last couple of weeks. She just *knows* Ryan keyed her car, but there's no way she can prove it. Today though, Ryan's nowhere to be seen.

At five past twelve, the bell rings to end morning lessons. Raks and me put our pens and pads away and head off round the curve towards the dining hall, stopping off on the way to put our bags in our lockers. We've beaten the rush at the canteen, and we're straight to the front of the queue, loading up our trays with all the essentials. Chips, a hot dog, a doughnut and a can of Pepsi for me. Chips, beans, sausage and bacon, a Coke and an éclair for Raks.

As we walk out into the hall, someone whistles. I look up and see Gary Simmons waving at us. He's sitting with Rob and Jerome, at a table over by the noticeboards.

We start to cut across the hall in the direction of Gary's table. Glancing to my left, I see a big lad coming towards us. He looks familiar. Tousled hair. Spots. Army jacket. It's the bastard who helped himself to one of my chips a few weeks back.

I nudge Raks with my elbow.

"Look who it is," I say, nodding in the direction of

Army Jacket Boy.

Raks grins.

"Wonder if he likes the look of your dinner today?" he says.

"Dunno," I say. "I think I'll find out."

I come to a stop, out in the middle of the floor, right in Army Jacket Boy's path, turning my tray round so that he's got a full choice of food items to take his pick from. The thing is, he doesn't look so keen this time. He's seen me and he knows I've seen him. All of a sudden he's changing course, eyes glued to the ground, picking up speed and heading for the foyer.

I draw in a deep breath. I feel good. Powerful. People don't mess with me these days. I look at Raks and raise my eyebrows.

"Soft bastard," he says.

We both laugh, then we carry on across to Gary's table, pulling out a couple of chairs and unloading our trays.

"How you doing boys?" Gary says.

"Not bad," Raks says.

Jerome nods at us both and we nod back.

Rob stuffs a slice of pizza into his mouth.

"No sign of Dawkins?" he says.

I open my can and shake my head.

"Not seen him."

We spend the next fifteen minutes or so eating and chatting away, checking out the girls. Susie Black and Carly Watts are sitting at a table over to the right, and I've caught them looking in our direction two or three times. The Medstone chip shop girls are sitting by the double doors, next to the Christmas tree. Raks reckons they've been giving us the once-over too.

As I'm finishing my doughnut, I look up at the

noticeboards. It's all the usual stuff. Sports teams. Clubs and Societies. Flyers for events. Rules and regulations for this and that. Up in the top left hand corner there's a new note. Hand-written in chunky black pen on a red sheet of A4. *WARNING: All students are reminded that defacing toilet cubicles will not be tolerated. Anyone found to have been doing this, or to have been otherwise engaged in damaging school property will be subject to disciplinary measures.* I look at Raks and point to the note.

"Defacing toilet cubicles," I say. "Now, what sort of bastard would do that?"

Raks shrugs.

"Fuck knows."

We grin at each other.

Jerome starts looking over my shoulder. He smiles.

"What's up?" I ask.

"Look who's put in an appearance," he says.

I take a swig of Pepsi and turn round. Ryan's here. He's got a tray full of food and he's heading our way.

"Alright lads?" he says, sitting down, pulling out his earphones and stuffing them into his pocket.

We all nod.

Ryan unzips his jacket and gets a card out, tossing it across at me.

"Happy birthday," he says.

I'm quite shocked. I knew that Ryan knew it was my birthday. I just didn't have him down as the card-buying type.

I rip along the top of the envelope and get the card out. It's an old photograph. A cross-eyed woman with facial hair. *Carl resolved not to go on any more blind dates*, it says along the bottom. I laugh and show it around the table, then I open it to read the inside. *To Tom. Happy Birthday To Letchford Town's No. 2*

Hooligan. From Letchford Town's No. 1 Hooligan. I laugh again and put the card into my bag.

"Cheers mate," I say.

Ryan eats a chip and grins at me.

Raks starts drumming his knuckles on the table-top. He looks at Ryan.

"Didn't you fancy school this morning then?" he asks.

"Nah. Wanted a lie-in. Big night tonight."

"Don't they ever chase you up about all your skiving?"

Ryan laughs.

"Not at Parkway," he says. "The last place I was at, they had the EWO round every couple of weeks. Made me re-do Year Eight. They were always trying to get me and my mum to sign all these stupid fucking Home-School Agreements. Pointless. When my dad died, my mum went to pieces. Nowadays, she's always either pissed or stoned. Nobody can get any sense out of her. They certainly couldn't. They gave up in the end."

I nod. It's the first time I've heard Ryan talking about his home background. It doesn't sound too different to mine.

"Your mum's like my dad," I tell him. "Since my mum died, he's just been all over the shop. On benefits. Pissed every day."

Ryan looks into the distance. He rubs his nose with the back of his hand.

"How old were you when your mum died?" he asks eventually.

"Nine," I reply. "It was cancer. What about you?"

"Seven. My dad had cancer too."

I'm actually surprised. For some reason I thought Ryan's dad would have died with a bit more drama.

172

Killed by foreign riot police on an England awayday or something like that. Something spectacular.

Ryan shakes his head.

"It's a fucker of a disease," he says. There's bitterness in his voice. "You've seen Trev's picture of my dad, haven't you?"

I nod.

Ryan carries on.

"Massive bastard, he was. Six-two. Fifteen stone. By the time he died, he was down to seven and a half stone. I was too young to really understand. All I could see was that my dad was shrinking away to nothing in front of me." He shakes his head. There's a glazed look in his eyes.

I nod again. It's all I can do. An image of my mum, wasting away in a hospital bed, flashes through my mind. White sheets, vases full of flowers and the smell of disinfectant. I blow out a breath.

Gary's seen the way the conversation's developing and he pipes up, looking to lift the tone a bit.

"So anyway, what about tonight then?" he says. "Are we going to win?"

Ryan coughs. His face lights up again.

"Well, they're only a couple of places above us, and they've lost three in a row, so we should be in with a shout. There again, we're not exactly bang in form are we?"

Gary laughs.

"You could say that," he says. "Twentieth and sinking. At least we're still above Mackworth."

"Only on goal difference," I say. "And they've got a game in hand."

Jerome nods. He squints at the screen of his mobile, then looks up again.

"We badly need a win," he says. "I reckon if we

don't pick up soon, John Whyman's going to be getting the bullet."

I fiddle with my new T pendant.

"It's easy enough to get rid of him," I say. "But who's going to take over? It's not what you'd call a glamour job. We'd get some right donkey coming in."

Jerome puts one foot on the table. He's got Adidas Gazelles on. Green with white stripes. They're the cleanest trainers I've ever seen out of a shoe shop. Not a speck of dust on them.

"They couldn't be much worse than Whyman though, could they?" he says.

Gary smiles.

"I dunno. We might end up with Steve McClaren."

"If that ever happens," Ryan says, "I'm going to start supporting Mackworth."

We all laugh.

"It'd be nice to get one over on Whitbourne tonight though, wouldn't it?" Raks says. "Give them a bit of payback for 1990."

Ryan looks at Raks and blinks.

"Fucking hell Raks. You've been studying the history books, haven't you? I'm impressed."

Raks shrugs.

Rob looks confused.

"What's he on about?" he asks, picking at a scab above his left eyebrow.

Ryan shakes his head.

"Tell him, Raks."

Raks smiles. It's good to be in the know.

"Whitbourne beat us on aggregate over two legs in the 1990 Freight Rover Trophy Southern Area Final. We lost 1-0 at their place and then it was 1-1 at Southlands. If we'd have won, we'd have been going to Wembley."

174

Rob nods. He's finished picking now, and he's checking his finger ends to see if he's got anything interesting stuck under his nails.

"Oh right," he says.

Gary gives him a dig in the ribs.

"You fucking part-timer," he says.

Jerome puts his other foot up on the table.

"Should be quite interesting off the pitch tonight," he says.

Ryan puts his hands behind his head.

"Yeah," he says. "There's some bad blood there. It was pretty lively last year."

"Me and Raks were on the Internet the other night," I tell them. "Looking at the hooligan sites. All the previews were saying that Letchford-Whitbourne was going to be a bit interesting."

Raks joins in.

"And it's an important one for the Firms league table. We're 4th at the moment. Whitbourne are 5th. We can't let the bastards roll us over."

Gary shakes his head.

"Whitbourne are nothing to worry about," he says. "Bunch of old blokes. Fat bastards in their mid-thirties. Fucking Southern Softies."

I laugh. Whitbourne are from down on the south coast, so they're Southern Softies. Castleton are from up north, so they're Dirty Northern Bastards. That's the beauty of being slap bang in the middle of the country I suppose. There's nothing much else to be said for living around here.

I check my watch. Getting on for quarter to one. The dining hall's filled right up now. Everywhere I look, kids are wandering around with trays full of food, scanning for somewhere to sit. Around our table, we've all finished eating, but we're not in any rush to go anywhere. We're nice and comfortable. Nice and relaxed. People might want our seats, but they're just going to have to wait.

I lean back in my chair and watch the world go by. Jimmy and Scotty are sitting on the other side of the hall, Nike rucksack at the ready, waiting for customers. They see me and raise their hands in acknowledgement. A couple of chav lads in tracky bottoms and white Reeboks are having a bit of aggro over near the serving hatches. For a second or two it looks like something interesting is going to kick off, but it never really gets going. A bit of name calling, a bit of half-hearted shoving and then they're being pulled apart.

It's a week and a half until the end of term and the school dress policy looks like it's broken right down. Virtually no-one bothers with greys and blacks any more. The chavs are in their sports gear. The indie lot are in spray-on jeans and stripy cardigans like the one Zoe tried to get me to buy. The popular girls all look like they're just stopping off on their way to a nightclub. The hip-hop crew are wearing baseball caps around the place now. A couple of weeks ago, Mr Barnard imposed a ban on the wearing of headgear inside the school building. It's not worked.

Two tables over to the left, there's a gathering of emo kids. They've all broken out in huge jeans, to go with the big black jackets. The eye make-up application seems to have gone into overdrive. A couple of the Nocturnal Emission boys are having another squabble. Artistic differences again, by the sounds of it. I think about listening in, but decide not to bother.

I find myself thinking about the conversation I was having with Raks a couple of months ago. He was saying how the school was like a safari park, full of different species, and I was saying that I didn't know what species we were. We didn't fit in. Well, that's all changed now. I look around, at Raks, at Ryan, at Jerome, at Rob, at Gary. The short haircuts. The T-shirts and zip-up tops. The jeans. The Adidas trainers. There's no denying it. We look like a group. A gang. A species all of our own.

A couple more minutes pass. Gary gets his phone out and checks the time. He yawns and leans forward, pushing himself up against the table edge.

"I'm going to nip over to the newsagents," he says. "Get myself a packet of fags."

Jerome and Rob stand up. Me, Raks and Ryan stay sitting down.

Gary looks at us.

"You lot coming?" he asks.

"No. I think we'll give it a miss," Ryan says.

Gary shrugs.

"Okay," he says. "If we don't see you later on, we'll see you at Southlands tonight."

I nod.

"We'll be there."

Gary hooks his chair back under the table and heads off towards the foyer with Rob and Jerome in tow.

I run my hands over my hair. It's down to a number one again. Another £6.50 at Talking Heads last night. I didn't bother with a tip this time. It only took the woman about two minutes to do. Zoe didn't say anything about it this morning. Either she's getting used to me with short hair, or she's just given up on trying to talk me out of it.

Raks slowly sits up in his chair.

"What have we got this afternoon?" he asks.

I fish in my pocket and get my timetable out.

"Art and Design with Mrs Flanagan, then History."

Raks nods.

"Have you finished that Industrial Revolution assignment?"

I put my head in my hands.

"Shit." I knew there was something I was supposed to remember. I was a week late with the last assignment.

Raks rolls his eyes.

"Fucking hell. You're getting worse. Mr Richards is going to go apeshit."

I shake my head.

"Bollocks," I say. "How am I going to dig myself out of this one?" I squeeze my eyes tight shut and try to think of plausible reasons why I've got nothing to hand in.

Ryan starts laughing.

"There's an obvious way to get out of it," he says. "It's not rocket science. Let's just piss off into town."

Raks rubs his forehead.

"You've only just got here, you idle bastard."

Ryan waves his hand in the air. The fly-swatting gesture.

"It's been a good half hour," he says. "That's long enough for me."

I look at Raks.

"What do you reckon?"

Raks shrugs.

"I'm in if you're in," he says. "I mean, our attendance records over the past few weeks haven't been too impressive, have they? Another afternoon isn't going to make much difference."

Ryan beams.

"That's my boy." He puts his arm round Raks's shoulders and gives him a squeeze.

I stand up. Ryan and Raks do the same.

"Right then lads," I say. "That's sorted then. Let's hit the road."

thirteen

I squash my empty Red Bull can and shove it across the table.

"What time is it?" Ryan asks.

I push up my sleeve. It's quite gloomy in the Café Rialt, and I have to squint to see my watch properly.

"Half past five. Just over two hours until kick-off." I feel the familiar fluttering in my stomach.

We've been in the Ainsdale Centre for about four hours now. The whole afternoon. The time just seems to have flown by. We had a look round the shops, sat on the benches for a bit, spent a couple of hours in Harris's Amusements, wasting my birthday money, and for the last three quarters of an hour we've been sitting here in the Café Rialt. It was quite quiet when we came in, but now it's starting to fill up with people on their way home from work or getting geared up for some late-night Christmas shopping.

Ryan yawns.

"We'll get off then," he says.

Raks raises his eyebrows.

"It's a bit early isn't it? We need to kill a bit more time in here. They won't open the turnstiles until about half six."

Ryan shakes his head.

"We're not going straight to Southlands," he says. "We're going to be making a pit stop on the way. Thought we'd drop in at The Shakespeare, see the LLF lads. Trev won't be there, and Steve might not, but Dave and Chris will be. They practically live in the place."

We pile our cans and plates onto a tray, then head out of the café and down the back stairs. On the ground floor, pan-pipe music is blasting. *Careless Whisper*. Santa's Grotto has been shut down. According to the *Letchford Argus* last Thursday, they found asbestos in the ceiling. We go through the back doors and into the car park.

Outside, the Christmas lights are twinkling. The whole festive set-up was officially switched on a couple of weeks back. They roped in Paul Butterworth and some local bird who was on *The X Factor*. She was supposed to entertain the crowd with a medley of Christmas songs, but the PA broke down. Letchford Borough Council. *Working For You*. Again.

It's cold and dark in the side streets, and we're not hanging around. Before too long we're coming to the junction near the Industrial Estate and hanging a left down past the shops to The Shakespeare. Since the last time we were down here, Balti Towers Indian Takeaway has gone belly-up. The windows are covered with rough-looking chipboard, daubed over with posters. *Club Majestyk – New Year's Eve All-Nighter*.

The wind's really getting up now. The cross of St George on the front of the pub is fluttering out of control. It looks like it's about to take off. We cut through the car park and along the side of the *Family Beer Garden*, up to the door of the back bar.

Inside, the place is even gloomier and smokier than it was last time. The metal awning's wide open but it's not making much difference. The pub's busier than I remember too. All the seats at the bar are taken. My eyes are drawn down to something glinting around the legs of the stools. Chains, attaching them to the brass rail round the bottom of the bar. I'm sure they weren't there last time.

I nudge Ryan and point at the chains.

"What's that all about then?"

Ryan laughs.

"Just a little extra security measure they put in for match days."

As we're standing, just inside the door, a bloke wanders past with a black bin bag under his arm. He's a scrawny type, balding, wearing a stained white T-shirt and no jacket. Whatever is inside his bag, it's quite heavy. He gives the bag to the barman. Quick as a flash, the barman has a look inside, then whisks it away, out of sight. He nods his head and hands over a roll of tenners. Bin Bag Man counts the cash, smiles, then wanders back out into the night.

I start looking around for the LLF lads. It doesn't take me long. Ryan was right. Trev and Steve aren't here, but Dave and Chris are. They're sitting over in the corner, under the Spitfire. Dave's got a mauve polo shirt on. Chris is in an expensive-looking cream bomber jacket. Their table is covered in pint glasses and fag ash.

As we start to head over towards them, Dave and Chris see us coming. They both stand up, smiling, shoving their hands in our direction. They look genuinely pleased to see us. We all shake hands and sit down. Dave and Chris are still smiling. They're actually quite a tragic sight without Trev and Steve around. Like a pair of monkeys left behind when the organ grinders have gone home. Now we've arrived it's given them some purpose in life.

Chris gets his wallet out.

"I'll get them in," he says, rubbing the bridge of his crumpled nose. "Carling all round, yeah?"

Everyone nods.

Chris sets off to the bar. Dave starts looking at the front of Ryan's jacket. He's squinting his eyes, wrinkling his forehead. His eyebrows are almost touching his hairline. He reaches out with his finger, pointing at something.

"Got a little fuckin' spot there," he says.

As Ryan looks down, Dave whips his finger up and tries to touch Ryan's nose. He's too slow though. Ryan grabs his hand and puts it back on the table.

"Dave," he says. "That's the oldest and shittiest trick in the book."

Dave looks a bit sad.

Raks laughs.

"It makes a change from poking holes in beer mats though."

Pretty soon, Chris is back. He's got four pints wedged between his hands and a fifth one balanced on top. He puts them all down on the table without spilling a drop.

Raks looks amazed.

"Fucking hell Chris," he says. "How did you manage that?"

Chris grins.

"Years of practise."

The first pint of the evening goes down very nicely. As I drain the last dregs, I cast my mind back to the way I felt when Ryan first brought us to the pub. It seems like a long time ago now, but it's actually less than three weeks. I think about how anxious I was. How self-conscious. It's not like that this time though. It just feels right.

By quarter past six we're onto the next round. Dave got it in. He paid for it with a fifty-pound note. Whatever it is Dave and Chris do for a living, it certainly pays well. The hours are nice and flexible too. I once asked Ryan what it was. He was a bit non-committal. Just said it had something to do with import and export.

My phone starts beeping. I take it out of my pocket. I've got a text. It's from Colin, the assistant manager of Thurston Dynamo. *Where r u?* it says. I stare at the screen for a few seconds, thinking about making something up, texting back to say I'm ill, but all in all, I just can't be bothered. I push the phone back into my pocket. I take a swig of my pint and blow out a breath.

Ryan raises his eyebrows at me.

"What's up?" he asks. "Woman trouble?"

I shake my head.

"I'm supposed to be at football training tonight," I tell him. "I've just got a text asking me where I am. I'll be getting it in the neck on Sunday."

Ryan shrugs.

"Tell them to shove it. It's kids' stuff. I stopped playing years ago."

Raks has been listening in.

"Were you any good?" he asks.

Ryan looks down.

"I was OK. I was on the books of the Letchford Town Youth Academy in my last couple of years at primary school. Went to the School Of Excellence, stuff like that."

"Shit," I say. I'm impressed. The Letchford scouts have been to loads of games where I've been playing, but I've never had so much as a sniff of interest. Ryan must have been a pretty decent player.

"So why did you give it up, then?" Raks asks.

"I didn't, really. I got sent off playing for my school in Year Seven. Some bastard kept kicking me, so I butted him. Broke his nose. Ended up getting banned from all representative matches for two years."

"Two years?" I say. "Fucking hell, that's a bit harsh. In our Sunday League I've seen lads punch refs and only get banned for a couple of months."

Ryan pulls a face.

"It'd have been a lot less than two years, but there was this teacher who had it in for me. Mrs McDowell. She got onto the Schools FA. She just wouldn't let it lie until I'd been properly punished."

I nod. I take another swig of my pint.

"So what did Letchford Town do?"

Ryan places his hands flat on the table. He looks at his fingernails.

"They let me go."

"Shit," Raks says. "I'm surprised you still support them, after that."

Ryan shakes his head.

"It wasn't Letchford's fault. They'd have kept me on, but there was no point if I couldn't play for two years. They appealed on my behalf, went cap in hand to the Schools FA, but the Schools FA are just a bunch of old twats in blazers. They weren't going to change their minds. So I just said fuck it."

"And that was the end of that?" I ask.

Ryan nods. He downs what's left of his Carling and slams the glass on the table.

"And that was the end of that."

We all go quiet. I take another sip of beer, glancing across at Ryan. There's sadness in his eyes. I try to think of something to say, but nothing seems appropriate. From the expression on Raks's face, I can see that his mind is working in the same way as mine. The whole mood has gone right down. Suddenly there's a flash. A lighted match bounces off the rim of my pint glass. The match lands on the table-top and fizzles out in a patch of spilt beer.

I look up. Dave's smirking. He shakes a box of Swan Vestas in the air. It's his latest prank. He pushes the box open, lights another match and lobs it across at Ryan. Before the match has even had a chance to land, he's lit a third one and chucked it at Raks.

"Come on you miserable fuckers," he says. "You've got faces like a row of fuckin' smacked arses."

Everyone laughs. Just for once, Dave's need to entertain has been put to some use.

I reach into my jeans pocket and get out a twenty-pound note.

"I'll get the next round in," I say. "It's my birthday today, so I'm a bit more flush than usual."

Dave holds his hands up.

"Don't be fuckin' soft. If it's your birthday, the fuckin' drinks are on us."

Chris stands up. He looks at Dave.

"Pints and chasers, yeah?"

Dave nods.

Chris makes two trips to the bar this time. He's back with five Carlings first, then he follows it up with five tumblers of neat whisky. As he sits down, he raises his pint glass.

"Happy birthday to Tom, then, yeah?"

We all pick up our pints and take a mouthful.

"Happy birthday Tom," everyone says.

I'm touched.

"Cheers."

Chris smiles. He puts his pint down and picks up his whisky, shoving the other tumblers across the table towards the rest of us.

"Come on then, Tom," he says. "Lets see what

you're made of, yeah?" He downs his whisky in one, and sits grinning at me.

I've been feeling quite nice and mellow, but now I'm on edge. This is a challenge. I pick the tumbler up and raise it to my mouth. The smell of the whisky makes my eyes water. I take a breath, then knock it back in one gulp. I swallow, then put the glass back on the table as the whisky burns down my throat.

Dave and Chris start to clap.

"Fuckin' hell," Dave says. "The lad's a fuckin' natural."

I laugh. I can feel the whisky going to work inside me.

"You could say it's in my genes," I say.

Dave puts his whisky away in one, then laughs at Raks and Ryan as they struggle to keep up, coughing and spluttering, eventually draining their glasses. He shakes his head slowly.

"You two are fuckin' piss-poor," he says. He lifts my arm by the wrist. "Tom's the champion."

I grin. I know he's only arsing around, but it still feels good. I check my watch. It's nearly ten to seven. Fifty-five minutes to kick-off. A nice little burst of adrenalin courses through me. I take a swig of my third pint and look around. Over at the bar, something dodgy is going on. A couple of lads in McKenzie sweatshirts are counting out a wad of notes, passing the money across to the barman. He ducks under the counter for a second or two then reappears with the black plastic bag we saw earlier. It's handshakes all round, then the lads are off, the one in front carrying the bin bag.

Chris has another swig of Carling. He looks at Raks, Ryan and me.

187

"Whitbourne tonight then," he says. "They're usually up for a bit of aggro. You boys ready, yeah?"

Raks nods.

"Too right." He's pissed and he's brimming with confidence. "We fucked up the Castleton mob, we bricked the Ashborough buses. I shouldn't have thought we'll have too much trouble tonight. We're on a roll. Someone will write a book on the NLLF one day."

Dave smiles.

"Funny you should fuckin' mention that," he says. "A bloke *was* going to write about us once."

"Oh yeah?" I say. It sounds like a piss-take, but from the look on his face, I can see that he's not joking.

Chris joins in.

"Yeah," he says. "That's right. It was back in 1990. The start of the season after the World Cup in Italy. Football was dead popular – Gazza and all that shit, yeah? – but there was quite a bit of aggro going off on the terraces. It was all over the newspapers."

Dave nods. He adjusts his identity bracelet and takes up the story.

"This fuckin' journalist latched himself onto us. Jeremy something, his name was. Wanted us to call him Jez. Fuckin' bright lad. Public school, just out of Oxford. You know the sort. Some geezer had told him we were the top brass in the LLF. He wanted to follow us around for a season, see how it really was for lads like us, then write a book about it."

Ryan looks up from his phone and scowls.

"A posh kid slumming it, then."

Dave carries on.

"He told us he was going to produce a fuckin' *serious anthropological study*. Whatever that means. We just said fuckin' yeah, okay. Whatever. Thought there might be a few quid in it."

Chris starts laughing. He lights a fag.

"He didn't last long though, old Jez, yeah? He tried a bit too hard to be one of the boys."

Dave's laughing his Muttley laugh again, shoulders jogging up and down.

"First game of the season he got a right fuckin' kicking from some Mitcham fans. The next weekend he got arrested for being drunk and disorderly when we went to Peterborough. The week after that, someone pinched all his fuckin' stuff. Tape recorders, microphones, electrical bits and pieces. The works."

Chris taps his fag into the ashtray. He frowns, looking thoughtful.

"To this day, I can't imagine who'd have pinched his gear, yeah? Can you think who it might have been, Dave?"

Dave's laughing so hard now, he can hardly speak.

"Fuck knows," he splutters.

Chris grins.

"Well anyway," he says, "Jez pissed off after that. He'd rented himself a shitty flat down in Blue Gate Fields, but when we went over to see him, he weren't there, yeah? He'd cleared all his clobber out and gone back home to Mummy. Never did get round to producing his *serious anthropological study*."

I smile, nodding my head.

"I bet you wish he'd gone ahead with the book now though, don't you?" I say. "You could be one of these celebrity hooligans. On the telly talking about cracking heads back in the day."

Chris laughs.

"I'll survive."

I stand up and nip to the toilets for a piss. As I'm

coming back, I have another look round the pub. The place is packed with Letchford fans now. It's mainly the replica shirt and woolly hat-wearers, but there's also a fair number of our sort of people, the short hair and sports gear mob. There's no sign of Gary, Rob and Jerome, or Jimmy and Scotty, but there are plenty of lads I recognise. It's pretty cramped in the back bar, but people seem to be happy enough, standing together in groups, drinking and laughing. The atmosphere's quite relaxed.

I sit back down and take a swig of my pint. I'm just about to say something to Ryan when I notice him straighten up in his chair. He looks past me and narrows his eyes.

"What's up?" Raks says.

Ryan's got a stern expression on his face.

He nods towards the other side of the pub.

"Whitbourne lads," he says.

I look across. A bunch of four blokes, in their late twenties or early thirties has just come in. They're standing halfway between the door and the bar. They're all quite thick-set. Short hair and zip-up jackets. There's no visible clue that they're Whitbourne lads, no green and white scarves or replica shirts, but if Ryan thinks they are, I'm not going to contradict him. It's like Gary Simmons said. Ryan's got a nose for trouble. As I carry on watching, four more men come through the door. There's quite a posse growing.

Dave and Chris are instantly on the alert. They've noticed what's going on and they're sitting upright, casting glances across the bar.

Raks lifts his pint glass and watches the bubbles rising to the surface.

"They can't be Whitbourne lads," he says. "It's

190

only five past seven. The away coaches don't usually come until fifteen or twenty minutes before kick-off. Half an hour at most. It's too early."

Chris adjusts a couple of his sovereign rings. He shakes his head.

"Raks, lad," he says. "Let's be honest, yeah? You might get the odd one or two, but the proper lads don't come on the bus. That's the bobble hat brigade. The proper lads come under their own steam."

Raks still looks confused.

"But when we ran the Castleton lot, they headed straight for the buses."

Ryan rolls his eyes.

"They were just trying to get out of the way," he says. "They'd have got into an ice-cream van if there was one standing there."

I have another swig of beer, fiddling with my T pendant. I look back across towards the door. There's a gang of about ten there now. Some of them have been served at the bar, and they're standing around holding pint glasses and bottles. They're all flicking their eyes around, sussing the place out. Any remaining doubts I might have had that they were Whitbourne lads are disappearing. They couldn't look any shiftier if they tried.

The atmosphere in the pub is changing. The juke-box has been playing quietly in the background for all the time we've been here, but now it's run out of credits. As the music fades away, a sort of ominous silence comes down. The only sound is the wind howling outside, whistling through the hole in the wall and making the awning rattle. All eyes in the room are turning towards the group by the door.

Dave and Chris are grinning from ear to ear. It's like all their Christmases have just come at once.

They're not allowed to cause trouble at football matches any more. But now the trouble looks like it's come to them. As I watch their grins get wider and wider, I feel my own face breaking into a smile. My heart thuds against my ribs. I'm starting to feel dry-mouthed and out of breath, tingling with nervous energy. Dave and Chris aren't the only ones who live for moments like this.

The silence is stretching on and on. I'm just about to reach out for my pint again when there's a whistling followed by a sound like an explosion. Instinctively I duck down, hands over my head. The next thing I know, I'm covered in beer and fragments of glass. I peer up at the wall behind us. Beer is cascading down the *Stripers* poster. A piece of green glass is sticking out of the propeller of the Spitfire. Another bottle comes hurtling through the smoky haze towards our table. It ricochets off the wall and ceiling and hits a bloke standing just over to our right.

Suddenly there's blood everywhere. The bloke who's been hit by the bottle crashes to the ground and all around him people start diving for cover, crushing into the corner near the fruit machine and the toilets, shouting and screaming. In the blink of an eye, a big space has opened up in the middle of the floor. The Whitbourne crew are up at the far end, jeering, trying to yank the chained-up stools away from the bar, beckoning, inviting us to come and have a go.

We don't need to be asked twice. Dave and Chris are the first onto their feet, hurdling the table and charging across the room. Ryan and me are right behind them and a load of other Letchford lads are bringing up the rear.

192

Immediately I've sobered up and I'm at absolutely 100% of my full capacity. My brain is operating at warp speed. In the couple of seconds it takes to get to the other side of the bar, I've sized everything up, calculated all the possible angles of attack, selected a target, assessed the danger. You name it, I've done it. As I pile in, I'm as prepared for combat as I possibly could be. It's becoming second nature now.

Like the skirmish with the Castleton fans, the whole thing is over in a few seconds. As soon as they realise we're up for it, the Whitbourne boys don't want to know any more and they make a bolt for the door. I manage to land a couple of punches on my target, a fat bloke in a denim jacket, and I get a kick in at another lad as he jumps out of the way of a right-hander from Chris, but that's about it. Nobody manages to lay a finger on me. In a funny sort of way I'm slightly disappointed.

We chase the Whitbourne mob out across the car park and into the street but they're running like rabbits, skittering through the traffic on the main road and heading down into the Industrial Estate. There's no point going after them.

I nod at Ryan. He smiles.

"Advantage Letchford," he says.

I look towards the Industrial Estate again. The Whitbourne lads have vanished. In the distance, the lights of Southlands are filling the sky with a white glow. My pulse rate is coming down. I feel an odd mixture of satisfaction and frustration. We've scored a victory, but it wasn't enough. I'm like a junkie who's been given just a little taste of gear. I want more. I need it. I touch my T pendant, puff out a breath and follow Ryan, Dave and Chris back into the pub.

Inside, the clear-up operation has started. Nobody really seems bothered that there's just been a near-riot. Everything's calm again. The bloke who got bottled is sitting at the bar with a Fosters towel clamped to his head. I think of the cover of *Terrace Warfare*. By the looks of him, he's OK. He's probably going to need a few stitches though. Most of the broken glass has been swept away and the splashes of blood have been wiped off the furniture.

We head back to our table and sit down. Raks is still there, looking dazed, picking bits of glass out of his hair.

"Sorry lads," he says. "It all happened a bit too fast."

Chris laughs.

"Don't worry about it," he says. "I think you need to cut down on your booze intake though, yeah? It's interfering with your hooliganism."

Dave leans back in his chair. The grin on his face shows no signs of going.

"That was fuckin' great," he says. "Just like the good old days. Away fans trying to take over our boozer, getting sent off with their tails between their fuckin' legs."

I look down at my trainers. There's a scuff on the left one, but it's just superficial. I lick my finger and it wipes straight off. The first two knuckles of my right hand are red, and there's a little indentation on one of them. It could be a tooth mark. I smile. Scars of battle.

"Do you think that's it from the Whitbourne lads?" I ask.

Ryan shakes his head.

"No," he says. "That was just a minor squabble. A run-in with the scouting party." He finishes his pint and puts the glass down. "After the match. That's when the real battle begins."

fourteen

The first thing I notice, arriving at Southlands, is that there are a lot of Police around tonight. As we come round the corner of the Family Stand and head along towards the North Stand turnstiles, there's one everywhere I look. They all seem twitchy and on-edge, as if they're expecting some bother. Word has probably reached them that there was a bit of trouble at The Shakespeare. They're taking people at random out of the queues, patting them down for concealed weapons. They don't seem to be interested in us.

As I go through Gate 20, I notice Comb-Round Man's having a night off. In his place there's a fat bloke with stubby little fingers. He's red-faced and sweaty and his breath's wheezing in and out like he's got a punctured lung. I hand over a twenty-pound note and get twelve quid change, then I meet back up with Ryan and Raks inside Gate 19.

We don't bother hanging around in the concourse. Kick-off's in less than five minutes. We head straight across and up the steps to the top of the terracing. *Ready To Go* by Republica is on the PA. Perhaps it's just the alcohol making me sentimental, but there's something magical about the way the stadium looks this evening. Everything seems to be gleaming. The grass seems greener, the pitch markings seem whiter, the floodlights seem brighter. There's a good crowd in tonight. At least 7,000, I'd say.

Looking over to the right I see that Whitbourne have brought a pretty decent travelling support, too. At least as many as Castleton. Maybe more. The fans are evenly spread out across the concrete slope. St George flags with *Whitbourne* and *Seasiders* painted onto them are attached to the Perspex panels at the back of the stand and are hung over crush barriers near the front.

"Evening boys," a voice says.

I turn to my left and see Gary Simmons. Another one of his sudden appearances. He's with Rob and Jerome, as usual.

"Gary," I say. "Fancy seeing you here."

Gary laughs. He points over to the Whitbourne fans. One or two are already rattling the fencing separating them from our lot. Doing their best to stir up trouble.

"They look lively," he says.

I smile and nod.

Gary carries on.

"I've heard there's already been a bit of a barney tonight. Down The Shakespeare. Some Whitbourne lads tried to smash the place up and got a good hiding for it."

I smirk, scratching my nose.

Gary does a double-take.

"Fuck me. It was you lot wasn't it?"

Ryan pats him on the shoulder.

"Gary," he says. "I *could* tell you, but then I'd have to kill you."

We leave Gary and the lads laughing and set off down towards our crush barrier. As we get there, all the usual punters are standing around, present and correct. Pessimistic Granddad hasn't started moaning yet, but it won't be long. Twitchy Bloke is chewing his fingernails. Big Fleece Woman has got her phone in one hand and a cup of hot chocolate in the other.

I peer through the mesh into the Whitbourne section. A couple of stewards are trying to persuade the fence rattlers to pack it in, but they're not having much success. I start scanning faces, trying to pick out the lads who were at The Shakespeare. I can't see them, but it doesn't really matter. There's something in the eyes of all the Whitbourne fans. They know some of their boys got a kicking earlier on. They want to even the score. One lad has seen me looking, and now he's trying to stare me out. I wink at him and blow a kiss, mouthing *wanker* at him as he does his best to look threatening.

On the PA, *Ready To Go* fades out as *The Boys Are Back In Town* fades in and the teams run out. There's no confetti tonight, but in the Family Stand there's an outbreak of black and orange balloons. The wind's getting stronger, and it doesn't take long for the balloons to start blowing around on the pitch, swirling in circles with bits of paper and crisp packets.

All the Letchford players are applauding the fans this week. Tony O'Neill and Tommy Sharp are pumping their fists in the air, trying to get the crowd worked up. To be fair, we're being as enthusiastic as anyone could be, preparing to watch Letchford Town on a freezing cold Tuesday night in December.

It's getting very close to kick off now. The tannoy announcer has given out the teams and Carl Butterworth has shaken hands with all the hangers-on in the centre circle. I'm expecting us to start the match defending our end, but Jimmy Knapper is collecting his stuff from the goalmouth and heading towards the halfway line.

"Fuck," Ryan says.

"What's the matter?" Raks asks. It's the first thing he's said since we got here. I think his pissedness is gradually wearing off.

"Those bastards must have won the toss," Ryan says. "We're kicking the wrong way. We always lose when we kick this way in the first half."

As the Letchford players trot up to the far end, the Whitbourne team trundle into the half in front of us. They're wearing garish green and white hooped shirts and white shorts, like a down-market Celtic. As they start getting into position, it looks like they're going with some sort of Christmas tree formation. It's either 4-3-2-1 or 4-4-1-1, but the number 13 on the left hand side doesn't seem to know how far up the pitch he's supposed to be playing.

Raks scratches his head.

"What sort of line-up's that, then?" he asks. "Do you think we'll try to change the way we set our team out? Push a defender out and fill up the midfield?"

Ryan laughs.

"Don't be soft. If John Whyman even thinks about a formation more technically advanced than a 4-4-2 he has to have a lie-down."

Billy Scanlon, the Whitbourne keeper, has finally arrived in our goalmouth. He's quite a big-boned chap, and the first choruses of *You Fat Bastard* fill the air. Everyone's in their places now. Leroy Lewton's got his foot on the ball, waiting for the whistle. When it comes, he rolls the ball to the side for Carl Butterworth to knock it forward in the general direction of Leon Marshall's head. It's not one of his better passes. As it sails into the upper tier of the Main Stand, a groan goes up. The scoreboard timer says we're six seconds in.

The first quarter of an hour is fairly aimless. It's more or less what you'd expect of two teams down at the bottom of League Two. Misplaced passes, mistimed tackles, a couple of offside flags every minute. Nothing to write home about. As the timer ticks over to 16:00 though, things take a turn for the worst.

Martin King, the Whitbourne number 19, picks the ball up in the centre circle and heads out to the left. Before he gets very far, Mark Sheedy barges into him. King goes down, doing a passable imitation of a dying fly, and the referee summons Sheedy over.

Twitchy Bloke is shaking his head.

"Don't book him ref," he shouts. "He only makes about three tackles a season."

But the ref isn't booking Sheedy. He's sending him off. As the red card appears, people start looking at each other in disbelief. The Whitbourne fans start to cheer. Carl Butterworth's arguing, but there's no point. Mark Sheedy heads for the tunnel.

It's taken a few seconds, but gradually it's sinking in. We've had someone sent off for nothing more than a badly-judged challenge. Against Ashborough, Dave Nicholson only got a booking for a much worse one. A proper clattering. And we *wanted* him to get sent off. To really round things off, Martin King is back on his feet, looking very sprightly for a man who seemed to be in agony a few seconds ago.

"It's a miracle," someone yells from behind, showering me with spittle. "He is risen."

A barrage of boos and whistles cascades down from all parts of the ground. We start a chant of *Cheat Cheat Cheat* and follow it up with *Who's The Wanker In The Black?* However loud we shout though, it's not going to change the facts. We're down to ten, and we're not much good when we've got eleven men on the park.

The free kick after the sending off comes to nothing. It's a half-arsed punt into our area that Jimmy Knapper collects without any trouble. Two minutes later though, and we're 1-0 down. Tony O'Neill nearly has his head taken off by a ball from Dave Nicholson, and before he has the chance to control it, Martin King has nipped it off his toes. O'Neill tries to bring him down, but King skips out of the way and sends a ball through to Andy Miller, who's got a clear run on goal.

Miller looks about half a mile offside. Tommy Sharp and Paul Hood put their hands up to signal to the assistant, but the flag stays down. Jimmy Knapper comes off his line, but it's too little, too late. Miller takes the ball round him and sticks it into the empty net.

The Whitbourne fans explode in celebration and we start booing and whistling again. We're being cheated. *1-0 To The Referee* rings out, blending into *You've Only Got 12 Men*. Already though, there's a sort of hopeless feeling in the air. It's just not going to be our night.

As the Whitbourne fans' cheering dies down, there's a surge on their side of the barrier. A bit of gesticulating and name-calling kicks off, and a few of our lads start advancing towards the fencing. The stewards have seen what's going on, and they're marching up the steps, trying to keep people apart.

My heart leaps. I'm ready get involved. I look across at Raks and Ryan.

"Here we go," I say, grinning.

Raks smiles, but Ryan shakes his head.

"Leave it for now."

I pull a face, confused.

Ryan jabs his finger in the direction of the fence.

"It's not just stewards tonight."

I look across. He's right. Interspersed with the stewards are police officers in helmets and visors. They were outside last time, but tonight they're inside, and there are lots of them.

"We're not going to go steaming in now," Ryan says. "Because if we do we're going to get our collars felt, and we'll be out of the action before it's even started."

I nod. Ryan's made his point.

The rest of the half is garbage. The minor outbreak of hostilities after the Whitbourne goal only lasts a few seconds, and apart from that, all we've got to keep us entertained is what's going on out on the pitch. The referee's coming in for some real flak now. *You're Not Fit To Referee. The Referee's A Wanker.* All the old favourites.

When we're not barracking the referee, we're giving Martin King a hard time. Every time he touches the ball, a chorus of jeering goes up. It doesn't seem to be having much effect though. At one point the little bastard cups his hand to his ear so he can hear us better. In the meantime, our players are flapping around like headless chickens. Fat Boy Scanlon in the Whitbourne goal hasn't had a shot to save yet.

We're already going down the steps when the half-time whistle goes. Another round of booing erupts. *Let Me Entertain You* starts up on the PA while I head for the toilets and Raks and Ryan join the food and drink queue.

When I've finished in the toilets I stand watching the TV screens in the concourse. It's not *Sky Sports* tonight, it's *LTTV*, the Letchford Town closed-circuit channel. They're showing replays of the Whitbourne goal, over and over again. It's just the way it seemed from the Kop. Andy Miller was yards offside. The only two people in the ground who didn't spot it were the ref and his assistant. Next up it's the sending off. From this angle it doesn't even look as if Sheedy made contact. Martin King fell over the ball.

Pessimistic Granddad is standing next to me. He's not happy. He points at the nearest screen.

"Corruption," he says. He has a slug of his hip flask and wanders off.

Raks and Ryan are finished at the kiosks. Raks has got a hot dog. Ryan's got a cup of coffee and one for me. He hands it over then we all go back out to see what's going on.

Apparently we're having a fancy dress competition tonight. The contestants are making their way onto the pitch, where Letchy The Lion is waiting. We've got four Santas, an Elvis, a pantomime cow, two girls with flashing orange reindeer antlers (one ninety-nine from the club shop), and a man in a blue leotard with an Irish flag draped over his shoulders. I'm not sure what he's supposed to be.

The tannoy announcer is asking the crowd to cheer for each of the contestants in turn. The *Cheerometer*, he calls it. The contestant who gets the loudest cheer wins the prize. A ten-pound voucher for the club shop. Generosity knows no limits in Letchford.

When the punters have lined themselves up, the *Cheerometer* gets under way. The Santas and the pantomime cow get a bit of half-hearted applause. The bloke in the Elvis costume has made the mistake of thinking he's some kind of personality and he gets booed. When the bloke in the leotard steps forward, the silence is so total, you could hear a pin drop.

Finally, the girls with the reindeer antlers take their bow, to the nearest thing we've heard to a cheer all evening. The prize is theirs. They have their photographs taken with Letchy and then *The Final Countdown* comes over the PA.

I check my watch. The second half should be starting any minute. The tannoy announcer fades down the music to give out a message.

"A date for your diaries," he says. "The match against Mackworth, scheduled for Saturday December 16th, has been switched to Friday December 15th, kick-off 7.45 pm. This is to allow live coverage on *Sky Sports*. Letchford Town would like to apologise for any inconvenience caused."

I sip my coffee and turn to Ryan.

"Should be good, playing Mackworth on a Friday night," I say.

Ryan nods.

Then it hits me. Friday December 15th. Eight o'clock in the Alderman Richard Martin drama studio. *Oliver*. I slump forward against the crush barrier and close my eyes. A horrible sickly taste starts clawing its way up my throat. Letchford Town or *Oliver*? Or more to the point, Letchford Town or Zoe Gifford?

I open my eyes. I know I really shouldn't have divided loyalties. It's Zoe's big night. A once in a lifetime thing. I've just got to go haven't I? I've got to do the right thing. The problem is, I've got a nasty feeling that this time the idea of doing the right thing might be going straight out of the window.

I'm still feeling sick when the game kicks off again. If the first half was bad, the second half is terrible. Letchford start quite brightly, and we get behind them with a few blasts of *Come On Letchford*. Five minutes in though, and we're 2-0 down. Martin King sends in a corner from the left, our defenders don't bother to challenge for the ball and Andy Miller nods it in at the far post.

Twenty more minutes of headless chicken football and there's mutiny in the air. We've stopped giving Martin King and the referee gyp and we're turning on John Whyman. Chants of *Johnny Johnny, Sort It Out* go up. The consensus is that Danny Holmes is the man to save us. A couple of goal scoring substitute appearances and he's the new Messiah. We want Danny up front with Leroy Lewton, but Whyman takes Leroy off and puts Patrick Agamoa on, to the strains of *You Don't Know What You're Doing*.

The substitution's not popular but it almost pays off perfectly. A cross from Tony O'Neill flashes through the Whitbourne six yard box and finds Agamoa unmarked, two yards out. He's got time to control the ball, sit on it and light a cigar, but instead he swings at it and sends it over the top of the scoreboard and out of the ground.

People are literally howling in anguish. For some of them it's the final straw. A steady trickle starts heading for the exits, even though there are still twenty minutes to go. Big Fleece Woman has had enough. As she comes past us, there are tears in her eyes. The Whitbourne fans are loving it, pissing themselves laughing, singing *Cheerio Cheerio Cheerio* and *Can We Play You Every Week?* Up at the back of our section, someone starts chanting *Whyman Out*. Plenty of people join in.

As the timer hits 83:00, things are looking desperate. If we're going to get anything out of the game, we're going to have to score now. Sean Andrews has won a corner out on the right. Instead of just banging it into the box, Carl Butterworth and Tony

O'Neill are having a discussion about what to do.

"For fuck's sake," someone screams. Another shower of spittle sails by. "We're two fucking nil down. Stop fannying about and get it in the fucking mixer."

It's all pointless though. To no-one's great surprise, we try a short corner routine and lose the ball. John Whyman comes out into the technical area, arms waving, but he gets so much abuse he retreats back to the dugout.

Raks puts his hands over his eyes.

"I can't watch," he says.

Ryan shrugs. He's resigned to the outcome. He's seen Letchford lose a lot more times than we have.

"Told you we'd be fucked if we started off kicking this way," he says.

Everyone knows the game's effectively over now. The Family Stand and The Main Stand are virtually empty. The only part of the ground still packed is the Kop. And nobody on the Kop is paying much attention to what's happening on the pitch any more, because the ritual manoeuvring of the troops is getting under way. It's the familiar pattern. The non-combatants are moving out of the way and the soldiers are getting into position.

Looking through the wire mesh, it's pretty clear that Whitbourne have come prepared. Castleton had a firm of fifty or sixty. Ashborough only had thirty or so. Whitbourne look to have at least eighty. We probably outnumber them, but there's not much in it, and they're all big bastards. Grown men. It's like it said on the Internet. *Should b tasty*. I start to grin. The hairs on the back of my neck are standing on end. I'm nervous, but in a good way. I know, I just *know* that when it all goes off, I'm going to be ready. I'm not going to let anyone down.

A few of the Whitbourne fans have broken through the cordon of stewards and police along the side of the fencing and they're gripping the mesh, shouting abuse, going through the motions of pretending to climb into our section. It's just a show of strength, a big *Fuck You* to us, but plenty of our lads are rising to the bait, trying to get at them but being held back.

I glance across at Raks. He's been a bit subdued this evening. I think he's upset that he missed out on the action at The Shakespeare. There's a glint in his eyes that tells me he's ready to make up for it. He watches another couple of lads try to go through a gap in the line of green jackets and get pushed away.

"Pussies," he hisses. "Come on. Let's show them how it's done."

Before he has a chance to make a move though, Ryan has laid a hand on his arm. Not for the first time tonight, he's the voice of caution. It goes with being a general in The NLLF army, I suppose. It's not just about fighting. Sometimes it's about tactics. Strategy.

"Now's not the time or the place," he says. "Use your brain. It's swarming with Old Bill in here. Same as I said to Tom. You'll be out of the action before it even gets going."

Raks shakes his head. He's feeling gung-ho.

"I bet they're not even real coppers," he says. "They'll be these Community Support Officers. Hobby Bobbies."

Ryan nods.

"Probably. But they're the worst sort. Real bastards. Ready to run you in for anything, just to get one over on the regular lot." At that moment, as if to illustrate Ryan's point, two coppers pounce on a

Letchford lad just to our right. They bundle him down the steps, over the wall and along the front of the stand, past the jeering Whitbourne fans. His feet don't even touch the floor.

I shake my head and glance out onto the pitch. The timer is showing 88:00. We've finally brought Danny Holmes on, but even he's not going to be able to rescue this one. We should be throwing everything at Whitbourne, but they're the ones on the attack. It's not really important though. My mind is on other things.

I look at Ryan.

"What are we going to do then? How are we going to kick it all off?"

Ryan zips his tracky top right up under his chin.

"Well," he replies. "We want to ruck. Whitbourne want to ruck. It's just a case of giving the Boys in Blue the slip. It's all about timing."

I look into the Whitbourne section again. Hardly any of their boys are watching the game. They're watching us. Waiting for us to make a move.

Ryan sniffs the air. He looks at me and smiles.

"Come on." He starts making his way up to the exit.

Within seconds, the message has spread. The army is on the march. A whole battalion of us is heading up the terracing, down the stairs and over the dusty concrete floor of the concourse, picking up speed, shouting, chanting, our voices booming out. Raks and Ryan are beside me. Gary and the lads are on the left. I notice Jimmy and Scotty coming down from the right. The gates are open, but because the match is still in progress, only a few stewards are on duty down here. We've caught them on the hop.

We go straight out into the car park, wheeling to

our left just as the Whitbourne lads burst through their exit gates. They're not pissing around. They're out for revenge. Earlier tonight, in The Shakespeare, there was a stand-off before the action got under way. Now it's just heads down and charge. There's hardly time to think about anything, take in all the emotions, all the sensations. And it isn't a time for thinking anyway. It's a time for instinct.

A big black lad is coming straight for me. He throws a right-hander but I sway to my left and he stumbles past. Next up it's a white bloke with receding hair and a goatee beard. He makes a grab for the front of my coat but I drag him forward and he falls to his knees then onto his side, curling into a ball as I launch a couple of kicks at him. All around me bodies are hurtling about, arms and legs are flailing, blood is spattering onto the tarmac. The wind is almost blowing a gale now, and somehow it makes things seem wilder, madder, more dangerous.

Somebody hits me in the back, and I spin round in time to see a red-faced bloke in a beanie hat swinging another punch at me. I duck down and feel his fist crack into the top of my skull. As I look up, he's screaming in pain, shaking his hand like it's on fire. I smile at him. He's had his go. Now it's mine. I dig a left hand into his guts then crack a right over the top, sending him crashing.

It's difficult to gauge how long the fighting's been going on for. It could be seconds, it could be much longer. But one thing's for sure. We're starting to get the upper hand. The Whitbourne crew are tough blokes, up for a scrap, but we're eating into their territory, like an army advancing across a battlefield, and we're coming out on top in all the skirmishes. One-on-ones, groups of lads piling into each other, every time it's Whitbourne giving ground.

We've driven them right back past their exit gates now, and the first couple of lads are making a break for it. A split second later, and they're all running. It's a fantastic sight. The Whitbourne boys are scarpering like scared rabbits. They won't be leapfrogging us in the Firms league. The battle's over and the NLLF boys are victorious. I start to laugh. I feel invincible. Untouchable. Made of steel.

But then there's a pair of arms tightening round my waist and I'm being pushed forwards, stumbling down to the ground face first. I stretch an arm out in front of me, trying to push myself up, but there's a weight on my back holding me down. I feel my other arm being wrenched up until my hand is between my shoulder blades. A jolt of panic goes through me. This shouldn't be happening.

I manage to force myself up on one elbow, looking around in disbelief. Everyone's running now. It's not just the Whitbourne lads. It's Letchford too. And the reason they're running is that suddenly there are police everywhere. I see Rob and Gary sprinting towards the corner of the Main Stand. Scotty and Jimmy and Jerome are doubling back in the other direction. I see Ryan bombing across the car park and clambering over the perimeter fence.

I roll slightly to my right. And then I see Raks. He's face first on the tarmac too. A policeman in riot gear is sitting on his back. My heart feels like it's stopped. With one last big effort I wriggle myself around so that I can see who's pinning me down. In all honesty, I already know.

The policeman pushes up his visor and looks at me.

"I suggest you stop struggling son," he says. "You're under arrest."

fifteen

The next five hours are surreal.

By ten o'clock we're sitting in the police detention room at Southlands. It's down in the bowels of the Main Stand, fifteen feet square with a concrete floor and pale blue walls. Someone's punched a hole in the door. There's me and Raks and seven other lads. I vaguely recognise a couple of them, but the others I've never seen before. They're probably Whitbourne boys. There's no hostility now though. We're all in the same boat.

Me and Raks are the youngest in the room. The coppers speak to us first. They make sure we know we're under caution. They tell us why we're being held.

On suspicion of committing offences contrary to the Public Order Act 1986, namely the offences of Threatening Behaviour and Affray.

They take away our mobiles and jot down our details. Addresses, home phone numbers. Raks starts to cry. I just feel numb.

By twenty past ten we're in the back of a transit van heading for Letchford Central Police Station. There are metal grilles over the windows and a set of bars inside the back doors. It's like a cage on wheels. It's only a five-minute journey, but it's not pleasant. Nine of us are squashed in side-by-side, hot and bothered, jostling for elbow room, gagging on the smell of beer and aftershave, sweat and puke.

By half past ten we're at the station. It's been a busy night in Letchford. The reception area is full of shouting drunks, red-eyed women and fidgety druggies. Ten minutes later it's just me and Raks, alone in a room, waiting for our dads to get here. It's a nicer room than the one at the stadium. Pink walls, grey chairs, a low table in the middle of the floor. A WPC is checking up on us every few minutes. She's quite fit. I smile at her, try to get her on our side, but she's not having it. She's completely expressionless. I talk to Raks, try to keep him going. Tell him to keep cool. Admit nothing. Raks just keeps crying.

At half past eleven, Dad and Raj Patel turn up. Dad's pissed as usual. He's had to cadge a lift from Raj. Raj is just seriously pissed off. We're allowed to speak to them for a few minutes, and then we're whisked away to be photographed, fingerprinted and to have DNA swabs taken. After that we're back into the room with pink walls to sit in silence with Dad and Raj, their eyes boring holes into us.

Just after midnight two duty solicitors arrive. A man and a woman. Raks and his dad go off into another room with the bloke. Me and my dad stay put. My solicitor is a pretty Chinese lady in her mid to late twenties. She wants me to call her Suki. Dad thinks I should call her Miss Chang. We talk for forty minutes. She clarifies the reasons why I'm being held, tells me about the interview process and all the possible outcomes. Bail. Custody. Court appearances. Banning orders. Dad starts to look ill. He goes off to get a cup of coffee. I tell Suki what happened earlier on. I'm fairly economical with the truth. We decide on a strategy. It's not too original. Basically I'm going to say *It wasn't me guvnor*.

At half past one it's time for the interviews. Raks,

his dad and his solicitor go through one door. Me, Dad and Suki go through another. We're in a small, claustrophobic room with a low ceiling. We sit across a table from two officers. PC Andy Crowe and PC Alan Cushing. PC Crowe does most of the talking. He's thin-faced, bald, Yorkshire accent, white spittle in the corners of his mouth. For the third time tonight I'm reminded that I'm under caution.

You do not have to say anything. But it may harm your defence if you do not mention when questioned something which you later rely on in Court. Anything you do say may be given in evidence.

For the second time tonight I'm formally notified of the reasons why I'm being held.

I'm still numb and detached from what's going on around me. It's like being stuck inside an episode of *The Bill*. The uniforms, the stern faces, the neon strip lights, the Formica table-top, the upright chairs, the polished floor, the tape machine, the paper cups of water. I've seen them all before, hundreds of times on my TV. The procedures I'm going through, I know them off by heart. The legal jargon and police-speak I'm listening to, I can almost recite it word-for-word before it's said to me. Everything is oddly familiar. But it's also very very weird. Because it's not a fictional character trying to talk his way out of charges of *Threatening Behaviour and Affray*. It's me.

The interview lasts three quarters of an hour. Dad stays silent while I go through my version of events outside Southlands. I was trying to make my way out when I got caught in the crossfire. I was struck several times and only raised my hands in self-defence. My breathing is steady. My voice is steady. I'm surprised at how calm I am. I find myself thinking about

Ryan, Gary, Dave, Steve, Chris, Trev and the other lads. They'd be proud of me. The police officers try to pick holes in my story. Suggest to me that perhaps my recollection is wrong. That I, in fact had a role to play in instigating the violence. Prompted by Suki, I deny this.

At quarter past two, me and my dad go back into the room with pink walls. Raks and Raj are already there. Suki, Raks's solicitor, the interview teams and the custody officer are locked away in another room.

The next fifteen minutes seem to drag on forever. Raks looks shell-shocked, chewing his fingernails and staring at the floor. Raj is pacing around like a caged tiger. Dad's drinking another cup of coffee. His hands are shaking. I'm completely numb now. Totally switched off.

Just after half past two, the custody officer comes in, flanked by the solicitors. He's a big bloke, six foot two or three, grey hair and black eyebrows, wire framed glasses. He's holding a clipboard. I'm holding my breath. Raks stands up, but I stay sitting down. The custody officer blows his nose on a blue handkerchief. He starts to read.

It is the opinion of the Interview Team that there is insufficient evidence in either case to provide a realistic prospect of conviction in a Court of Law. For this reason you are to be released without charge. It is my duty to inform you that a record of your arrests will be held on the Police National Computer until you reach the age of seventeen. Once you have collected your personal effects, you are both free to leave.

I suck air back into my lungs. I can almost feel the oxygen returning to all the different parts of my body, a tingling sensation. The numbness is wearing off. I rub my chin with the back of my hand. I look at my dad and grin. He's not amused. Raks bursts into tears. The custody officer leaves the room. I stand up and thank Suki. She smiles, but there's no real warmth in it. Getting scrotes off the hook is just a job she does.

Five minutes later we're all at the front desk. The reception area has emptied right out now. Raks has had his mobile returned and I'm just collecting mine. The desk sergeant pushes a form across the counter for me to sign. I scribble my signature and hand the form back. I shove my phone into my pocket.

The desk sergeant looks at me, then he looks at Raks.

"From what I hear, you two have had a very lucky escape tonight," he says. "And if you want a word of advice, I'd keep well away from Southlands for the foreseeable future."

It's cold outside in the car park. The wind that was blowing earlier on has died down and it's raining now. Miserable, drizzly rain that makes a start on soaking through my clothes the second I step out into it. We crunch across the gravel, heading for Raj's Mondeo. He and Dad are out in front. Raks and me are bringing up the rear. Raj pushes the button on his key fob and de-activates the central locking. We all get in the car, slamming the doors and pulling our seatbelts across. The interior light goes out and Raj slowly reverses out of the parking bay, nosing the car towards the exit.

The centre of Letchford is pretty deserted. There are a few women in miniskirts and vest tops staggering along the pavements and looking for taxis, and a stray dog sniffing at a discarded kebab in Town Hall Square, but that's about it. We keep on going, heading out of town. I sit and stare into the night, at the

Christmas decorations, the shop fronts and billboards sliding past. Glory Hole Antiques. Poundland. Magic Valley Chinese. Wisla Polish Grocery. Big posters for mobile phones and underarm deodorants. The silence in the car is deafening.

As we pull onto the ringroad, Raks starts to cry again. Little hiccupping sobs, with his finger and thumb pressed into the top of his nose and his head on his shoulder. I reach a hand out and squeeze his elbow, but he shrinks away into the corner of the seat. Shrugs me off. I pull my hand back and rest it on my knee.

I take a breath and look out of the window again. I think about everything that's happened to me, try to make sense of it all. I feel strange. Different. Like I've been through a rite of passage and lived to tell the tale. And there's one sentence that just keeps going round and round in my head. *We got away with it.*

The roads are empty at this hour of the morning, and it doesn't take us long to get back to Thurston. We go through the centre of the village, past the shops, weaving through the streets until we're on Wolverton Road, hanging a right into Dale Road and pulling up outside our house.

Dad unbuckles his seatbelt.

"Thanks Raj," he says. "I really appreciate this."

"That's alright Tony," Raj replies.

Dad gets out of the car. I lean across towards Raks. I grip his shoulder.

"Chin up mate," I whisper. I tap my nose. "And not a word to Zoe, right?"

Raks doesn't say anything.

I undo my seatbelt, pull my door open and step out onto the pavement. The rain is really coming down

216

now. In the distance a dog howls. I duck my head back into the car.

"Thanks Mr Patel," I say.

Raj nods, but he doesn't look up.

I slam the door and follow Dad down the path. Inside the house we hang our jackets up and go into the living room. I slump into an armchair and Dad heads for the sofa, stopping off on the way to flick the TV on. Force of habit. It's *The Jeremy Skinner Show*. A young bloke with acne and a baseball cap is sitting on a stage next to an old woman in a leopard print top. There's a caption in the bottom left hand corner of the screen. *I LEFT MY PREGNANT FIANCEE — AND MOVED IN WITH HER MUM*. Dad looks at me. We've not said a word to each other since we left the police station, but I get the impression that's about to change.

"Well?" Dad says.

I shrug.

He has another go.

"What have you got to say for yourself?"

I rub the top of my head. There's a slight lump there, where the geezer with the red face wrecked his fist earlier on.

"Not much," I reply. "They took me in, they weighed up all the evidence, they let me go. End of story."

Dad shakes his head.

"That's not the end of the story. This is serious stuff. You were *arrested*. That's terrible. Shameful. Nobody in our family has ever been arrested. And that'll stay on your record forever."

"No it won't," I tell him. "You heard what that copper said. Once I'm seventeen, it gets wiped off. Forgotten about."

Dad holds his hand up.

"Don't you believe it. It'll always be there. Employers check things like that." He takes a breath, then carries on. "Anyway. I want to know what's *actually* been going on."

I shrug again.

"You were there during the interview. What else do you need to know?"

"Well," Dad says. "I heard what you said. What the solicitor advised you to say. Just an innocent bystander. In the wrong place at the wrong time. It got you out of trouble. But is it the truth?"

"Oh right. Now I'm a liar."

"So innocent bystanders have DVDs called *Terrace Warfare* in their bedrooms, do they?"

I look down at a stain on the carpet. The question's still hanging in the air, but I'm not going to answer it.

"Listen Tom," Dad says. "I watch the news. I read the papers. I know there's been some trouble at Letchford games recently. Fighting, stone-throwing, general thuggery. Is that you and your stupid mates? Arseholes like this Ryan?"

"Not really," I say.

Dad laughs.

"Right. So it *is* you and your stupid mates." His voice is rising. All the pent-up frustration of the evening coming out. "At least we've got that cleared up. Well, I'll tell you now. You're not going to any more games. You lied to me. Just this last weekend you told me that nothing was going on, and I believed you. Never again. No more Letchford Town."

I say nothing, but my mind's in overdrive. No more Letchford Town? We'll see about that.

Dad starts getting himself properly worked up.

"I mean, what do you think you're going to get out of this?" He spreads his arms out wide. "Punching people. Kicking people. Is it some sort of shortcut to being a man? Do you think it's big? Do you think it's clever?"

I smirk. Part embarrassed, part defiant.

"No."

"And getting Raks involved," Dad says. "What do you think Raj Patel thinks, seeing his lad being led astray by his oldest friend?"

"Hey, back up. What makes you think I've led Raks astray? Don't you think he's big enough to think for himself?"

Dad ignores me. He's on a roll.

"Just look at the state of you," he says. "You look like a yob. Your prison haircut. The clothes you've got on. I'm not an idiot. I know you don't wear your school colours any more. I've seen you, sneaking out with your jeans and trainers in your bag."

I snort.

"I won't bother trying to hide them in future then."

"Oh right." Dad nods his head sarcastically. "I thought I'd get that. Backchat. Cockiness. Just what I'd expect from you these days."

I swallow. It feels like he's trying to goad me. Tempt me into a massive bust-up. I stare at the TV and try to stop myself rising to the bait. The couple on stage have had their say and Jeremy Skinner's out in the crowd, canvassing opinion. An old bloke with slicked-back white hair and a moustache is saying his piece. He's taken their behaviour as a personal insult. The pair of them should be utterly ashamed. They should bring back the birch. He's getting more and more incensed. Ten seconds after he's finished

219

venting his spleen, his jowls are still jiggling with indignation. Up at the front the happy couple are smiling. They've started holding hands.

Dad flops back into the sofa and lets out a deep breath. He shakes his head. It looks like he's calming down.

"Tom," he says, voice softer now. "You used to be such a nice lad. What's gone wrong? Just tell me. I'll try to understand."

I don't know what I'm supposed to say. I pick at a bobble of fluff on the side of my chair and avoid eye contact.

"All the good things in your life – fishing, Thurston Dynamo – you don't seem to care about them any more. And what about your schoolwork? I never see you doing anything these days."

"I get by."

Dad pulls a face.

"You should be doing more than just getting by. I said this to you the other night. You've got a good brain. Natural ability. But you can't just coast along on natural ability forever."

I sigh. I glance back at *The Jeremy Skinner Show*. The pregnant fiancée has been brought on stage. She's about eight months gone and she's not happy. She's trying to attack her mum, but she's being held back by a couple of security guards.

Dad's seen that my attention's wandering. He gets up and switches the TV off. The only sound now is the ticking of the mantelpiece clock.

"Tom," he says. "You've got to get yourself back on track. Don't go off the rails. Start enjoying the good stuff again."

"Like what?" I ask.

He rubs the stubble on his chin.

"All the things I've said. Fishing, school, playing football. Seeing Zoe. What's she going to say about this?"

"She's not going to find out."

Dad raises his eyebrows.

"Well that's between you and your conscience," he says. "But anyway, what I'm saying is get your priorities right. Put your energy into proper things. Even your paper round – you only seem to do it nowadays for the money it gets you."

I can't help smiling at that. I look up.

"What do you expect me to do it for? My health? To meet nice people? Who like? Mr Curran on Blakely Road, phoning up to complain if I'm a couple of minutes late or I've left his gate open?"

"That's not the point I'm making," Dad says, angry with himself for getting sidetracked.

"Anyway," I go on. "I have to earn my own money. I hardly ever get anything out of you."

He runs a hand through his hair.

"There's a reason why I don't give you money," he says. "It's because I know the sort of things you'll spend it on. I know you've been drinking. I've seen the cans in your room. I could tell you'd had a few this evening too."

I put my hands on my head. I'm too tired for all of this.

"You're the last person in the world who should be lecturing me about drinking. You were completely plastered at the police station. You stank like a brewery. What do you think they thought about that? They just looked at you and thought *piss artist*. It's no wonder his son's such a fucking twat."

Dad's suddenly furious, shocked at what I've said, shocked at the words I'm using.

"Watch your language," he says.

I'm straight back at him.

"Don't change the subject. You wanted to talk about boozing. What about last Saturday at Raks's? What a performance that was."

Dad sits up straight. He moves across the sofa so that he's nearer to me, invading my space. His eyes are blazing.

"Don't try to turn all this round so that you can take potshots at me, you rude little sod. You obviously don't give a shit what I say, but think about Mum. What would she have made of all of this?"

I roll my eyes.

"Oh, how did I know you'd bring Mum into it? That's just low."

Dad shakes his head.

"No," he says. "It's a valid question. What would Mum have thought, seeing her only child growing up to be a lout with a criminal record?"

"Oh piss off. Don't give me all that emotional blackmail bollocks."

Dad's wagging his finger at me. He's been rattled and now he's fighting dirty.

"I'll tell you what she would have thought. She'd have thought you were a big, big disappointment."

It's a cheap shot. Way below the belt. At first I don't know how to respond. But then I can feel the anger flaring up inside me. I'm getting that strange metallic taste in my mouth. The one I get at football matches when everything's about to turn nasty. I start to laugh, but there's no humour in it.

"You're fucking priceless. I'm a big disappointment? Then what are you?"

Dad says nothing.

I'm on the front foot now. It's my turn to throw the

cheap shots and I'm really going for it.

"What would Mum have thought of you? Pissed as a fart every night. Lying unconscious in the living room. Dossing around on benefits for years. Not washing. Not shaving. Dressing like a tramp. Showing me up in front of my friends. Is that your idea of being a role model?"

His mouth drops open. He can't believe what he's just heard. In truth, I can't believe what I've just said. But it's not like it hasn't been coming. It almost burst out on Saturday evening when we had to leave Raks's house. Tonight, after all that's gone on, I just couldn't hold it in any more.

Without warning, Dad jumps to his feet, standing over me. He's tried everything else, now he's trying intimidation.

"My old man would have thrashed me for speaking to him like that," he says.

"Oh yeah?" I stand up and look him in the eye. "Well why don't you have a go then? See what happens?" My heart rate has shot right up. It's another surreal moment in a night full of them. I'm ready to chin my own father.

Dad blinks. There's uncertainty in his expression. Fear, even. I'm as big as he is, but I'm a lot younger. A lot fitter. His eyes flick to the side, away from mine. He takes a step backwards, then sinks into the sofa again. All the fight has gone out of him.

I sit back down. I look at my watch. Quarter to four. I've been up for nearly twenty-one hours. I seem to have gone through a couple of years' worth of shit in that time. I've pissed Zoe off again. I've skived school. I've been in a fight in a pub. I've got a big dilemma hanging over my head with the Mackworth game date-switch. I've got arrested at Southlands. I've been photographed, fingerprinted, swabbed, interviewed, interrogated. And now this. I'd almost forgotten I turned fifteen yesterday. Happy birthday to me.

For the next few minutes, Dad's got his head in his hands. It's a strange, awkward scene. Everything's silent, except for the clock ticking on and on. My pulse has slowed down, but I'm still on edge.

Random thoughts are popping into my mind. I'm thinking that me and Dad have said more to each other in the last twenty minutes than we've managed in the last couple of years. I'm thinking about the moment I was arrested and comparing it with the moment when the custody officer told me I was going to be released without charge. I'm thinking about the other night at Raks's again. The way I felt as Dad staggered up the garden path. Knowing that I should give him some sympathy, put things right. But I couldn't do it. I couldn't do it then, and I can't do it now. Not that it's an option now, anyway. We've gone way beyond that.

Another couple of minutes pass. Dad still shows no sign of doing or saying anything.

I clear my throat.

"Are we finished, then?" I ask.

He doesn't look up. Eventually he grunts.

I take it as a yes.

"Right then." I stand up, yawn and stretch. "I'm going to bed."

sixteen

The bloke next door is banging around again. Saturday morning and he's hard at it. He started a bit later than usual today. Ten to eight, instead of twenty-five past seven. He's making up for lost time now though. Quarter to twelve and things seem to be reaching a crescendo. He's making such a racket that I'm not actually sure if I've just heard the doorbell ring.

I push myself up onto the edge of my bed, leaning across to turn down the volume on my stereo. I listen for a couple of seconds. There's a whining sound like a high-speed drill, but no bell. Perhaps I'm imagining things. I'm just about to turn my music up again when I hear ringing. This time there's no mistaking it. We've got visitors.

I stand up and head out onto the landing. Dad's downstairs, but there's not much likelihood of him getting up. He's crashed out on the sofa again. I start to go down the stairs. I'm wondering who's at the door. It might be Jehovah's Witnesses. They're quite often in this neck of the woods at weekends, suits on, briefcases in hand. I think they were round last Saturday though, so it probably isn't them. I can rule the postman out because there's already a pile of junk mail on the mat. So that leaves Raks or Zoe.

As I reach my hand up to turn the catch, I make a prediction. Raks. I've not seen him since Tuesday night. He's not been at Parkway and he hasn't been

225

returning my texts or calls. He'll have been under the cosh big-time at home, but now he's coming round to tell me all about it. I've got lots to tell him, too. It's been a pretty interesting week at school. I open the door. I'm half right. Because it is Raks. But Zoe is there too.

I blink, surprised.

"Alright you two?" I say.

They both give me nervous smiles.

I step aside to let them in, but they're hesitating. I feel a little flicker of anxiety. Something's going on. I hope it's not what I think it is. Surely Raks wouldn't have given the game away? Not after I specifically told him not to.

"What's up?" I ask, trying to brazen things out.

Zoe looks at me. She steps up into the hallway and puts her arms round my waist, squeezing me tight. It's just a hug, but there's something strange about it. It feels more like sympathy than affection. It's the sort of hug I remember relatives giving me at my mum's funeral. She loosens her grip, then kisses me on the cheek.

I laugh.

"This is all very formal," I say. "What's going on?"

Zoe takes a breath, composing herself.

"Tom," she says. "I haven't got long. I've got to get the twenty past twelve bus into school for a dress rehearsal. Let's not mess around. Why didn't you say anything?"

I swallow. I decide to play dumb. I'm pretty certain I know where this is leading, but there's always a chance I might have got it wrong.

"Say anything about what?"

She shakes her head.

"Tom. I know about Tuesday night."

Instantly I feel like all the air has been knocked out of me. I rub my nose, thinking about what I can say.

Zoe carries on.

"Raks told me. He feels really bad about it, like he's let you down. But he did it because he's your mate and he wants what's best for you. He thinks you need to talk."

It's a totally inappropriate response, but I get a sudden urge to laugh. I'm in the middle of what Americans call *An Intervention*. I glower over Zoe's shoulder, trying to catch Raks's eye, give him the look of death. If he thinks I think he's betrayed me, he's spot on. Raks just stares at the ground. My mouth is dry. I swallow again.

"Do you both want to come in then?" I ask.

Raks looks up.

"I'll tell you what," he says. "You two have got a lot of things to talk about. Why don't I leave you to it, and go down the Rec? Tom, you could come down when Zoe goes into town."

I shrug.

"Whatever you want," I reply, offhand.

Raks heads off up the path and I pull the door closed.

Zoe gives me another nervous smile.

"Shall we go for a chat then?" I ask.

She nods and follows me up the stairs.

In my room I sit on the bed. Zoe stays standing up. She's in her indie kid gear again. Converse, skinny black jeans. Her army jacket isn't zipped all the way up and I can see that she's wearing the Mickey Mouse T-shirt she bought last month on our trip into Letchford. She brushes dust off my chest of drawers and picks up a DVD case. *Terrace Warfare*. My heart sinks. I keep forgetting to give it back to Ryan.

Zoe tuts and puts the DVD down. She comes across to the bed and sits next to me.

"I don't know how to start," she says. "I knew something was going on, that you were changing, but I never thought you'd get yourself into anything like this. *Arrested for football violence*." She shakes her head.

I clear my throat.

"It's not as bad as it sounds," I say. "We've not been charged with anything."

Zoe laughs. It's a hollow sound.

"Only because you denied it all. Raks told me you were both in the thick of it. And that you'd done other stuff before."

My mind is in a whirl. I flatten out a section of my quilt cover with the palm of my hand.

"Sorry," I say. But as I say it, I realise I don't really mean it. Why should I? It's not like I got myself arrested to spite her. She's just trying to make me feel guilty.

She ducks her head down to look into my eyes.

"Why, Tom? What's happening to you?"

I pull a face. There's not really an answer to that. Or if there is, it's too complex to put into a few sentences.

Zoe flicks hair out of her eyes, looking around, searching for the right words.

"Come on Tom. You know what football hooligans are like. They're scumbags. Wanting to hurt people, making people's lives a misery. You're not like that."

I shake my head. There are things I could say to her. Like how there's more to it than just hitting people. It's about pride. About belonging. But I don't think she'd believe me. I'm starting to feel annoyed

228

now. Irritated at being put on the spot and having to justify myself when there really shouldn't have been any need.

"I suppose Ryan Dawkins is behind all of this isn't he?" she asks.

"Not really."

She isn't convinced.

"I asked you what Ryan was like and you wouldn't tell me anything. But I've heard stuff now. There are people at my school who know about him. He was sent down a year, basically for being a complete nutter. Did you know they call him ASBO Boy?"

I laugh. I've not heard that nickname for a while.

"It's not funny," Zoe says. "Do you really want to be known as someone who hangs around with people like that? You'll get a reputation as an idiot, too. *Yeah. Tom Mitchell. Good bloke to know if you need someone headbutted or slashed with a Stanley knife.* Either that or you'll get yourself killed."

I blow out a breath and flop back onto the bed. I can't get a word in edgeways.

Zoe leans over me. There's a sad look in her eyes now.

"The thing is, "she says, "I can't help feeling like I'm somehow to blame."

I prop myself up on one elbow.

"In what way?" I ask.

Zoe looks down.

"Oh, you know. I just haven't been there for you over these past couple of months. What with all this time spent on *Oliver*. I've given you a load of grief about your hair, drinking, about the people you've been hanging about with, stuff like that. Maybe I've driven you to this."

I actually *do* feel a twinge of guilt now. I reach out

my hand and stroke Zoe's face. Her skin feels smooth and soft.

"Don't be silly," I say. "It's not you."

She tries a smile and touches the T pendant around my neck.

"Well, I don't know," she says. "I'm really sorry if I've been giving you a hard time."

I ease myself back down. Zoe lies next to me and we stay that way for a while. It's starting to occur to me that this might be a good moment to get one or two things off my chest. It looks like I might just have landed on the moral high ground by accident.

"I haven't really seen much of you recently," I tell her. "It's like I've seen you, but I haven't *seen* you."

"Yeah," she says. "I know what you mean."

"And I know that you think it's me that's changing, but maybe it's you. I think maybe I've been a bit worried about that. You're dressing differently and spending time with different people. Sometimes I feel you might be leaving me behind."

There's a pause while Zoe lets this sink in.

"No," she says eventually. "You're just being paranoid. You're the one that's changing. Look at the evidence. I'm growing up. There's a difference."

I nod. The moral high ground has just collapsed under my feet. I keep my mouth shut.

Another couple of minutes pass. Zoe looks at her watch. It's nearly five past twelve.

"Anyway. I've got to go. I've said what I needed to say. I just want you to know that I'm here for you, yeah? And I'll do everything I can to help you put this Letchford Town episode behind you."

My stomach lurches. Zoe thinks I'm done with Letchford Town. I'm shocked for a second or two, but then the shock subsides. Of course that's what she thinks. It's obvious from the way she's been acting. I can hardly believe I didn't suss it out for myself. Raks must have given her the full run-down of what was said on Tuesday night. The desk sergeant advising us not to show our faces at Southlands for a while. That was just an unofficial warning though. Nothing binding. As far as I'm concerned, the Letchford Town episode isn't behind me. Not by a long way.

Zoe kisses me.

"I just want to have the old Tom back," she says, sitting up.

I cough.

"So what do you reckon?" Zoe asks. "Fresh start?"

"Fresh start," I say. I'm completely cornered. Unless I want a big flare-up, there's nothing else I *can* say. Another twinge of guilt goes through me. And this time it's a killer. Because I know all of this is bollocks. There's not really going to be a fresh start between us. Not if it means giving up Letchford Town. And after next Friday night, with the small matter of the clash between *Oliver* and the Letchford-Mackworth derby, there probably isn't even going to be an *us* any more.

Fifteen minutes later Zoe has gone and I'm walking along Hill View Drive, on my way to meet Raks. I've gone through a pretty big range of emotions in the last three quarters of an hour. Surprise, annoyance, irritation, guilt. Now I'm feeling pissed off and angry.

There's been a hard frost overnight and there's no sign of a thaw yet. As I go through the gate and head across the Rec, the grass is white and brittle, crackling under my feet. In spite of the weather, the usual punters are out in force. The dog walkers, the two big blokes in England shirts whacking golf balls around,

231

the kids on quad bikes and mopeds, number plates wrapped in plastic bags in case the coppers turn up.

I can see Raks. He's sitting on one of the few un-vandalised swings in the adventure playground, swaying to and fro, squinting at his mobile, breath coming out in white clouds. I hadn't noticed it before, but his hair's getting long. He didn't get it cut the last time I did and it's quite bushy now. He's wearing a short brown pilot jacket with a fur-trimmed hood. He doesn't look like an NLLF boy any more. I keep walking. As I get closer, Raks glances up. He's spotted me. I can see that he's smiling. And he can see that I'm not.

"What's up?" he asks, stuffing his phone into his pocket. It's a fairly pointless question. He knows what's up.

I pull myself onto a swing next to him. The chains are icy cold in my hands. I shake my head.

"I don't fucking believe you. What did you have to tell her for?"

Raks looks like he's going to say something, but then he thinks better of it.

I look down at the ground. Frosted bark chippings, broken glass and fag ends, muddy scuffs worn away under each of the swing seats. I shake my head again. I've got so much I want to say but I don't know how to start. I look up at the sky. There's a plane cutting its way through the clouds. The cobwebs in the corners of the swing frame are frosted white like cake decorations.

"What did you have to tell her for?" I ask again.

Raks says nothing.

I launch into a rant, everything spilling out at once.

"You really fucking dropped me in it. I kept quiet

about Tuesday night all week. I just carried on as if everything was normal. I even went to school on Wednesday morning after I'd only had a couple of hours sleep."

"Tom…" Raks says.

I cut him off.

"Zoe didn't have a clue that anything had gone on. That was exactly what I wanted. But then you went and opened your big fucking trap. You did exactly what I told you not to do."

"Tom, I was trying to…"

"Just leave it. The damage has been done."

We sit in silence. It's probably only a minute or two but it feels longer. I swing slowly from side to side. I'm still feeling pretty wound up, but the real hostility is dying down now. The anger's not gone, but it's directed more at myself and at the world in general than at Raks. I blow out a breath.

"Anyway," I say. "How've you been? Everyone's been asking about you. What've you been up to?"

Raks looks relieved. He rolls his eyes.

"Shit man," he says. "You don't want to know."

I chuckle.

"I bet your mum and dad went ballistic, didn't they?"

Raks stares out past the cricket square.

"Ballistic's not the word. It was beyond ballistic."

I raise my eyebrows.

"I thought you might have been in some deep shit when you weren't at school."

Raks is still gazing at a point somewhere in the distance. The thousand yard stare.

"I tell you man, it was touch and go whether I'd ever be going back to Parkway."

"Really?"

"Yeah. My mum's never liked the place. She thinks there's too many bad influences there. She was straight on the phone to Letchford Grammar on Wednesday morning. Got me a place all sorted out. It was only my dad that stopped her going out and buying me the uniform. He talked her round. Now they're going to give me one more chance. If I fuck up again, that's it. Bye bye Parkway."

I whistle.

"Shit."

I dig the toes of my trainers into the bark chippings and push myself backwards. The frame of the swing groans and creaks as I swish forwards through the cold air.

"So what about you?" Raks asks. "How's things with your dad?"

I bring the swing to a halt.

"We haven't really spoken to each other since Tuesday night. Probably just as well. Quite a lot of stuff was said."

Raks nods.

"And how do you feel about it all now? You know, after the dust has settled?"

I shrug.

"It's just one of those things isn't it?" I say. "It's an occupational hazard, getting arrested. In time we'll look back at it and laugh, feel a bit nostalgic, like the lads at The Shakespeare do when they think about Italia 90 and The Battle Of Southlands."

Raks looks uncomfortable.

"I feel a bit ashamed," he says, voice low. "Like I've let my family down."

"Oh come on. It's no big deal. It's just what happens from time to time when you do the sort of things we've been doing. It's a validation, really. And

234

anyway, we were released without charge."

Raks mumbles something under his breath. He twists his swing seat through three hundred and sixty degrees then spins back to his starting position.

"How's school been?" he asks. "Does anyone know about what happened?"

I laugh.

"Too right they do. It's the bush telegraph again. Word was right round the place by the time I got there on Wednesday morning. I don't know how it happens. It just does."

"And what are people saying?"

"They love it. You wait till you get back. See the way everyone acts around you. We're heroes now."

Raks shakes his head.

"Heroes for getting ourselves arrested? That's not right."

"Get real," I tell him. "You know how it goes. Have a bit of a brush with the law and people treat you differently. It's like you've got an aura. And here's the bit you'll like — the girls are well into it. Susie and Carly and all their mates. Nice girls like bad boys."

Raks furrows his brow.

"But we're not bad boys," he says. "We're good boys who've got ourselves into something we should have steered well clear of. It's all got to end."

I can hardly believe what I'm hearing.

"You're joking aren't you? It's only just getting started. We can't let Ryan and the rest of the lads down."

Raks goes quiet, thinking. I look across at the cricket pavilion, reading the graffiti. It's pretty crude stuff. Nobody's ever going to mistake it for urban art. Badly sprayed tags and random insults. *SARAH IS A SLAG. MARTIN SUX COX.* Beyond the pavilion there's a row of trees, abandoned crows nests dotted about through their bare branches, black against the slate grey sky. I swing sideways, gently bumping into Raks.

"Come on mate," I say. "Don't quit on me. We're well on the way to being the top boys. We got a mention in the *Argus* and everything. No names, but when it said *nine arrests at Southlands*, everyone knew it meant us. Giving up now would be like selling a load of shares when their value is about to go through the roof. You do Business Studies. You know how stupid that would be."

Raks sighs.

"Do you know why I told Zoe about last Tuesday night?" he asks.

"Not really." I've not really had the time to think about it.

"It's because I knew you'd be like this. No regret, no remorse. I knew you'd ignore what the police said to you, what your dad said to you. I knew you'd just carry on like nothing had happened. I thought that she might be able to make you see sense."

Things are slowly clicking into place in my brain.

"So you didn't send her round because you thought I needed to talk then. You sent her round to bully me into not going to Southlands any more."

"I suppose you could put it that way," Raks says. "It looks like I was wrong."

"Well yeah." I'm starting to get annoyed. "You *were* wrong. Until the law actually says I can't go and watch Letchford Town, I'm going to keep on doing it. Why shouldn't I? I'm in the clear. We're both in the clear. We were lucky, but we got away with it. I don't get what the problem is."

Raks looks exasperated.

"No, that's right," he says. "You don't get it. I mean, what did Zoe say when you told her you were still going to go to matches?"

I scratch my chin.

"She doesn't know. She's just assumed I've packed it in and I've not told her any different."

Raks's mouth curls into a sneer.

"Oh, I get it. You're a big hard football hooligan, but you haven't got the bottle to tell your missus the truth about things."

There's tension in the air now. He's narked and I'm narked. I decide to go for the jugular.

"So come on then. What are you saying? That's it? You're finished with the NLLF? Finished with Letchford Town?"

Raks nods.

"Exactly. I've had time to think about things. It's all wrong. It's not us. Well, it's not me anyway." There's determination in his voice. He's not pissing around. He means it.

I try a different approach.

"You're a hypocrite. A few days ago you were right into this. Letchford. The NLLF. The Firms league. We sorted Whitbourne out. Do the same to Mackworth and we'll be top of the table. You understand what it all means. And now what? A bit of a run-in with the Old Bill and you give it all up? That's fucking sad."

"Tom," Raks says. "Even if I wanted to go again, I couldn't do it. My dad's banned me. He says no more Letchford games while I'm living under his roof."

I laugh.

"My dad said the same thing. So what? I don't care what he says."

Raks shakes his head sadly.

237

"You should respect your dad."

I pull a face. It's easy for him to say. I brush my hand across my hair. I'm not having much success breaking his resolve. I try yet another angle of attack.

"So what about Friday night then? Mackworth at home. Imagine the tension. The nerves. The danger. Won't you be getting a bit of an urge then?"

Raks laughs.

"Friday night's out for you anyway," he says. "It's *Oliver*, you daft bastard."

I sniff.

"Raks. It's Mackworth. Do you honestly think I'd miss it?"

He looks horrified. He wasn't expecting this.

"But what's going to happen about *Oliver*? You promised Zoe you'd go, man."

"Well, you'll be there won't you?"

"I can't go," Raks says. "I'm grounded. In before five every night. But anyway, that's not the point. She's your girl. You've been together for years. How would you explain yourself?"

I shrug.

"I haven't thought yet." It's true. I've just sort of blanked it out of my mind, assumed something will occur to me eventually.

Raks puts his hand on my shoulder. He looks deadly serious.

"Tom. You've got to go to Zoe's play. It's going to be bad enough when she finds out you're still going to Letchford games. Imagine the shitstorm if you miss *Oliver* to go to a match. She'll finish with you. You know she will."

"Maybe."

Raks tightens his grip.

"Look," he says. "Letchford-Mackworth is live on *Sky*. You go to the show and I'll record the football for you. You could watch it on Saturday morning. I'll bring it round. Just avoid finding out the score until then."

I rub my hands over my face. I take deep breaths.

"Raks, I see what you're saying, and I appreciate what you're offering, but it's pointless. I've got to go to Southlands. It's not just for the football. You know what I mean. I'll just have to face the music afterwards."

He lets go of my shoulder. He's run out of patience.

"I don't understand you any more," he says. "You've turned into an arsehole." He stands up.

"What are you doing?" I ask.

"I'm going to leave you to it," he says. "This conversation's going nowhere."

I shrug.

"Right. Suit yourself."

Raks looks like he's about to go, but he's hesitating.

"I'll see you around then," he says.

I glance up at him.

"Suppose so. Can I trust you not to blab your mouth off to Zoe about Friday night?"

"You needn't worry about that, mate," he replies. "I'm saying nothing. If you want to fuck your life up, that's your business. But if I was you, I'd be thinking hard about things before I came to any decisions."

Before I can say anything else, Raks is gone, marching away across the white grass towards the gate on the other side of the Rec. I stay sitting down, watching him go. Pretty soon he's out of sight.

I try to take a breath, but it's difficult. There's a lump in my throat. It feels like an era of my life has just come to an end. For a brief moment I'm struggling to hold back the tears, but then I get a grip of myself. I remember where I am. I remember who I am. And I remember I don't do crying.

seventeen

I couldn't face getting the Preston's bus into college this morning. It wasn't so much that I didn't fancy the journey. It was just that I didn't want to stand outside the Bulls Head yakking away to Zoe about how much I was looking forward to *Oliver* this evening. It just wouldn't have been right. Because I'm not going.

It's not as if I haven't thought about it. To be honest, I've not really thought about anything else this week. *Zoe or Letchford Town? Letchford Town or Zoe?* Round and round in my mind, morning, noon and night. But the answer I'm coming up with every time, is Letchford Town. It's like tossing a coin and always getting heads. Letchford are playing Mackworth tonight. I have to go to Southlands. The guilt is churning me up inside, but there's nothing I can do about it. I don't even feel like I've got a choice.

Because I wasn't getting the school bus this morning, I had a lie-in and got the twenty past eleven number 84 into town. It's quite a walk to Parkway from Letchford bus station. Thirty-five or forty minutes. Sometimes it's nice to be out alone in the fresh air, having a bit of a think. Today, though, it's not doing me any good at all.

I'm trying my hardest not to go off the deep end, but there's no getting away from it. After tonight, a lot of things are going to be very different. If I go to Southlands, instead of *Oliver*, the shit is going to hit the fan in a big way. My relationship with Dad will hit rock bottom, if it isn't there already, and Zoe will probably never speak to me again. Don't get me wrong. I don't want it to happen. In an ideal world it wouldn't happen. But this isn't an ideal world.

According to my watch it's coming up to twenty-five to one now. The school building is just rolling into view up at the top of the hill. There are some roadworks on the bridge and I keep to the right, past the line of orange cones. Someone's chucked a *Men At Work* sign into the river. The top is just sticking out of the murky water. I shake my head and keep walking.

A couple of minutes later I'm coming through the Parkway gates and heading down towards reception. My mind's still churning away like a hamster on a wheel. It's the last day of college before the Christmas holidays, and judging from the broken eggshells and splashes of flour on the path and the grass on either side of it, there hasn't been too much in the way of academic endeavour going on during the morning.

I push my way through the main doors and go left across the foyer, towards the dining hall. Someone's put a Christmas CD on. *Step Into Christmas* is just fading out and *Walking In The Air* is starting up. I'm a bit of an authority on Christmas songs at the moment. I sat through an hour of them on *Top Of The Pops 2* a couple of nights ago. There was nothing better on. I scan around for familiar faces, but the place is rammed. Jimmy and Scotty are sitting in the corner, but they've not seen me. They're too busy dealing with the last minute rush on ropey block-busters.

A lot of the teachers are in the hall today. Mr

Dickinson's over on the far side, sitting with a group of Year Ten girls. Nita Parmar and Cassie Morton and a couple of others. He's in his *US ARMY* T-shirt again, and he's had his fin hairdo sprayed with silly string to show what a zany guy he is. Mr Gillespie has broken out in a replica Newcastle top. Mrs Wetherall is on her own, picking away at an orange Tupperware bowl of salad. Just to my right, Mr Green is sitting with Sophie Reed and Tanya Fielder. They're not friends. Someone's been shit-stirring again. It could just be the light in here, but they both look like they're about four months pregnant, which might go some way towards explaining what their problems are all about.

I head for the canteen to get something to eat. I grab a tray and I'm just about to tag myself onto the end of the line when I hear someone calling my name. I look up. Green Adidas top with yellow stripes. It's Ryan. He's near the front with Gary, Rob and Jerome, beckoning me over. I go straight across, jumping a good thirty places in the queue. I wouldn't have done that a couple of months ago, but nowadays I don't think twice. In any case, nobody complains. If they've got anything to say, they're keeping quiet about it.

"All set for tonight?" Gary asks.

I squeeze myself in front of two Sixth Formers and give Gary a half-smile.

"Yes and no," I say.

Ryan looks at me and raises his eyebrows.

"Problems?"

"Kind of." I leave it at that.

I push my tray along the runners, seeing what's on offer. The cooks have laid on some festive stuff today, slices of dry-looking turkey breast, stuffing balls and

Brussels sprouts, but they're not finding many takers. I pick up portions of chips and beans and get myself a couple of sausages. I finish things off with a doughnut and a can of Coke and then I cut across to pay for it all. It's the usual woman on the till. She's got tinsel in her hair and baubles for earrings, but she's not looking any more cheerful than she normally does.

Back in the dining hall, *Walking In The Air* has finished and *White Christmas* is oozing out of the speakers. I stand next to Ryan and we survey the area, checking for seats. There aren't any. There's one space at a six-seater table over to the left, and apart from that, nothing.

But then I notice who's sitting at the table with the single space. It's the Budget Homeboys hip-hop crew. I look at Ryan. He smiles.

"Aren't they mates of yours?" he says.

I grin and nod my head. Then we set off to get our dinner places sorted out.

The pudgy Homeboy with the handcuffs bracelet is the first to see us coming. His hair has grown a fair bit since I last saw him, and he's had it braided into a feeble set of cornrows. As we get closer he nudges the Asian lad sitting next to him. They both look at us for a second or two and then tilt their heads down. They know who we are. It would be safe to say that a confrontation isn't at the top of their list of priorities at this moment in time. When it was five-on-two, they were all for it. Now it's five-on-five, they've gone all coy.

It only takes us a few more seconds to get to the Homeboys' table. I'm leading the way.

"Afternoon lads." I park my tray next to Cornrows Boy. "Just going, were you?"

Cornrows Boy doesn't say anything. He swallows hard and stares at the table-top. His big fleshy ears are going bright red. The Asian lad next to him starts scrabbling around, shoving half-eaten stuff onto his tray, trying to keep things low-key, but one of the white kids is looking a bit edgy, like he wants to have a go at standing his ground. He takes a bite of his hot dog and tries to give Rob the eyeball. Rob laughs. As the kid with the hot dog carries on staring, Jerome comes up behind him and snatches the *NY* baseball cap off his head.

Hot Dog Boy stands up and tries to take his hat back, but Jerome holds it out of his reach. Smiling, he pulls it onto his own head, back to front, pulling a gangsta pose, forearms crossed over his chest.

We're all pissing ourselves laughing now. The Budget Homeboys have well and truly got the message. Time to beat the retreat. They're filling up their trays as quickly as they can with whatever they can put their hands on, standing up, trying to get out of our way. I barge past Cornrows Boy and sit in his seat. Rob and Gary hustle a couple of the other lads out of their chairs. Ryan's just standing there grinning. Proud that he's trained us so well.

Jerome sits down and starts eating his hamburger. He's still wearing the *NY* cap.

Hot Dog Boy stretches his hand out.

"Give us the cap back," he says.

Jerome frowns. He puts his burger down.

"Give us the cap back *please*."

Everything's gone really quiet. People on the tables around us are glancing across, seeing what's going on. The rest of the Budget Homeboys are standing around like spare parts. Some of the teachers have noticed that something's happening but it doesn't seem like they want to get involved. Bing Crosby's finished now and Cliff Richard is launching into *Saviour's Day*.

Hot Dog Boy looks like he wants to cry. His carefully-cultivated hard man image is falling to pieces around him. There's not much chance of him taking a swing at Jerome. And there wouldn't be much point anyway. It would be like firing a peashooter at a tank.

"Give us the cap back please," he says.

A couple of girls giggle.

Jerome smiles. He's enjoying this.

"Give us the cap back please *sir*," he says.

There's no hesitation this time.

"Give us the cap back please sir."

Jerome smiles again. He looks across at Ryan, but Ryan shakes his head.

"Let him have it now."

Jerome pulls a face, like a kid who's just been told he's got to come in for his tea. He takes the cap off and hands it over.

Hot Dog Boy puts it back on his head, takes his tray and goes to stand with the rest of his crew. As they start trudging towards the canteen, Ryan calls out after them.

"Lads."

The Budget Homeboys turn round.

Ryan pulls his features into the most sincere expression he can manage.

"You make sure you have a very Merry Christmas and a Happy New Year."

My dinner goes down very well after that. It feels like a score has been settled. For the next half an hour or so my mind is nicely blank. The urge to keep thinking about things has faded right away. Around our table we sit and chat, take the piss out of each other. It feels good. It feels comfortable. At one point I make eye contact with Susie Black and she gives me a little wave. The Christmas CD rumbles on and on. *Wonderful Christmastime. I Wish It Could Be Christmas Everyday*. The songs are all old and cheesy, but somehow it doesn't matter.

There's a happy atmosphere in the dining hall. Everyone's getting into the spirit of the season. People from different groups and gangs are letting their guards down, talking to each other, laughing and joking. Popular kids are sitting with chavs. Smartly dressed townies are on the same tables as scruffy indie kids. Snoop is giving high-fives to the Dalton twins. I've even seen one or two of the emo kids smiling.

Ryan takes a swig of Sprite and then lobs the can onto his tray. He looks round the table and grins.

"So tonight's the night then lads," he says. "The big one. League Two Armageddon. Letchford versus Mackworth."

I smile. A little shiver of excitement goes through me. In the build-up to the last few matches I've been full of nervous tension for days beforehand. This time, with the whole *Oliver* thing hanging over my head, I've just been feeling blank. Out of it. Finally though, the adrenalin seems to be kicking in.

Gary rubs his hands together.

"It's going to be cracking," he says. "Local derby. Lots at stake. Give the bastards a spanking on the pitch, then a good shoeing in the streets afterwards."

Jerome nods.

"We should get three points this evening. Mackworth are shit."

Rob shakes his head.

247

"Can't take it for granted," he says. "They've got one point less than us after we got the draw at Rochdale, but they've got a game in hand. And if they beat us tonight and Mitcham and Torquay win tomorrow, we could be bottom of the table going into Christmas."

I wave my hand in the air.

"It's not that table you want to be interested in. Mackworth are top of the Firms league. If we see them off tonight, we'll be out in the lead."

"Is that right?" Gary asks.

"Yeah," I say. "And Mackworth know it. The hooligan messageboards on the Internet are full of postings from Mackworth lads. All sorts of threats about what they're going to do to us. You can tell they're running scared."

Ryan starts folding his empty crisp bag smaller and smaller until it's just a triangle of green plastic.

"It got a bit wild against Mackworth last season," he tells us. "They're a pretty decent firm. Mixture of young lads like us and some older blokes. They all know how to handle themselves though."

I nod.

"They reckon they might be bringing a hundred plus tonight. I don't know how many we can pull in, but it can't be too many more than that."

Ryan shrugs.

"No. It'll be pretty evenly matched."

We all go quiet for a few seconds, thinking things over. Then Rob chips in.

"Do you think there'll be a lot of coppers there this evening?"

"For definite," Ryan says. "They know what's likely to go down. It could be a full-scale riot. The Battle Of Southlands Part II. Coppers are going to be all over the place."

Jerome puts his arm round my shoulders.

"So we'll just have to make sure that Thomas here doesn't get himself arrested again," he says.

Everyone laughs. I just look at my hands and smile. But when I look up, I see something that wipes the smile right off my face.

Over by the noticeboards, alone, head hanging down, looking more miserable than I've ever seen him before, is Raks. He's only fifty yards away from me, but it might as well be fifty miles. Or fifty thousand. It's like we're in different worlds now.

Two seconds ago I was pretty content. Pretty much at one with things. Now there's a horrible empty feeling in the pit of my stomach. I look across at Raks again. It's not the first time I've spotted him on his own. Throughout this whole week we've been avoiding each other as much as possible. We're not really speaking any more. Even so, it's still a shock to see him like this, so isolated, so vulnerable. It seems strange. Wrong.

Because it's Raks. My pal. My mucker. My right hand man. I might be pissed off with him now, but we go right back. We've been best mates since the very first day of Rising Fives at Thurston Primary. Out in the mobile with Miss Handel. Raks had brought half a packet of Refreshers for his break time snack, and he let me have one of them. It was pink. I gave him a bite of my apple. And now look at the state of us.

I take a breath and shake my head, trying to clear my mind. All the problems that were crowding in on me earlier on are back again. I'm trying not to think, but it's the same as trying not to breathe. Sooner or later, you're just going to have to do it. I check my watch. It's nearly quarter past one. Five minutes until afternoon registration.

Ryan, Gary, Rob and Jerome start loading up their trays with empty plates and rubbish, standing up and getting ready to make a move. I know I should be doing the same, but I can't be bothered.

Ryan looks at me.

"You alright?" he asks. Gary and the other lads are already making for the canteen, but Ryan hangs back, waiting for an answer.

I nod and smile, not too convincingly.

"Yeah."

Ryan cocks his head to one side, seeing if he can suss me out. I'm giving nothing away.

"Right then," he says, after a while. "I'm off. I'm going to show my face this afternoon, just remind Sankey who I am. What about you? What lessons you got?"

"Maths and History."

Ryan whistles.

"A thrilling end to the academic year then."

I laugh.

Ryan zips up his Adidas top.

"So are you coming?" he asks.

I shake my head.

"Not yet. I'm just going to sit here for a few more minutes."

Ryan shrugs.

"Suit yourself. I'll see you later on, yeah?"

"Yeah," I say. "Later on."

Ryan heads off, and I stay sitting down.

The dining area is emptying right out, but the Christmas songs keep on coming. *Do They Know It's Christmas? A Spaceman Came Travelling*. I put my hands over my face and rub my eyes with my fingertips until I see stars. I take my hands away and look across to where Raks is sitting. Only he's not there any more. He's gone.

A couple of minutes pass. I just stare into space. I eventually summon up the energy to start piling stuff onto my tray, but then my phone starts to beep. I reach into my pocket and take it out. It's a text from Zoe. *Hp u r lkng 4wd 2 2nite c u l8r txt me?*

I feel sick. I want to text her back, but I can't. The fallout from tonight is going to be hard enough to deal with as it is, but at least I've not lied so far. At least I've not categorically said that I'm going to be at the show. Well, not in the last few days anyway. I've somehow managed to avoid the subject all week. But if I send a text, actually put into writing that I can't wait to see her do her stuff, I really will be setting myself up for big, big trouble. Any chance of keeping things going with Zoe will be gone for good.

I decide on a compromise. Something non-committal. I key in *Gd lk 2nite brk a leg! Tom X*. As my thumb flicks across the numbers I notice that the power on my phone is getting low. There's only one bar lit up. I reach inside the collar of my jacket and touch my T pendant. I read the text through, and take a deep breath.

As I hit *SEND*, another wave of guilt sweeps over me. It's becoming a bit of a theme with me this week. I've not lied to her, but I've not told the truth either. In some ways, what I've done is even worse than lying. It's the lowest of the low. It's like being all nice to your Granny, lulling her into a false sense of security, on the day you know you're sending her off to the Care Home.

I slump into my chair, putting my phone back in my pocket. My palms are wet with sweat. I shut my eyes. My brain is spinning out of control. There are just too many thoughts to deal with. It's complete overload.

I open my eyes again. The hall is virtually deserted now. The kitchen staff are out and about, clearing trays, picking up food from the floor, sweeping and polishing. A couple of them are casting suspicious glances in my direction, as if I'm up to something. The bell for registration starts to ring, drowning out the sound of Slade doing *Merry Xmas Everybody*.

I slowly get to my feet. I've come to a conclusion. There's no way I can stay here today. I mean, I've not even brought a pad or a pen. But that's not the real reason. The real reason is I can't spend the afternoon sitting in classrooms with Raks, seeing the look in his eyes. I need to get away. It's pointless trying to keep the thoughts at bay. I've got to let them all out. See if I can put them in some sort of order.

I start off across the dining area, slaloming through the tables and pushing through the double doors into the foyer. I go out through the main entrance and head up the path to the gates, turning right and crossing the road, then going left down towards the parade of shops.

Booze Brothers Off-Licence is the third unit along, past the newsagents and The Golden Plaice Fish N Chips. A bell rings as I enter. The old bloke behind the counter looks up from his paper. It's the *Argus* I was delivering last night. He's looking at the sport on the back page. *Whyman Rallying Cry : Win It For Fans*. A smaller column along the side has the heading *Police Warn Troublemakers To Stay Away*. The radio is on. It's Letchford Sound. *The Richie Bowser Lunchtime Jam*. Richie's playing some Level 42. *Running In The Family*. I get myself a four-pack of Carling from the fridge and take it across to pay.

"You eighteen?" the old bloke asks.

"Yeah," I tell him.

The old bloke looks at me for a second or two.

"Got any ID?"

I shake my head.

"Nope."

The old bloke carries on staring for a bit longer. He's seeing if I'm going to bottle out. I'm not. He knows full well that I'm nowhere near eighteen, but if he only ever sold alcohol to over eighteens, instead of schoolkids, he'd be bankrupt inside a couple of months.

"That's four fifty-seven," he says, putting my cans into a cheap-looking blue and white striped carrier bag. He looks at me like he's doing me a big favour, but I don't give him any acknowledgement. I'm not in the mood. And anyway, it's me that's putting money into his hand, not the other way round.

I shove a twenty over the counter and collect my change. Then I leave the shop, go back up to the road and turn left, away from Parkway and out of town.

About a mile up, I come to a bridge. There's a footpath running under the road in both directions, the course of an old railway line. I cut down the steps and head left. Another four hundred yards down, there's a bench. It's daubed with graffiti and someone's tried to set it on fire at some point, but apart from that it looks reasonably clean and dry. I sit down, fish a can out of my bag and crack it open.

The first swig of beer makes me grimace. It's so cold I can feel myself gagging as it sinks into my stomach. I suppose al fresco drinking isn't really the order of the day in the middle of December. I pull my Letchford scarf up out of my jacket, tightening it round my neck, trying to fight back against the chill of winter weather and icy Carling. It seems to work. The second and third swigs are much better. By the fourth, I'm coming up to speed, gearing myself up for some serious thinking.

I look out across the fields. In the distance I can see the Letchford skyline. Dirty tower blocks, church spires, chimneys, cranes pulling things down and building them up again. Over on the far left I can just make out the clock tower at Alderman Richard Martin High School. In the middle there's the Ainsdale Centre, and further out to the right, the Industrial Estate and Southlands Stadium, flood-lights stretching into the grey sky like little black twigs.

I take another swig of Carling and turn my thoughts back to the matter in hand. *Zoe or Letchford Town? Letchford Town or Zoe?* The same question, over and over again.

All this week I've been resigned to the fact that I don't have a choice about what I'm doing tonight. Like Letchford Town is an addiction I've got no hope of breaking away from. Maybe I'm wrong. Maybe I do have a choice. It's up to me to weigh up the pros and cons and come to a decision. Nothing's set in stone yet.

I could kick the Letchford habit and go to the play. Then I wouldn't lose Zoe. We could work harder on our relationship, get it back to the way it used to be. I could patch things up with Raks and Dad.

But that would mean missing Letchford's biggest match of the season. Missing the buzz, the adrenalin surge. Missing Mackworth. And where would that leave me? Looking like I'd pussied out. I'd lose my rank. I'd lose my status, everything I've built up over the past couple of months. I'd lose Ryan and Gary and the rest of the lads, and I'd be back at square one. Bottom of the Parkway pile. Down with all the deadwood.

I finish off my first Carling and put the empty can on the bench next to me. I hoped the alcohol might loosen me up a bit, help me to see things more clearly, but it's not working yet. I feel like I'm being pulled in one hundred different directions. And whichever direction I go in, I'm going to upset someone or something will be gone forever.

I get another can out of the bag. I check my watch. Half past two. I'm not going back to Thurston this afternoon. Dad thinks I'm staying in town then heading straight to Zoe's play. So I've got about four and a half hours to make my mind up, and still have enough time to get to Alderman Richard Martin or Southlands. Four and a half hours to come to a decision that could change the whole course of my life.

eighteen

It's just gone seven o'clock when I start walking back into Letchford. The sky over the town is orange with the glow of streetlights and there's a full moon away to the right.

I've made my decision. It's probably been the hardest decision I've ever had to make. I've agonised over it. In the end though, three and a half cans into my thinking session, things started to come into focus. Going to *Oliver* is the most sensible option all round. The consequences of not going hardly bear thinking about. I could just bullshit Ryan and the other lads. I got taken ill. Explosive diarrhoea. Water-pistol arse. Absolutely no way I could go to Southlands.

And yet here I am, just before twenty to eight, coming past the *Sky* outside broadcast trucks and the teams of police doing body searches, ducking into Gate 20 and handing my eight quid to Comb-Round Man. It doesn't matter what the most sensible option is. The pull of Letchford Town is too strong to resist.

Comb-Round Man presses the button that releases the locking mechanism on the turnstile. A buzz of excitement runs through me. I'm still fairly pissed, but I know this is an important moment. The point of no return. Even now, if I turned tail and legged it, I could just about get to Alderman Richard Martin in time for curtain up. As the turnstile clangs shut behind me though, I know that's not going to happen.

Kick-off is getting close and the concourse is almost deserted. I head past the bookies and up the steps as the sound of the crowd gets louder and louder. Airhorns are blasting and *We Are The Mackworth Haters* is booming out.

The teams are already on the pitch. Carl Butterworth and Ian Seaman, the Mackworth captain, are shaking hands while the ref, Letchy The Lion and the match officials look on. There's a cameraman in the centre circle, another one just to the left of the goal at our end, and two more up in the gantry at the back of the Main Stand. Because we're on the TV, there are electronic hoardings along the front of the Family Stand, flashing up adverts for Littlewoods Pools, Coke and Internet poker. Silk And Satin Table Dancing Club doesn't get a mention.

I start looking for Ryan. There's something different about the Kop tonight. There's a definite distinction between the civilians and the soldiers this time. The ordinary punters are down to the left. I can see Twitchy Bloke, Pessimistic Granddad and Big Fleece Woman a good thirty yards further across than they normally are. They know something's in the air. Something it's probably best to keep away from. Down to the right, it's Lad Central. There's not going to be any need for the NLLF army to join together before the final whistle. It's already happened. And we're out in force.

I head down the terracing, scanning across the sea of shaved heads and sports gear, hoping to pick out someone I know. I'm halfway down when Ryan steps out into the gangway in front of me. His face breaks into a huge smile.

"Fuck me," he shouts. "Look who it is." He grabs my arm and pulls me into the crowd.

257

There's a crush barrier up ahead. Gary, Jerome, Rob, Jimmy and Scotty are already in position. They've not seen us coming. I barge in amongst them, arms round Gary's and Jerome's necks.

"Evening lads," I say.

Suddenly everyone's all-smiles. I'm having my hand shaken, Jerome's giving me a bear hug, people are ruffling my hair, patting me on the back. I'm being treated like the returning hero. It feels good. It feels like I've made the right decision.

Gary shakes his head.

"Thought you weren't turning up," he says.

"Never doubt me," I say, grinning.

I look around, getting my bearings. We're about five yards from the fencing separating us from the away section. The police and stewards are on full alert tonight. They're already in place, more than I've ever seen before, a wall of green jackets on both sides of the wire.

Pushing myself up on the metal bar in front of me, I peer over the top of the human barrier, trying to get a glimpse of the Mackworth mob. Seeing what we're up against. The whole area is solid. Wall-to-wall bodies. Every time anyone steps to the side, ripples go off in all directions. My stomach twists, a mixture of anxiety and anticipation. Maybe it really could turn into The Battle Of Southlands II tonight.

Ryan squeezes in next to me. He nods in the direction of the Mackworth support.

"Not bad, is it?"

"Mmmm," I say. "How many do you reckon?"

Ryan shrugs.

"Difficult to tell. Definitely into three figures."

I nod.

"Do you think we've got the numbers to deal with them?"

Ryan grins.

"We'll be OK. We've got a reputation to uphold. The legacy of 1992." He rubs his hands together, trying to keep the cold out. "Anyway, I texted you earlier on, but you didn't get back to me. Where have you been?"

"Just around," I say. "Few things needed sorting out."

"Yeah?" Ryan raises his eyebrows.

I change the subject.

"How long have you been here?" I ask.

"Fifteen, twenty minutes," he replies. "All sorts has been happening this evening. Police escorts for the Mackworth buses. Coppers marching fans down from the town centre. Bit of naughtiness outside."

I nod.

"Any action down The Shakespeare?"

Ryan shakes his head.

"Couldn't even get in. Old Bill everywhere. It's like I said earlier on. They know what's likely to go down."

I flex my legs. My knees are starting to ache. I've done a lot of walking today. The noise of the crowd around us starts to build. I look towards the pitch. The players are getting into position. We're kicking the right way. The ref raises his hand. He's got his whistle in his mouth now. One shrill blast and we're under way.

Right from the start it's pretty frenetic. A typical derby. A lot of steam is being let off. Tackles are crashing in, there's an outbreak of handbags between Kevin Taylor and Danny Lee, the Mackworth number 6, and two yellow cards have been brandished.

A lot of steam is being let off on the Kop too. Chants are bouncing back and forth between the two sets of fans. Mackworth are singing *You're Going To Get Your Fucking Heads Kicked In*. We're responding with *You're The Shit Of Lincolnshire*. I thought there was vitriol in the chanting at the Castleton game, but compared to this, it was nothing. Vicarage tea party stuff.

Dave Nicholson is coming in for a torrent of abuse from the Mackworth fans. They've never forgiven him for defecting to the enemy. Our lot would probably like to sing a song for him, show him that we accept him as one of our own, at least for tonight, but we haven't got a song for Dave. He's got too many syllables in his surname.

There's another coming together near the halfway line. Jeff Hawkins scything into Eddie Banks of Mackworth. The ref looks across, then waves play on, even though Banks is lying pole-axed. The Mackworth section is incensed, but we're loving it. A chorus of *Get Into Em, Fuck Em Up* rings out.

As the chanting dies down, I try to get my breath back. I glance up at the scoreboard. Fifteen minutes gone. Kick off was at 7.45. I look at my watch. Eight o'clock. *Oliver* time. A hot flush of guilt and shame goes through me. I wonder how Zoe's feeling, looking out into the audience, realising I've let her down. I turn to say something to Raks, hoping he can give me a bit of moral support, but of course he's not there.

The rest of the half passes me by. I'm in a daze. I'm thinking about Zoe. I know her scenes are in the first act. I hope she's doing OK. Out on the pitch, the pattern of the game is changing. It's not blood-and-thunder now, it's nervous, niggly football, players terrified of making mistakes. It's only December, but already the match has the look and feel of a relegation 6-pointer.

Everyone's being affected by the tension, on the field and off. It's spreading like a contagious disease. All the chanting of earlier on has died away. The hostility that was threatening to get out of control at the start has gone back down to a gentle simmer. At times the stadium is as quiet as a church. Individual heckles are coming across loud and clear. *Come on Sharp you big stiff. Get stuck in Butterworth you nonce. Compete for the fucking ball Leroy.*

Gary and the other lads have already seen enough by the time the whistle goes to bring the half to an end. Me and Ryan head for the concourse. It's the usual routine. I go for a piss, Ryan gets the coffees. When we've both finished, we nudge through the hot dog and pie eaters until we're standing under one of the TV screens.

It's the *Sky* coverage of our match. They show a montage of highlights from the first forty-five minutes and then cut to George Gavin, sitting in one of the executive boxes at the other end of the ground. Next to George is Mark Sheedy, hair gelled, shiny pinstripe suit on. He's not playing tonight. He's serving his suspension for the sending off against Whitbourne. He reckons Letchford have clearly been the better side.

Ryan tuts.

"What fucking game has he been watching?" he asks no-one in particular.

We listen to a bit more chit-chat from George and Mark and then we head back out onto the terracing. The Mackworth section is virtually empty, but the police and stewards are still on guard along the fence. They're taking no chances.

There's a brass band out on the pitch, in front of the Family Stand. They're a load of kids, the local Boys Brigade, something like that. At first I wonder why they're not playing anything, but then it dawns on me. They *are* playing. It's just so quiet you can't hear it more than twenty yards away.

A bloke behind us laughs.

"They're doing *Silent Night*," he says.

Two minutes later, the teams are back out. The crowd roars again, trying to get the players going, but almost as soon as the sound of *The Boys Are Back In Town* fades away, we're back to the way things were for the majority of the first half.

The whole match seems to be taking place in the middle third of the pitch. Nobody's risking anything. Mackworth win a corner but only send four men up into our box and Jimmy Knapper claims the ball without any trouble. Up at our end, Leroy Lewton has a shot from thirty-five yards but it sails high and wide.

The tension is getting uncomfortable. A few of our fans at the back start a chant of *Come On Letchford*. Nobody joins in. Letchy The Lion is down at the front of the stand, kissing the badge on his shirt and raising his arms, geeing us up. It's a waste of effort. We're all too tightly wound. Nobody wants to sing. Nobody even wants to talk. I've not said a word to Ryan or Gary or anyone since half-time.

The timer ticks over to 69:00. Danny Holmes starts warming up. After a couple of minutes of sprinting and stretching, he's ready to come on. Leon Marshall makes for the dugouts and Danny jogs out into the middle.

Ryan shakes his head.

"It's a red-letter day," he says. "Danny Holmes

plays twenty minutes of a match. They'll be giving him a testimonial if he makes it to the end."

Danny's immediately into the game. He takes a ball from Paul Hood on his chest and runs at the Mackworth defence, forcing a throw-in over on the right. A ripple of excitement goes through the crowd. Jeff Hawkins takes the throw, finding Danny Holmes again. Danny spins to his left, away from his marker, and starts weaving towards the Mackworth penalty area. Two defenders are blocking his path. Danny dummies to the left, does a step-over and falls on his arse. Straight away he's waving to the bench, clutching his face. He's tweaked something. Thirty seconds after coming on, he's finished for the night.

Ryan sighs.

"I knew it was too good to be true," he says.

Danny Holmes departs on a stretcher. The game never really gets going again after that. As we head into the last ten minutes, we're back to extreme caution, the odd cynical foul and nothing in the way of goalmouth action. It's like the teams have signed a truce. They'll both be happy with a point. The crowd is hushed again. The only way the deadlock is going to be broken is if there's a piece of stupendous skill or an absolute howler.

And on eighty-seven minutes, Tommy Sharp provides that howler. A long, aimless punt heads towards him, twenty yards out from our goal. He brings it down, turns and knocks it back to Jimmy Knapper. Only Jimmy's come right off his line, Tommy's overhit the back pass, and the ball's bouncing into the corner of our net.

The Mackworth fans' celebration is so loud, I swear I feel the ground shaking. The cheering seems to go on forever, and even when it dies away, they're still going mad, stamping their feet, banging on the Perspex panels at the back of the stand, chanting *Going Down, Going Down, Going Down.* They're probably right.

In a few seconds, the atmosphere has changed beyond all recognition. The tension holding everyone back has evaporated and there's danger in the air. The hostility that's been bubbling quietly in the background has just boiled over in a big way. A huge surge starts on our side of the Kop, lads climbing over one another, trying to get at the Mackworth fans. The green jacket mob along the fence know they've got trouble, and they're linking arms, advancing forwards, trying to drive people back. A couple of boys are wrestled to the ground, dragged down to the front and led away, struggling.

Choruses of *Whyman Out* reverberate around. The stadium is emptying rapidly. People have concluded that the game is lost, and they've seen what's brewing behind the goal. The tannoy announcer is giving out warnings from the Safety Officer, pleading with people to calm down, but no-one's listening. The Mackworth fans are baiting us, singing *Who The Fucking Hell Are You?*, jumping onto one another's shoulders to flash wank signs. They're charging at the fence too, and one or two of them are breaking through the line of green jackets on their side, snarling at us, spitting, throwing coins and stones and cups of lukewarm coffee.

My body is suddenly filled with electricity. It's like all the tension of the evening has been charging me up like a battery, and now I'm up to full power. And if I don't find a way to release some of the voltage that's built up, I'm going to explode.

I look at Ryan. There's a sort of smirk on his face.

Instinctively, I know what he's thinking. The result on the pitch isn't important. It's what happens outside that really counts. I remember all the stuff the Mackworth lads posted on the Internet. All those words. *Mackworth rule supreme over Letchford scum.* It'll soon be time to ram those words back down their throats. And I can't wait.

The scoreboard timer is showing 90:00. The fourth official has signalled there's only one minute of stoppage time. The Mackworth fans are whistling. The game is virtually over.

Ryan grips my shoulder.

"Now," he hisses.

He doesn't have to explain what he means. I know exactly what's coming next. The NLLF is moving as one, bigger and stronger than ever, steaming up the steps and down through the concourse. I'm right at the front, Ryan and Gary next to me, Rob, Jerome, Jimmy and Scotty just behind. The police and stewards are lined up, bracing themselves, trying to hold us back, but it's useless. We're knocking them flying, charging through the exit gates, picking up momentum. We're unstoppable.

The Mackworth boys meet us head-on. There's even less time to think than there was after the Whitbourne game. Seconds after getting into the car park I'm grappling with a short-haired bloke in a black leather coat, turning him round, throwing him down. I step to the side, but the bloke in the leather jacket is back at me. He grabs my legs and I feel myself losing my balance. The next thing I know, my skull is bouncing off the floor and I'm staring up through a forest of bodies, blinking against the glare of a searchlight shining from a police helicopter clattering fifty feet overhead.

I spring back up, but my equilibrium is all shot. I can hardly hear myself think over the sound of the helicopter engine, and it's hard to stand in the down-draught of the whirling blades. Dust and rubbish is spiralling up into the air. Savage fighting is going on everywhere I look. I take a step forward and walk straight into a right-hander from a big skinhead in a green check shirt.

I've been hit before and I've quite enjoyed it, but this time I'm dazed and hurt and I'm starting to sense that something's wrong. There are too many Mackworth lads. More and more of them are pouring out through the exits. The whole Mackworth away support seems to be piling in. The NLLF is outnumbered and we're starting to cop a beating. I can't believe it's happening. This wasn't in the script. But it's happening all the same.

A few more seconds of coming off second-best and the NLLF army is scattering. Deserting. And wounded comrades are being left behind. Ten yards over to my right, Rob is down on the ground with two Mackworth boys kicking the shit out of him. Gary and Jerome have seen what's going on, but they're backing off, eyes wide. Jerome might be built like a nightclub doorman, but this is one dispute he's not going to try to sort out.

I start to head across, see if I can do anything, but the big skinhead hasn't finished with me. He grabs my head and pulls down, locking my neck between his elbow and his side. It feels like I'm trapped in a vice. My necklace is cutting into my skin like cheese wire. I'm coughing and spluttering, fighting for air, twisting my head side-to-side. There's a sensation like something snapping and then I'm free. I straighten up, putting a hand to my throat, feeling

266

for my necklace, realising that it's gone. I feel cold. It's too symbolic. A link to Zoe, broken forever.

It's complete mayhem all around me. The police and stewards are everywhere, but they're powerless. The helicopter is no help at all. Riot vans are screeching into the car park, but it's too little too late. The Mackworth mob is rampant. They're roaming about in gangs, lashing out in all directions. They've done what they couldn't do in The Battle Of Southlands. They've come onto our patch and taken over. Rob has finally managed to get to his feet and he's running away across the car park, chased by a lanky Asian kid. Gary and Jerome have disappeared. I've not seen Jimmy and Scotty since the fighting started.

I'm just about the last Letchford boy standing and I'm in real danger now. Three Mackworth lads are heading straight at me, eyes filled with hate. The big skinhead, a bloke in a black coat and a smaller lad in a cream bomber jacket. Everything's spinning out of control. My heart is racing. My breathing is shallow. My palms are sweating. I've got the metallic taste in my mouth again. My body is tingling all over. I'm experiencing all the sensations that first got me hooked on Letchford, on the NLLF, but it's not bringing me any pleasure. It's not excitement. It's terror.

I look around for someone to help me out, to back me up. I'm just starting to think it's useless when I see Ryan. He's over by Gate 20. He's seen me, and he's seen the mob closing in on me. He looks me right in the eye and shakes his head. He's not bothered about the legacy of 1992 any more. He's saving his own arse. Leaving me to it. I've been betrayed. A split second later Ryan has gone and I'm under attack.

I've only really got one option. I duck down and start running. I head to the left, round the corner of

267

the Main Stand and keep going, hurtling through the car park. I stop when I get to the main road, checking behind me, making sure I'm in the clear. It's looking good at first, but then the crowd parts and the three Mackworth lads come careering through, knocking people over like skittles.

In a flash, I'm off again, darting across the road and heading up to the right, aiming for the maze of passages through the Industrial Estate. It's a risky strategy. I'll be OK if I manage to shake the Mackworth boys off, but if I don't, I'll be fucked. I head right, left, right, trying to remember the route Ryan took us on after the Ashborough match. I come to another corner and spin through one hundred and eighty degrees, stumbling, nearly losing my footing, swivelling my eyes around, trying to see if I'm still being chased. I can't see anyone, but I can hear footsteps running, voices shouting, getting closer.

I put my head down and keep going, zigzagging along the metal walls of deserted factories and warehouses, desperately hoping that I'm not going to run into a cul-de-sac, almost praying that I'm on the right track. There are streetlights up ahead. As I come out between two buildings I realise where I am. Morrells is down to the left and the wasteland is in front of me. And on the other side of the wasteland is the main road, The Shakespeare, the bright lights, safety.

I stand still, holding my breath, listening for the sound of footsteps. In the distance I can hear the wail of sirens and the steady hum of helicopter blades. But no footsteps. I think I've escaped.

I start off across the wasteland. Fifty yards into the darkness and the churning fear inside me is starting to die down. Over on the main road, past the pylons,

I can see the flashing blue lights of more police vans racing towards Southlands. A huge sense of relief is spreading through me, and I can feel my body coming down off red alert.

But then a fist cracks into the side of my head and I sprawl onto the hard muddy ground. A split second later, kicks and stamps are raining down on me. I haven't escaped at all. I stagger to my feet and try to run, but someone's got hold of me. A forearm smacks me on the bridge of the nose, punches start crashing in from all sides. I'm getting a proper working over. I'm dizzy, winded, feeling sick. I'm not sure how much more of it I can take. A foot sinks into my stomach, and then something thuds into my back, low down on the right.

Instantly, pain shoots up my side. Not a dull ache, like the pain from the punches and kicks, but a sharp, cold pain, like someone pushing an icicle into my body.

The arms that have been holding me loosen and let go. The three blokes disappear into the night and I'm on my own again. I sag to my knees. My head is starting to clear. My nose feels twice its normal size, my left eye is closing, but it looks like I've survived. I run my tongue along my teeth. They're all still there. That's good. The pain in my back and my side just isn't going away though. That's not good. I reach my hand round, gently pressing the area. It doesn't feel right.

Looking down, I see that there's something black and glistening, spreading around the leg of my jeans. As I take my hand away from my back, I see that whatever the black, glistening stuff is, it's all over my fingers now. Only it's not black. It's red. Blood. I've been stabbed.

I start to panic. I try to stand but my legs are gone. My body is beginning to feel numb. But it's not the sort of numbness that I felt at the police station, the numbness that kept me calm and helped me talk my way out of everything. This is bad numbness. *About-to-pass-out* numbness.

I scrabble in my inside pocket and get my phone out. I flip open the front. The screen is dead. The power was low at dinnertime. Now it's gone completely. There's no way to call for help. I'm at least a hundred yards from the main road. I look down at the leg of my jeans again. It's absolutely black. Saturated. The ground around me is coated in my blood, steaming in the freezing night air.

A million and one thoughts start tumbling through my brain. A horrible realisation is dawning on me. This is what the whole Letchford Town thing has been leading towards. I think of all the people who tried to stop me, warned me about the dangers. Dad. Raks. Zoe. Even Steve Fisher at The Shakespeare. I didn't listen to any of them. I just kept ploughing on and on, getting deeper and deeper, even though it meant lying to and letting down the people who loved me the most. I put Letchford Town and the NLLF in front of everyone and everything. And now I'm going to pay the price.

I'm getting weaker and weaker. I try to crawl, but my arms won't keep me up. I unwind my scarf from around my neck, the black and orange scarf my mum knitted for me when I was a little lad, and I hold it into my side, trying to put pressure on the wound, trying to soak up the blood, trying to stop it pouring away.

Images are flickering in and out of my mind. It's a slideshow of memories. No order, just a mish-mash.

Kite flying with my dad on Great Yarmouth beach. Raks grinning, holding up a fish. Scoring for Thurston Dynamo. The first time I kissed Zoe, next to the conifers on Hill View Drive. A hot still night in my garden, moths on the honeysuckle. The smell of Samsara perfume. Mum's perfume.

I start to cry. I'm finished. I know I am. The blood's coming out too fast. I'm going to bleed to death. And for what? There's no honour in this. I'm not a soldier, laying down my life in a noble cause. The NLLF army was all a sham. A bunch of thugs who could dish it out but couldn't take it when it came back at them. I'm just an idiot. A fucking idiot.

I sink down onto my back, gasping, looking up at the full moon.

"Sorry Dad. Sorry Mum," I whisper.

And then everything goes black.

nineteen

It was my scarf that saved my life. By pressing it onto the hole in my side and keeping it there even when I passed out, I managed to stem the flow of blood just enough to keep me going. Otherwise I'd have died, out there on the wasteland amongst the old car batteries and shopping trolleys and bicycle frames.

Even with the scarf in place, I'd lost two and a half pints and was hypothermic and in deep shock by the time I'd been found and was in the back of an ambulance heading for Letchford General. If it hadn't been for the paramedics stuffing my wound with gauze, filling me up with blood volume expander, getting my circulation going and the pressure in my system back up to something like normal, I'd have pegged out there and then.

When I first arrived at the hospital I was unconscious and bleeding internally. I was assessed straight away and then rushed into theatre. I'd been stabbed between my eleventh and twelfth ribs, and the blade had passed through the muscles of my body wall. Beyond that, nobody could really say without opening me up. When they did, it wasn't good news. My right kidney was so badly lacerated, it had to be removed.

I cried when I woke up on Saturday morning and they told me my kidney had gone. I was groggy, zonked out, pumped full of antibiotics and painkillers, and in that split second an *emergency nephrectomy* sounded

272

pretty serious shit. I thought I'd be spending the rest of my life strapped to a machine. Doctor Konje put me right though. It's not so bad. You can live perfectly normally minus a kidney, assuming that the one you've got left is up to scratch, and everything looks alright on that front.

I felt a lot happier after that. I felt even better when he told me how lucky I'd been. According to Doctor Konje, if there's any such thing as a good stab wound leading to the removal of a kidney, then this was it. First of all, the knife didn't catch my renal artery, so my rate of blood loss was relatively slow. Nick the artery and it's *Goodnight Vienna*. Secondly, although the blade went almost four inches into me, it somehow managed to avoid damaging my peritoneum or my diaphragm. Thirdly, despite the knife being shoved upwards and twisted into me, it missed cutting into my liver, my duodenum and my ascending colon. All things considered, I've had a bit of a result. Maybe I don't deserve it, but I've been given a second chance.

The biggest result of all though, was being found in the first place. And that wasn't too far off being a miracle. Because it wasn't just anyone who found me. It was Dad and Raks and Raj Patel.

A lot of things were going on while I was standing on the Kop on Friday night. Zoe realised I wasn't at *Oliver* and phoned my dad during the interval. That was about quarter past nine. Dad phoned Raj Patel. Raj spoke to Raks. Raks said he didn't know where I was. Two minutes of wrestling with his conscience later, the truth came tumbling out. He knew I was at Southlands and he knew what I might be getting myself into afterwards. Raj phoned my dad, and five minutes later all three of them were on the way into

273

Letchford in Raj's car, ready to confront me outside the ground.

But the trip into town took longer than they thought. By the time they'd arrived, at about ten o'clock, parked at the side of the road near The Shakespeare and started heading down into the Industrial Estate, the match was finished, the fighting was finished and the area around the ground was deserted apart from the police and a few stragglers. At that point, the most logical thing they could have done was head for home. But they didn't. And what happened next was spooky. Because Raks just became convinced I was on the wasteland. He set off into the darkness with Dad and Raj in tow, certain he was on the right track. And the rest, as they say, is history.

It's Sunday afternoon now. I've been in Letchford General for the best part of two days. I've never been in hospital as a patient before. I visited Mum when she was in here, but I don't remember much about it. Just a few sights and sounds. This is the first time everything's really registered on me.

I'm in The Devonshire Ward. It's a long narrow room. The walls are cream, the floor tiles are grey. There are ten beds along each side of the central gangway. I'm up at the end furthest from the doors. The curtains are navy blue and the sheets are white. The whole place looks exactly the way you'd imagine a hospital ward to look. If my night at the police station was like being trapped inside *The Bill*, then now I'm having a turn in *Holby City*.

According to the clock on the wall opposite my bed, it's just coming up to two o'clock. The afternoon visiting hour. Dad was here all the way through from Friday night until yesterday evening, and he's going to be back again this afternoon. Raks is coming with him.

Right on the stroke of two, the double doors over to the right swing open and people start filing into the ward. A fat Asian bloke in a grey hoody. The three middle-aged daughters of the old man in the corner bed. An elderly couple. Two tall thin black lads in blue and red baseball jackets. I gently push myself backwards along the mattress, propping myself up against two pillows. The doors open again and Raks appears.

As he comes towards me he's smiling, but I can see the shock in his eyes. He saw me on Friday night of course. But that was before the bruising on my face came out. When I still looked relatively normal.

Raks pulls up a chair. He plonks a copy of *Nuts* and a bag of green grapes onto the bed next to me and shakes his head.

"Fucking hell, Tom," he says. "You look like the Elephant Man."

I know what he means. I caught sight of myself in the washroom this morning. Eye closed, nose, cheek and jaw swollen, skin tight and purple, lips like a goldfish.

"Broken nose, fractured eye socket," I say. "You should see the state of the other bloke."

Raks laughs, but it's a nervous sound. With all that's gone on over the last couple of weeks, he doesn't really know where we stand any more.

"So how are you then?" he asks. "Your dad says they took a kidney out. You going to be OK?"

I shrug.

"Doctors think so," I tell him. "I'm pissing blood at the moment, but that's normal, they reckon. I'm already up and about. I should be out of here in a few days. A week at the most."

He nods. He breaks off a sprig of grapes and starts pulling them off one by one.

"Where's Dad?" I ask.

Raks pops a grape into his mouth. He jerks his thumb back over his shoulder.

"Just out there. He thought we'd want a bit of a chat."

I nod. I look at Raks and grin.

"What?" he says.

"The bruises on my face are pretty good, yeah?"

"Mmmm."

"Well check this out," I say. I pull the sheets down and my pyjama top up.

Raks's mouth drops open.

"Shit, man," he says.

There's a huge white bandage around my midriff. Above and below it the skin is literally black and blue. It looks like someone's taken two buckets of paint and loosely mixed them together, adding in a few splodges of red just to liven things up.

"Not bad, eh?" I say.

"Not bad at all," Raks says. "I like your corset too."

I smile. We're both loosening up now. I reach down and get a couple of grapes.

Raks clears his throat.

"So what went wrong?"

I close my eyes, reliving the experience.

"Too many Mackworth."

Raks scratches his forearm.

"What happened to Ryan and the rest of the gang then? Where were they when you were getting turned over?"

"Don't ask," I tell him.

276

Raks understands my drift. He has another grape.

"Have the coppers spoken to you yet?"

"No," I reply. "Not yet. But I expect I'll be getting a visit in the next couple of days."

Raks nods.

"Can you describe the lads who attacked you?"

I shake my head.

"Not really. It's all a bit of a blur. I get flashbacks but nothing definite."

"The coppers are going to want to know why you were at Southlands again aren't they?" Raks asks.

I laugh.

"Yeah. I'm going to have a bit of explaining to do."

"Just a bit."

We both go quiet for a while. In the next ward a baby is crying. I look at the cover of *Nuts*. It's some bird from last summer's *Big Brother* in a polka-dot bikini. I take a deep breath, composing myself. There are things I need to get off my chest.

"Raks," I say. "Thanks for Friday night. You saved my life, mate. Literally."

Raks grins, embarrassed.

"All part of the service," he says.

I shake my head.

"How did you know where I'd be?" It's been playing on my mind. I just can't work it out.

Raks rolls his eyes.

"I've got no idea, man. It must have been some sort of telepathy. Vibes in the air. Something like that. I just *knew* you were out there."

I puff out my cheeks.

"Well, anyway. You saved my life. For real. And after the way I acted…" My voice trails off. I'm too choked up to carry on.

Raks grips my hand.

277

"Don't be stupid man," he says. "There's been all sorts of stuff going on recently. I shat on you, you shat on me. It's gone now. Forgotten."

"Thanks," I say. "And we're mates again, yeah?"

"Definitely," he says. "Mates though, nothing more. Just because we're holding hands now, I don't want you getting any funny ideas."

We both laugh, and suddenly, despite the surroundings, it feels like old times.

I edge a bit higher up the bed, flicking a glance over Raks's head. The doors of the ward are opening again. I'm wondering if it might be Dad. It's not. It is a visitor for me though. Zoe.

My heart leaps into my mouth. She's striding across the polished floor in slow motion, holding a big bunch of blue and white flowers. As she gets closer, her expression is changing. Forty feet away she's looking determined. Thirty feet away she's forcing a smile. At twenty feet the smile starts to fade. By the time she's ten feet away, her eyes are widening in horror. As she arrives next to me, the colour is visibly draining from her face.

"Oh, Tom," she whispers, putting her hand to her mouth. She wasn't prepared for this.

I try to smile, try to look reassuring, but I'm nervous, tensing up.

Zoe dumps the flowers on the bedside cabinet and sinks into a chair.

Raks stands up.

"Right then," he says. "I'd best get going. I've got to get a few Christmas bits and pieces."

"Okay." I know he's not really going Christmas shopping. He's just being diplomatic. "Come and see me again, yeah?"

"Course," he says. He gives me the thumbs up,

grabs a last sprig of grapes, pats Zoe on the arm and makes his exit.

When Raks has gone, me and Zoe look at each other. Neither of us knows what to say. I'm burning up with shame and guilt. Zoe looks torn between sympathy for the state I'm in and anger for the way I've treated her.

"Oh, Tom," she says again. There are tears in her eyes now.

I try another rigid smile. My mouth is bone dry. I swallow.

"It's OK," I tell her. I point to my face. "This is just superficial. It'll be gone in a week or two. Even with the kidney, I'm not really in any pain. I'll be back to normal before you know it."

I reach out with my right hand. Zoe shuffles her chair closer to the bed, linking her fingers with mine. We look at each other again, and for a few seconds I think everything's going to be alright. But then she starts to cry. And I know she's not just crying because I've been stabbed and beaten and left for dead. She's crying because she knows I'm not the lad she thought I was. Because everything has changed. She hunches over, letting go of my hand, blonde hair spilling across her face, sobbing.

I feel completely helpless. I want to put my arms around her, hold her, tell her sincerely that I'll never deceive her again, never let her down again, but I can't. Too much movement like that and I'll rip my stitches. And besides which, she wouldn't believe me anyway. Why should she?

"Zoe, I'm sorry." It's all I can really say.

She looks up. Her eyes are red. She reaches inside her army jacket and gets out a blue tissue, dabbing at her nose. She stuffs the tissue back into her pocket.

279

She takes hold of my hand again, looking straight at me.

"I just don't understand," she says eventually. "How could all of this have happened? How could you have got so deeply into all this Letchford Town stuff that you ended up like this?"

I shake my head, looking down at the sheets bunched up around my waist, the red track marks on the inside of my elbow, where the IV drips were put in on Friday night. I'm lost for words. In the cold light of day, the whole thing is so illogical it's pointless even to try to explain.

Zoe leans forward, pulling my hand towards her, kissing my knuckles. It feels like she's letting me know I can stop struggling for answers. I'm just starting to relax when she tilts her head slightly to one side, narrowing her eyes, looking at the open collar of my pyjamas.

"Where's your necklace?" she asks.

For a split second I feel a jab of panic. It's another question I just can't answer. I remember being trapped in a headlock. I remember the chain cutting into my skin. I remember a horrible snapping sensation. But then I remember something else. The other bit of luck that Dr Konje told me about. The jingling sound one of the nurses heard as I was having my clothing cut away before my operation. The necklace and pendant, that had broken off and fallen down the front of my T-shirt, sliding onto the table next to me.

"It's in the top drawer of the cabinet," I tell her.

Zoe shoots me a sideways glance. She pulls the drawer open a fraction. She nods to herself.

I allow myself a little grin. The crisis has passed.

She stays for about another fifteen minutes. It's nice to spend some time together. The ward is busy and we watch people coming and going. A nurse takes Zoe's flowers away and brings them back in a chunky glass vase. We finish off Raks's grapes. We crack jokes, talk about all sorts of silly things. But all the time, there's a kind of undercurrent. We both know there's still a lot of serious stuff to discuss. Maybe not here, maybe not today, but soon.

As the clock on the wall ticks towards twenty to three, Zoe straightens up in her chair.

"I'm going to have to go now," she says. "Your poor dad has been waiting ages to see you."

I nod.

"Right," I say. "Well, thanks for coming. I really appreciate it."

Zoe smiles. She stands up, leaning over and kissing me on the forehead.

My stomach churns. Now isn't the time for big deep discussions, but there's something I need to know.

"So are we still together?" I ask. I'm coming straight to the point. It seems like the only thing I can do.

She pushes hair out of her eyes. Her smile is fading. She strokes my arm. She takes a breath.

"We'll just have to see," she says.

I feel deflated, but in truth, it's the best I could have hoped for.

Zoe kisses my forehead again, then heads for the doors.

A few seconds after she disappears from view, Dad comes into the ward. Even at this distance I can see there's something different about him. The nearer he gets, the more obvious it becomes. He's had a shave. He's washed his hair. He's in a pair of dark blue jeans and the lilac shirt I bought him for his last birthday.

He made an effort the night we went to Raks's party, but this is something else entirely. It's the smartest he's looked in years.

As he gets to my bedside, he smiles. A bit nervous, a bit self-conscious. He's got aftershave on, and this time it's not just to disguise the smell of Stella.

I shake my head.

"Bloody hell Dad," I say, grinning. "Look at you. Are you on the way to meet a woman?"

"You cheeky sod," he says.

We both laugh. It feels strange. I can't remember the last time we shared a joke.

Dad sits in the chair, dumping a carrier bag on the floor. He squeezes my arm.

"You OK?" he asks.

"Not bad."

He runs a hand through his hair and reaches down into the carrier bag.

"I've brought you some stuff," he says, lining things up on the side of the bed. A bottle of Lucozade. A big bag of Haribos. Today's *News Of The World*. Steven Gerrard's autobiography. My portable CD player and four discs.

"Nice one," I say. I'm amazed. I've never known him so organized.

"Didn't want you getting bored," he says. "Hope the CDs are OK. I just picked up whatever was next to your stereo."

I nod, shuffling through the plastic cases. Oasis. Arctic Monkeys. Kasabian. And lurking at the bottom of the pile, Level 42. *The Ultimate Collection*.

I shake my head.

"This wasn't next to my stereo."

He grins.

"Thought a few days in hospital was a good

opportunity to further your musical education," he says. "It's a 2-CD set. Keep you going for hours."

I laugh. I might actually listen to it. Or there again, I might not.

Dad pulls open the bag of Haribos and helps himself to a green fizzy dinosaur. I get myself a cola bottle and a couple of jelly babies and we kick off with some general chit-chat. How I'm feeling. What the doctors and nurses have said. How the painkillers are working. It's basic stuff but it passes the time.

"How's things with Raks and Zoe?" Dad asks, when we've exhausted all the medical banter.

I shrug.

"It's all sorted with Raks. With Zoe…" I hold my hand flat in the air and wobble it from side to side.

Dad nods.

"You've got a lot of work to do if you're going to get her to trust you again," he says.

"Yeah." I rub my chin. "I've got a lot of work to do with a lot of people, haven't I?"

He shakes his head.

"It's not just you," he says. "It's both of us. This whole episode has been like a wake-up call. Things haven't been right, have they?"

I raise my eyebrows. It's a bit of a rhetorical question.

Dad gets another sweet, then carries on.

"And I don't think we need a big inquest to work out where we've been going wrong. We both know, don't we?"

I nod.

"And we both know how we can sort things out," I say.

He smiles, relieved, glad that I'm on the same wavelength. He reaches out to squeeze my arm again.

"You're a good lad," he says.

Neither of us talks much after that, but there's no awkwardness in the silence. We've done all the talking we needed to do over the past couple of days. We've put all the bad feeling behind us. It's like we've wiped the slate clean and we're just waiting for the right moment to make a fresh start.

Three o'clock seems to come around very quickly. People begin to say their goodbyes, put their coats back on, get themselves ready to go home. Dad has a final rummage in the bag of Haribos.

"I'll be back in tomorrow, then," he says. "Is there anything I can get you?"

I shake my head.

"I think I'm all sorted now, thanks. I just need to get myself well again."

He nods.

"Yeah," he says. "You do that."

As Dad stands up, I can't help smiling. I've had time to get used to the transformation in the way he looks, but it's still hard to get my head round. It's not just that he's smarter than he's been in years. It's something more. It's that he looks the way he used to look. Back in the days when he was working, when Mum was alive, when he had a bit of faith in himself. When he was *Hollywood Tony*.

"See you then Dad," I say.

He looks at me and winks.

"See you mate."

A few seconds later, Dad's gone. I lever myself up against the back of the bed and pick up *The News Of The World*, reading the headline. *Soap Star's Gay Dungeon Shame*. I flick through to the middle pages and pull out *Score*, the football supplement. There's something that's started nagging away at me.

Something I need to find out. I skim the Premier League and Championship pages then keep going, through League One and down into League Two. I still don't know what happened in the games yesterday afternoon. The games affecting Letchford.

It doesn't take me long to find what I'm looking for. The League Two classified results. Page 18. I scan down the list. *Grimsby 1 Torquay 2. Mitcham 1 Wrexham 0.* Wins for Mitcham and Torquay. I know what that means, and a look at the table confirms it. Letchford are rock bottom. Bottom of our division. Bottom of the entire Football League. 92nd out of 92. As the old joke goes, we must be the strongest team in the country, because we're propping the rest up. My heart sinks. I somehow didn't think it would still be that important to me. Not now, not after everything that's happened. But it is. It hurts.

Letchford's next four matches are in brackets next to our points tally. Three awaydays in a row. Accrington Stanley on the 23rd. Wrexham on Boxing Day. Bristol Rovers on the 30th. And then on New Years Day we're at home to Mitcham. It's an important game, against another of the strugglers. A must-win game.

I close the paper and push it across the bed. I ease myself down under the sheets, staring up at the ceiling tiles. An idea is starting to form in my mind. Monday January 1st. That's more than two weeks away. I'll be well and truly on the mend by then. On my feet, building up my strength again. And what better way to get a bit of exercise and fresh air than taking a trip down to Southlands? Letchford need all the support they can get. I can't abandon them. They're my team.

I get a little tingle in my stomach. I wonder how

I'm going to break the news to people. To Raks. To Zoe. To Dad. They've probably all assumed I'm finished with Letchford Town. But I'm fairly sure I can swing it.

The last few people are leaving now. A pretty black nurse is holding one of the doors open, smiling, wishing everyone a safe journey home. As I watch, her expression changes and I see her shaking her head, talking to someone out in the corridor. The discussion's getting heated for a few seconds, but then the nurse is all smiles again. She pushes the door open and one final visitor enters The Devonshire Ward. I do a double-take. It's Ryan.

Everyone else who's visited this afternoon has been shocked to see the state I'm in. Not Ryan. As he gets closer to my bed, the grin on his face is growing wider and wider. It's almost unbelievable. He thinks this is funny.

Time has slowed to a crawl. I feel a bit woozy. I must have thought about everything under the sun since I woke up yesterday morning. Every aspect of my life, past, present and future. It's weird though. The one thing I hadn't thought about is how I'd feel when I next saw Ryan. Now I'm going to find out.

All sorts of emotions are swirling inside me. An image from the other night flickers into my brain. Me about to take a kicking. Ryan looking me in the eye, shaking his head and doing a runner. As the image fades, anger and resentment surge through my body. I'm sure the way I'm feeling must be registering on my face. But if it is, Ryan hasn't noticed. He's standing at the end of my bed now, chuckling quietly to himself, shaking his head.

And then something strange happens. It's like everything suddenly becomes clear. Ryan didn't betray me. It was just one of the things that can happen in the heat of battle. In all honesty, if our positions had been reversed, I'd have probably done the same thing to him. There's no problem between us. That's just the way it is. And in that instant, all my anger has gone. I break into a smile.

Ryan pulls out a chair and sits down.

"Alright, mate?" he says.